"Ever tattoo someone under eighteen?"

I arched a brow. "That's illegal, Detective."

"And you'd never break the law?" He slipped his hand into his jacket, then slid a photo across the desk. "This look familiar?"

Something in my gut tightened. Keeping my face blank, I looked down. My worst fear rushed up and smacked me in the face. The photo showed the tattoo on the small of a woman's back—a bear, paws outstretched and teeth flashing. My first early morning gift.

"Nice work," I commented, my throat dry, but my tone noncommittal.

He slid a second photo toward me.

I didn't really have to look, but I did—the leopard. I picked it up and tried to look at it dispassionately, as just a tattoo, not a piece of a once-living girl.

"Are there more?" I nodded at the pictures still in his hand. There were twelve main tribes, each with a totem. He'd only shown me two. I'd only found two bodies. Were there more? Had the killer left bodies on someone else's doorstep?

PRAISE FOR LORI DEVOTI

"Outstandingly exciting!"

—*Fallen Angel Reviews*

"Extremely talented and guaranteed to keep you reading."

—*Paranormal Romance Reviews*

Amazon ink

LORI DEVOTI

POCKET BOOKS

New York   London   Toronto   Sydney

Pocket Books
A Division of Simon & Schuster, Inc.
1230 Avenue of the Americas
New York, NY 10020

First Juno Books/Pocket Books paperback edition June 2009

JUNO BOOKS and colophon are trademarks of Wildside Press LLC used under license by Simon & Schuster, Inc., the publisher of this work.

POCKET and colophon are registered trademarks of Simon & Schuster, Inc.

For information about special discounts for bulk purchases, please contact Simon & Schuster Special Sales at 1-866-506-1949 or business@simonandschuster.com.

The Simon & Schuster Speakers Bureau can bring authors to your live event. For more information or to book an event contact the Simon & Schuster Speakers Bureau at 1-866-248-3049 or visit our website at www.simonspeakers.com.

Cover design by John Vairo Jr.
Front cover illustration by Timothy Wayne Lantz

Manufactured in the United States of America

10   9   8   7   6   5   4   3   2   1

ISBN: 978-1-4391-5427-4

To all the warrior women out there fighting for their kids.
Whether it's to feed and clothe them, to keep them healthy,
or to keep them safe, no battle was ever worth more.
I applaud you. Keep fighting.

Acknowledgments

Thanks for making this book a reality go to my editor, Paula Guran, who took a chance on something a little different, and to Holly Root, agent extraordinaire and professional Slurpee splitter. Next time, you get your own straw!

And thanks to Madison, Wisconsin, for being the perfect place for a family of Amazons to blend.

Chapter One

Not again.

My gaze darted around the old school yard, searching for whoever had left the dead teenager on my front porch.

I was hoping the intruder was still nearby, close enough to catch and deal with myself—right now and for good—but the acre of grass and trees that surrounded our home and business was quiet.

No more than a minute or two had passed since the rattle of stones thrown at my bedroom window had roused me. I knew—this time—to go to the front door. But there was nothing. No cars. No autumn wind. Nothing. Even at one in the morning, at least an occasional car should have been zipping down the street that lay only a football field's length away. My home was a little over a mile from the University of Wisconsin campus and it was a Saturday night, Sunday morning, technically; a few drunken students if no one else should have been traveling along Monroe Street, but the night was silent—deadly so.

I glanced down at the girl lying on her back on my front steps.

I almost stepped on her. There was something particularly disturbing about that. My hands shaking, I shoved the hair back from my face, tucked it behind my ears, and knelt next to her.

Maybe this one is different. A thin hope at best, but I clung to it, my fingers wrapping around the tiny wolf fetish that hung from a cord around my neck. The stone figure in my hand offered a small amount of reassurance, calmed me.

Maybe my first impression was wrong . . . maybe she was still alive. Maybe, unlike the first girl I'd found dead on my doorstep only weeks before, this one still lived.

I repeated the words in my mind: *maybe she is different. . . .*

A prayer to Artemis leaving my lips, I reached out, ready to lay my fingers against her throat. As I did, I couldn't help but take in her youth, her closed eyes. *So innocent. So like Harmony.*

My fingers curled back into my palm and my heart pounded; the words echoed through my head. Harmony. A flash of panic, then forced calm. It wasn't Harmony. My daughter was asleep, safe inside. I stood anyway, started to turn back to the wide double door of the old school behind me—to check—but I stopped myself. My need to see her was just maternal instinct pushed into overdrive. I had to stay calm, controlled. I couldn't leave this girl alone, not yet. I glanced back at her.

I took a deep breath and kneeled again, but even as I did, I knew I was lying to myself. There was no heart beating inside the body beside me.

Still, I pressed my fingers to the girl's throat.

Her neck was stiff, hard to my touch. I ran my fingers down her arm, met with the same cold, unresponsive feel. She wasn't alive, hadn't been for hours.

A curse formed in the back of my head, but I tamped it down. Whoever, whatever this girl had been, she'd suffered enough indignities. I had no right to add to them. My duty now was to ease her passage, not soil it with my own anger, frustration, and fear.

I lowered my chin to my chest, reflected for a minute, and tried to slow my racing mind enough to draw on my past, my training. I didn't practice the skills taught by my Amazon high priestess grandmother, but they were still a part of me, as impossible to deny as the horrible truth of this girl's death.

Pretending the moisture threatening to escape the corners of my eyes didn't exist, I took one more calming breath, then did the best I could to fold the girl's stiff arms over her chest, touched my thumb against the bridge of her nose, and murmured another prayer. This one asking for free and peaceful passage of her spirit—

that whatever took her life wouldn't hold back her journey from this world to the next.

I tried to steel myself for what came next, but it was just as hard this time as last. The girl's body sighed, not audibly, more of a feeling, a whisper of energy as her soul slipped from her form and wafted away, hopefully to join whatever loved ones had preceded her in death.

The ritual drained me, a piece of my own spirit leaving with hers, accompanying her. I'd recover, but not until her soul found peace. By performing the rites, I'd promised her that.

Normally, I would have been myself again in a matter of minutes, hours at the most, but I had yet to recover from the last one.

Which meant something was terribly wrong.

Like finding two dead girls on my doorstep wasn't wrong enough.

I rested my weight back on my heels and stared down at her.

Just like the first one, she was young—under twenty. Older than Harmony, but not enough that I didn't still fight the urge to go check on my sleeping child. I forced myself not to, though. Harmony was fine. No one had intruded our home. Only the yard . . . the steps. That was as far as my visitor had got.

After successfully reassuring myself, my attention went back to the girl.

Did the similarity between the two dead teens stop with their age? Only one way to know.

I gently rolled the girl onto her side and pulled her thin T-shirt up, baring her lower back to the night air.

A tattoo of a leopard snarled at me. What appeared to be a *telios,* the Amazon symbol of their family clan.

My lips thinned to nothing more than a line. Not the same, but similar. Now the hard part. I lowered the girl onto her back and again adjusted her shirt, this time to pull it low, down to the top of her right breast. A round circle of skin about the size of my balled fist was missing—the cut precise, even, and unending. Done with either great skill or care.

I stared blindly. The coincidence was too great. The tattoo on her back—a leopard, one of the twelve totems of the Amazon tribe. The other girl bore a bear. And both had the missing skin—exactly where a *givnomai,* personal power tattoo, would be. Removed either right before or right after their deaths.

Please, Artemis, let it be after.

The girl's blond hair caught in the breeze, tangling across her face, the motion in the dim light of my battery-powered lantern making her look alive for just a second.

I lowered my chin to my chest again and let emotion I'd denied earlier waft over me—sorrow, frustration, then anger. Someone was killing these girls . . . Amazon girls . . . and leaving them on my doorstep. A threat? Some kind of twisted gift? Or a warning?

Did the killer know the symbolism of the animals on the girls' backs and of the fetishes hanging from their necks? All Amazons did. Thoughts that had been nagging at me, that I hadn't let fully form in my brain, forced their way forward. Two dead girls, both Amazons. Could the killer be an Amazon—or just someone the tribe had angered? If another body were to show up, would it bear yet another of the twelve totems? Was there a plan to target each family? If so, it would mean the killer had to be an Amazon. No one else knew about the tribe and certainly not the significance of our totems.

Pure cold rage shot through my body and, like the first time, I fantasized about hunting the killer down, exacting revenge for the young lives unjustly ended. Vengeance was as much a part of being Amazon as our worship of Artemis. Within the tribe, a band of warriors would have been chosen and none would have rested until the killer was found and destroyed. Her soul released, but not in the gentle manner I'd used with these girls. No, it would be torn from the killer's body, then grounded to earth. Cursed to stay locked for eternity in one spot, her only conscious world the moments of her own death playing over and over.

But then reality settled down around me—again.

I was no longer part of the tribe. A fact I didn't regret, but for these girls' sakes, for my family's . . . for a moment I wavered. Amazon justice was hard and fast. A tempting resolution to this ugly dilemma. But I had left that world, and even if I wanted to return, they wouldn't accept me back easily.

In fact, they would view any approach from me with suspicion, perhaps even enacting their hard and fast justice on me before bothering to gather tiresome details. And they'd be back in my life, in my daughter's life. My daughter, who knew nothing of her heritage, didn't even know Amazons were real and that she was one.

It was why I hadn't done anything about the first girl—or not much anyway. I'd released her spirit, then left her body where the police could find it.

It had been something, but not enough. I cradled my face in my hands . . . not enough by a long shot. The dead body beside me proved that.

What now? Nothing had changed. I couldn't do any more this time.

But hard as I tried, I couldn't let it go. Couldn't just stand up and cart this body off like I had the last. Forget her . . . or try to.

What about their families? Their mothers wondering when their daughters would come home . . . expecting them . . .

Amazons were seminomadic. Here in the U.S., they traveled from one "safe camp" to another, much like gypsies. Also, like gypsies, Amazons tended to skirt the edges of the law—thinking nothing of conning the humans they encountered out of property and money— my grandmother was a prime example of that way of thinking.

And because of these tendencies, Amazons, even those still fully immersed in the tribe, might not see each other for months. A mother could easily not hear from her barely adult child for that long and think little of it . . . have no idea her daughter had been left, dead, on my doorstep. Their mothers could still be sitting at some safe camp, waiting, expecting . . .

My hands formed claws at my sides, my fingernails scraping against the concrete steps.

And what about the others—those not missing yet? Could my silence be endangering other young women? What if the Amazons had no idea they were being preyed upon—that there was a killer in their midst?

Two, then three fingernails broke down to the quick. I breathed out through my nose, ignoring the pain— forcing it and the nagging guilt building in the back of my brain out of my consciousness.

Flattening my fingers against the concrete until my knuckles glowed white, I forced myself to continue weighing my options. Choices—there had to be choices . . . something better than just ignoring all of this and praying it wouldn't happen again.

I focused, away from the current situation and the dead girl by my side, and toward the bigger picture: how to stop more girls from dying.

The next logical step, if anything about my life was logical, would be going directly to the police, but there were problems with that solution too.

I was an over-one-hundred-year-old Amazon. Something I hid, not only from society, but my own daughter. I'd spent ten years pretending, and so far I'd succeeded. But my mother and grandmother, who also lived with me, already raised eyebrows. They tried to hide their heritage, both to humor me and to protect the tribe I despised, but their efforts wouldn't hold up under close study. Not to mention that bringing the police into the picture would also mean bringing in my mother and grandmother. They would realize—just as quickly as I had—that the girls weren't normal runaways. They were Amazons. And they would insist on informing the tribe.

Bringing me back to problem number one.

So, calling the police, like any normal grown adult *human* would do when faced with a dead body on her porch, was out.

I was trapped by my own lies, and it pissed me off.

My gaze dropped to the body beside me, zeroing in on a thin strip of leather barely visible beneath the hair covering her neck.

I reached out and let the thong run over my cupped hand until the tiny stone figure I knew would be attached to its end landed in my palm. A leopard, black, his lips pulled into a snarl. I could almost feel anger pulsing in the tiny creature. This girl, like the first, like me, wore her family totem on her back and around her neck. It was the only piece of out-of-the-ordinary adornment aside from the tattoos that both girls had worn. I'd taken the first girl's for that reason.

I lifted her head and slipped the totem free.

With the tiny leopard tucked inside my pocket, I felt a little better. I had a plan, too late for this girl or the previous one, but maybe it would keep there from being a next.

Still, I muttered an apology as I pulled the corners of the old blanket on which the girl lay over her body and bundled her like a newborn infant. I would perform what Amazon burial rites I could and leave her corpse where the police would find it—hopefully, soon.

It wasn't much, but this time—I patted the lump of stone resting in my pocket—it wouldn't be *all* I'd do. I couldn't—wouldn't—reveal myself to the Amazons or the police, but I also couldn't sit back and do nothing, not again.

This time I'd do my best to let both know something was wrong, that someone was preying on teens.

I glanced at my watch—almost two A.M. I had three hours before my grandmother arose and addressed the sun. I could make it to Milwaukee—or close to it—and be back before anyone noticed my absence. But I wouldn't have time to complete the second task—not tonight. The Amazons would have to wait. I'd need a full night to make it to the northern Illinois woods where the closest safe camp was located and be back home before dawn.

After taking one last moment to mourn her death, I flipped the girl's body over my shoulder and trudged to my truck.

At some point I was going to have to try and interpret what message the killer was sending me by depositing the girls on my front steps, but for now I had an even more solemn job to complete.

Chapter Two

"*They found another girl's* body today." Mother spoke from over my shoulder. She was concentrating on the small TV perched on our kitchen counter.

The camera focused on a body bag being lifted onto a portable gurney and wheeled to the back of a hearse-type vehicle. I picked up the remote and flipped off the morning news.

"Unfortunately." I shifted my gaze to my bowl of Cheerios and waited for Mother to step away.

She didn't.

"Aren't you worried?"

My mind lurched. Had she seen me? I glanced up at her, searching for some sign that she'd witnessed my early morning mission, but she just blinked down at me, her gray eyes void of any accusation.

Worried—by the deaths, she meant. I inhaled and willed myself to relax.

"Neither of the girls were found here . . . in Madison," I replied, my eyes focusing on my cereal to cover my lie. A Cheerio slipped off my spoon and escaped back into the pool of milk.

"Yet," Mother countered.

I pushed the spoon to the bottom of the bowl, crushing the cereal trapped beneath the utensil to mush. Why couldn't she just let it go?

Harmony, my fourteen-year-old daughter, bopped out of her bedroom and bent over the oversized porcelain water fountain that dominated the entry to our unconventional home—a circa 1900 high school.

I took that chance to watch her, to breathe, relax. She was healthy, happy, and blissfully unaware her mother had been sneaking off in the middle of the night to tote a dead body far away from her protected little world.

The water fountain sputtered, spraying her blouse. Mumbling under her breath, she flounced off to the bathroom, but not before shooting me a "look." Harmony didn't appreciate the eclectic charm of the place as much as I did.

For once her teenage attitude helped me relax. I smiled, my eyes clocking each of her angry steps.

She popped into the bathroom, and I dipped my spoon into the cereal.

"She needs to be training." Mother nodded toward my daughter.

My tiny bubble of calm was instantly burst. I had

enough things to stress about right now—like dead Amazons being deposited on my doorstep, all but gift wrapped. I didn't need Mother bringing up this old chestnut.

Through the open door of the guest bath, converted from half of what used to be the girls' restroom, I could see Harmony rolling a line of lip gloss across her mouth. She pushed her lips into a playful pout, then smiled at her reflection.

"She is training—to be a girl." I gave Mother a *drop it now* look. As usual, it had absolutely zero effect.

"She's past puberty. Her powers . . ."

I narrowed my eyes, my fingers tightening around the spoon. "What powers?" At Mother's bland stare, I continued, "Priestess powers are supposed to skip one generation, not two. If anyone was going to get Bubbe's powers, it would have been me and, as you know, my priestess skills are more than just a little lacking." I held my gaze steady, just long enough to let Mother know I wasn't going to back down, then shrugged as I continued, "So far as artisan or warrior talents, if those appear we'll deal with it. She probably won't even need special training. Besides . . ." I smiled, just to tick Mother off. "She might be a hearth-keeper."

Mother huffed out a breath. Warriors had little respect for any of the other talent groups, but for hearth-keepers? Let's just say if Harmony showed skills in that area, I'd find myself fighting Mother with more than just words to keep her from dragging my daughter back to the Amazons to discover her "true" calling.

Not that I thought there was much chance of that. There hadn't been a hearth-keeper in our direct line for six generations. Besides, I was hiding more than the appearance of the dead teens from my family. I was hiding another discovery—that my own powers had grown. Maybe the ten years of non-use had done them some good. Twisted as it seemed, maybe ten years away from the Amazons was making me more of one.

"You don't work at it." Mother picked up the conversation like I hadn't even mentioned the hearth-keeper possibility.

"And neither will Harmony." I dropped the spoon on the table with a *thunk*.

"And neither will Harmony what?" My little pitcher strolled into the kitchen, a pink backpack slung over one shoulder.

"Make it to school on time if she doesn't get moving." I slid the box of cereal and a carton of milk across the table toward her and used my bare arm to wipe up a spill of milk.

"Not *Cheerios*. Lindy's baby brother eats them, for God's sake."

I turned my frown on my daughter. We might not worship mundane humans' God, but I believed in respect.

"Sorry, *goodness*' sake," she said, with a complete lack of remorse.

"Here. Eat." My gaze on Mother, I stood and plopped a bowl of cereal down in front of my daughter.

She stared at the bowl. "But I'll mess up my lip gloss."

"Eat," I demanded.

Mother arched one brow. I could read the gesture clear as day: *And this is what you want?*

I ran my hand over my head, my fingers tearing at my shoulder-length hair. I couldn't deal with all of this right now. The constant battle over telling Harmony about our past was hard enough to contend with at the best of times—but today, having so recently discovered the second girl, having carried her dead body in my arms—I wanted nothing more than to turn tail and run. Instead, I wrapped my hand around the wolf totem that hung from my neck and prayed silently for strength.

Tilting her head, Harmony studied us. "You weren't maybe . . . discussing . . ."—she shifted her blue gaze to Mother—"tattoos, were you?"

The prayer turning to a curse in my mind, I twisted around to face Mother more fully. Yet another old argument, and certainly not one I wanted to revisit today. Tattoos were more than body decoration for Amazons— a lot more. If done properly, they brought power to their owners. They were a blessing, and if the careful excision of the dead girls' *givnomai* tattoos were any indication, maybe a curse.

"It's not like *you* don't have any," Harmony continued, completely oblivious to the anger and frustration coursing through me. "Or like you'd have to worry about safety or anything. You could do it yourself." She unzipped her backpack and pulled out a catalog of standard tats my shop offered.

"Yes, Melanippe, it's time," a third voice chimed in.

Great, Bubbe was up. I closed my eyes a second, carefully slowing my heart rate, bringing my emotions back to a level that could pass for usual annoyance, then shot my grandmother a warning glare. If anything, it had even less effect on her than my mother.

Realizing I needed to put space between me and my too-observant grandmother, I picked up the milk and walked to the refrigerator.

"There's one right here." Harmony flipped open the catalog and placed a pink-tipped finger onto the page.

Bubbe shuffled closer and stared over her shoulder. By the grunt that followed, I guessed my grandmother didn't approve of Harmony's choice.

"It's a *hacekomoe*," Bubbe replied.

My Russian was rusty, but I could tell by my grandmother's tone whatever Harmony had chosen, it wasn't the source of mystical strength Bubbe had in mind.

"It's pretty," Harmony objected.

Another snort from Bubbe.

My emotions back under control—or at least well hidden—I wandered to the table and the open catalog. Harmony's carefully manicured finger was flattened over the image of a tiny pink-and-purple butterfly. I grinned, thoughts of serial killers being pushed from my mind for at least a few seconds as I enjoyed Bubbe's struggles with one of the world's most dreaded adversaries—a teenage girl intent on getting, well, anything.

"What, you don't like it, Bubbe?" I asked.

My response must have given Harmony hope. She beamed up at me, then jerked the neck of her mint-green T-shirt down to reveal the edge of a lace bra. "I was thinking I'd put it right here." She pointed to the top of her right breast.

My smile vanished. "I don't think so."

"You have one there," Harmony objected.

"Yeah, but it's . . ." I pursed my lips, struggling to suppress the image of two round patches of skin peeled back from a pair of young bodies.

"Not a *hacekomoe*," Bubbe burst into the conversation. "What strength will that give you? *Cobcem he*, I tell you." Sputtering, she stomped off.

"Harmony, a tattoo—" Mother began.

"Isn't for you." I jumped in, the words coming out unnecessarily terse. "You're too young. We've beaten this horse to death. End of discussion." I picked up Harmony's backpack, grabbing the catalog away from her when she moved to stuff it back inside. "Now you need to worry about getting to school." I gifted her with the look I'd tried on Mother and Bubbe. This time it worked.

With a huff, she flung her backpack across her shoulder and stomped down the steps to the front door.

"You have to tell her sometime." Mother pushed away from a pillar and strolled forward with feline grace.

I slipped the catalog into a junk drawer, then tramped to the nook where our upstairs computer sat. It was networked to three other computers, one in the basement where Mother worked out and Bubbe conned—make that *consulted with*, her clients—and two in my tattoo shop on the main floor, one in my office and the other at the reception desk. I'd given up the Amazons' nomadic way and with it their resistance to modern technology. Counting in my head to avoid screaming, I pulled out the chair and plopped down.

"Do I?" I asked.

"You know you do. Someday she's going to notice—"

I shot Mother a disbelieving look. "What? That she's stronger than the other girls? Or maybe more talented artistically? So? There's nothing unusual about either of those things."

"How about the fact that her great-grandmother is five hundred years old?"

"She doesn't look a day over seventy." I shook the mouse to snap the computer out of sleep mode, wishing I could snap Mother off as easily.

"At the very least, she should be working with me at the gym." Part of being a warrior, Mother didn't let go easily.

I gave up pretending to work. "Why? So she can learn to cleave a man's head from his shoulders with one swing of a broadaxe? Not a much-needed skill at West High— our property taxes get us that much, at least."

Mother wrapped a strong hand around my bicep, her gold snake bracelet brushing coolly against my skin. "The mothers of those other girls"—she nodded her head toward the TV—"probably thought that too."

I stared at the blue background of my computer's desktop, my shoulders tensing.

The grip on my arm changed to a stroke. "It would be good for her . . . she should know how to protect herself. Especially with what's going on. You may think we're protected because of who we are, but you can never be sure. Without training, who knows? Harmony might be too much the *girl* you want her to be—defenseless." Her hand dropped to her side and her voice hardened. "That last girl, the one they found today, she was just a couple of years older than Harmony."

A shiver passed over my skin and I closed my eyes. The dead girls delivered to me, the message—it couldn't involve Harmony. Could it?

Mother waited, a questioning expression flitting across her face.

Forcing myself to answer, I replied, "I'll think about it—there's no rush."

The buzzer sounded—signaling that my office manager and artist-in-training, Mandy, had arrived and it was time to get downstairs to the shop. We wouldn't open for a few hours, but I'd agreed to work with Mandy this morning on some basic skills like sterilization and making stencils. Glad for the escape, I deserted my computer and stood to leave.

"You never know how much time you have, Mel. Remember that."

Swallowing the lump that had formed in my throat, I turned on my heel and left the room.

Mother's words haunted me all day. I was stubborn and at times lied to myself, but I would never do anything to endanger Harmony. But had I endangered someone else's child? By keeping the discovery of the first girl from the Amazons, had I made it easier for the killer to take the second?

If so, I was going to rectify that tonight—at least somewhat.

It was after one in the morning. I'd driven two hours as fast as I dared—south from Madison, across the Wisconsin-Illinois border to a spot in the northern Illinois woods. It had taken me another fifteen minutes or so to find the rough path that led to the safe camp—an old farmstead surrounded by trees.

There were six such safe camps in the U.S. All were located in areas as remote as possible, never too close to a major city. The closest town to the camp I was visiting had a population under two thousand. There were cities of fifty thousand-plus within an hour's drive or so. The Amazons tended to go to one of them, where they could blend in more easily, for most of their business. The camps all had cover stories; they were explained away to any curious locals as church camps, vacation time shares, or charity operations that trained delinquent girls. And there were wards too, defensive spells that didn't completely hide the camps but made the entrances less noticeable and would lead any intruders on meandering walks that always took them back where they'd started. Luckily, the ward used here was a simple piece of magic. To outsmart it you didn't have to unwind it, just know it was there. Which I did.

The barn was closed up, horses left to wander freely inside the fenced area that included the house and over two acres of cleared pasture. I crept past a palomino mare, placing my palm flat against her side to calm her. Mother had the real talent with horses—came with the warrior skills—but I'd spent enough time with the creatures to at least be comfortable . . . and most important, to make the horses *think* I was comfortable. Just like Amazons—show a horse you were nervous and she'd push you as far as she could. That was the one horse skill I'd truly mastered—hiding absolutely any sign of discomfort, no matter how much the horse got in my space.

As if reading my mind, the mare turned to nose me. I shoved my hand against her velvety skin and pushed her face away from mine. With a soft snort, she wandered away.

I stood motionless, alone, staring at the dark house, wondering who was inside. Anyone I knew? Anyone I missed? Anyone I hated?

My heart began to beat loudly, my blood growing thick in my veins. My brows lowered and a growl formed at the back of my throat. At that same instant my hand brushed against the bulge in my pocket where I'd stored the two necklaces I'd taken from the dead teens. I shook my head, knocking aside the old resentments and past wrongs to concentrate on why I was here. I pulled the two figures free, holding one in each fist. A leopard and a bear: two of the most powerful totems.

Powerful or not, the totems hadn't protected the girls. A shudder shook my body and I clenched the small figures more tightly in my hands. My thoughts were wandering, my emotions taking over. There was no time for that. I had to leave these symbols so the Amazons would find them, so they would know something was wrong, and I had to do it quickly.

Focusing on my task, I crept toward the house. A few feet away I sensed magic—protective or destructive, I wasn't sure. I paced a few feet to my right, then my left, and quickly decided a second more intricate ward had been set up encircling the house. Perhaps the Amazons were aware they were being targeted, or maybe the current high priestess assigned to this safe camp was just more cautious than Bubbe had been when she held the position.

I paused briefly and noticed for the first time that the horses didn't wander within the warded circle. The animals probably worked as a first line of alarm. The ward was something more . . . disturbing, at least to whoever triggered it.

I considered my options. Disabling the spell was my gut instinct—more to prove I could than from need— but I quickly realized the folly of such a plan. If I unraveled the spell, the Amazons would know one of their kind had left the necklaces—one of their kind with priestess skills. They would not suspect me; I was only thought of as an artisan, but Bubbe would quickly come to mind.

With that decided, I looked for a likely spot to leave the fetishes. My first thought was to tie them onto one of the horses' manes, but I couldn't know which animal would be ridden first. Horses were an important part of Amazon life, but nowadays more tradition than necessity. There was no guarantee the animal I chose would be ridden or groomed today—and I wanted the necklaces found soon. Instead, my gaze traveled to the horses' replacements—a couple of battered trucks, a panel van, and a pair of ancient imports.

After selecting one of the imports, the one without a cracked windshield, I wrapped the two thongs around the driver's door handle. To make sure my trip didn't go unnoticed, I dragged a wooden bench from under a nearby tree and laid it across the hood.

After brushing off my hands, I was ready to go, except for one thing. I glanced back at the house. The priestess who had set the ward was experienced and obviously wary. And I'd had the necklaces in my possession for some time, close to my body, even. Odds were she would be able to detect something of me on the objects.

Made me doubly thankful I'd come prepared to erase all signs of myself from the scene. I reached into my jacket and pulled out a bundle of juniper and a lighter. Burning the herb and spreading the smoke would cleanse the necklaces and the area of my presence—completely, I hoped.

I tapped the light on my watch—after two A.M. I was running out of time. I knew nothing of the habits of the particular Amazons in this safe house. At least I didn't think I did. I hoped the major players had changed in the ten years since I had left. But nervous high priestesses and queens tended to be nocturnal. They could start moving around at any time. Not to mention I still had the drive back to Madison. The high priestess in my life, Bubbe, could very well be up before I returned.

Still, I had to do what I could. Pulling in a breath, I flicked the lighter and counted to myself as I waited for the herbs to crackle and catch. Within seconds, smoke streamed out of the bundle. Murmuring a prayer of forgiveness for my lie of omission, I waved the herbs around, paying extra attention to the car, bench, and necklaces. When I was done, I snuffed the herbs with a handful of dust and shoved the still-warm sticks back into my jacket.

It was then I noticed the horse. I could almost see the imprint of my palm shining back at me from where I'd placed my hand on her side.

Damn. Relighting the herbs was out—waving a bundle of smoldering sticks around a horse was never a good idea, especially when you were trying *not* to be noticed. The best I could do was rub the actual dried herbs over the spot and hope that did the trick. I broke off a few bits and walked toward the mare, empty hand held up.

She let me get within three feet before backing up and

letting out a whinny. Then, shaking her head, she began to buck—setting off a chain reaction that soon had fifteen horses stampeding around the paddock. The mare raced once around, then ground to a halt in front of me, the white spot on her nose dancing up and down as she tossed her head.

She was laughing at me, the bitch. *Wrong animal, but the sentiment held.*

A window flew up in the house and I knew Amazons would flow out the doors in minutes. With a curse, I wrapped my arm around the troublemaking mare's neck and threw myself onto her back. This time she played along; at a gallop we raced across the paddock. As we approached the fence, I prayed she'd been trained well—she had. Without breaking stride, she vaulted, clearing the gate by inches.

We rode on, down the gravel path, until I could see the spot where I'd left my truck. As I slid down her side, she stood patiently, waiting. Remembering the juniper, I reached in my pocket, only to find it gone.

I stared at the mare for another beat, wondering if the Amazons would sense me on her. She stared back, still waiting. Realizing I'd already wasted too much time, I shook off my uneasiness and smacked her once on her rump. Only then did she move, taking off down the path back toward the camp.

Definitely well trained. I stared after her . . . wondering. Then I shook my head and forced myself back in the present.

When I left the Amazons, I left everything about them, even my family, for a time. It was too late for regrets now. Besides, if the mare belonged to whom I suspected, she wouldn't let childhood friendships stop her from hunting me down—not if she learned I was the one who'd sneaked into the camp.

She would want answers, and she wouldn't be subtle about getting them. Just like she hadn't been subtle ten years earlier when she'd stood with the High Priestess against me.

Chapter Three

When I woke the next morning—three hours past my normal waking time—my first thoughts were of the Amazons: had they found my clues? Did they know what they meant? Would my small message be enough to save another teen? And had they sensed my presence? I'd dropped the juniper, but that would offer only the smallest of clues. My energy smeared all over the mare would be much harder to miss—by a high priestess as powerful as, say, my grandmother anyway. There weren't many as old as Bubbe, or as skilled, but it was a possibility. Were the Amazons already putting together a plan to drag me back to the council? To find out what I knew and how?

At that juncture I had no way of knowing the answers to any of those questions, but I was sure of one thing: hiding my unwilling involvement in the deaths was the right choice. If anything, my visit the night before, the roiling of my stomach when I'd first seen the house, remembering how even my best friend had turned against me, had confirmed that.

I'd done what I could to alert the Amazons, and the police were already investigating. It was enough; it had to be. I couldn't even share what had happened with Mother or Bubbe. Odds were they would feel they had to alert the Amazons directly, which would mean me facing the Amazons. It wasn't going to happen.

So, to keep up the facade of my carefully crafted world, I ignored the gnawing of my conscience, smashed aside all thoughts of Amazons, and went down the worn marble stairs that connected our living area to the main floor and my office.

The reception area was nothing but a couple of tall chairs in front of a barlike structure made of paneling and plywood. The shop wouldn't open for another hour, and I had no early morning meetings, so I had the place to myself. I walked around the reception desk/bar and opened the glass-and-wood door that hid my office. The room had housed the school's principal in its past life. My employees commented on that whenever I called them in to talk. Having been homeschooled myself or, more accurately, "road schooled," since I grew up traveling from place to place, I got no negative vibes when entering the space, but it didn't bother me that others did. There was nothing wrong with starting out with an upper hand—the principal thing did that for me.

A folder thick with papers sat squarely on the center of my desk.

Interview day. With everything going on, I'd forgotten.

Artemis bless Mandy for remembering.

My hand drifted down to the manila folder and rested there. Our business was growing—a good thing—and it was time to add an artist, also good. But I couldn't help question if now was the best time to be adding a new employee to the mix—another set of eyes to take note of whatever strange thing happened next.

This was no spur-of-the-moment decision. We'd talked about hiring another artist in our weekly staff meetings for months. If I backed out now, it would turn more than one pair of curious—make that outraged—eyes on me.

To make matters worse, even in the best times hiring an artist could be tricky. To work for me they had to be the absolute best at what they did, and they had to ignore little things like Bubbe's spell casting and Mother's weapon practice in the basement below the shop.

Oh, and female. They had to be female.

Female—like the dead girls. I shook my head and stared down at the folder. Putting the deaths to the back of my mind wasn't going to be easy, but somehow I had to—interviewing artists was as good a way as any. Resolved to the necessity, I heaved out a breath and flipped open the folder to see what my day had in store.

There were four applications inside, each with a time noted in the margin. My first was in ten minutes, a recent high school graduate with nothing more exciting to offer than a couple of art classes—and he was male. I shuffled his application to the side. I hadn't told Mandy about my gender preference for employees. I could do what I wanted, but I couldn't be obvious about it, which meant I'd have to interview any men who looked qualified. And while I didn't have to give them serious consideration, it had to look as if I did.

The next two were also male. One had twenty years of experience in one of the top shops in Miami. I frowned. Not hiring him would be hard to justify. Tapping my pencil against the table, I said a silent prayer to Artemis that he arrived reeking of booze.

Number three had only a couple years of tattoo experience. The woman could surely beat that.

Thankfully, she did—ten years of experience, numerous awards, and recommendations out of this world. Ding, ding, ding. We had a winner; now all I had to do was get through the other interviews as quickly as possible, making note of all the men's failings, and I'd be suitably protected from any potential legal problems.

At twelve thirty on the nose, my first interview arrived. He looked around nervously, obviously taking note when Mother stopped behind the reception desk dressed in Lycra shorts and a snug-fitting sport top. The old school's full-size gym was in a second building next door, but Mother had claimed a room in the basement for her weights. She was down there more often than not and had a better body than most twenty-year-old human aerobics instructors. The artist I was interviewing noticed. He was also young, cute, and easy to mark off my list without a trace of guilt.

The second, Mr. Experienced from Miami, seemed to have as many issues with working for a woman as I did hiring a man.

"I thought your name was Mel," he grumbled, reaching up to grab a cigarette he had stashed behind one ear.

"It is." I didn't bother explaining I was named for one of the original Amazons, Melanippe, a direct descendent of Ares and Otrera. Somehow I didn't think he would be all that impressed.

"It all women here?" He leaned to the side to see around my office door out into the shop.

I folded my arms over my breasts and smiled. Tattooing is a sacred business for Amazons—one exclusively performed by women, for obvious reasons. Men just don't have the same spiritual depth. I found it endlessly funny that in the modern world men had come to dominate the art. Of course, it also explained why most tattoos today no longer possessed the power they should.

"You have a problem with that?" I shifted my snake bracelet a little higher on my wrist, making sure the ruby eyes were pointed directly at my applicant, then smiled. I wasn't putting the mojo on him or anything, but I was thinking about it—hard.

He shivered. "No, I guess not—just weird, s'all."

"Yes, weird."

I was suddenly bored and antsy to get things moving. I still had one more fake interview to complete before the woman/*real* applicant arrived.

"Well, it's been nice. We'll call you." Or not. I ushered him out of my office.

A wave of surprise washed over his face, but he left. I followed him to the front, just to make sure. When he trudged down the steps to the front door, I wiped my hands together. Two down, one to go. Gotta love efficiency.

A man in his midthirties stepped inside as the second candidate left. He had dark hair and brows that drew attention to chocolatey eyes. He also had some impressive art on one arm, a quarter sleeve of mountains and stars. However, it was the portfolio tucked under said arm that led me to the ingenious assumption that he was applicant number three.

Kind of old for only a couple years of experience. I pegged him as a tattoo addict who thought he could do it himself.

This would be easy. I waved Mandy back to her spot behind the reception desk and held out a hand in greeting.

"You must be here for the interview."

He stopped two steps from the top, analyzing me from the tips of my well-used hikers to the top of my baseball-cap-covered head. I felt an insane urge to yank the hat off and run my fingers through my shoulder-length auburn hair.

Primping was not a usual Amazon urge. Irritated, I jerked my hand back and scowled.

"I'm here to see Mel," he announced.

Another one. "I'm Mel." I waited for the shock and outrage that he had been scammed by my masculine name.

"Really?" Confusion flitted through his dark eyes. "I was expecting someone . . ."

My scowl transformed into a smirk. I was starting to enjoy this; it was amusing and it kept my mind off the deaths . . . well, somewhat. "Yes, you were expecting someone . . ." I prompted.

He finished climbing the last two steps, stopping just inches from me. With the confusion still apparent on his face, he looked down at me.

"Taller. I thought you'd be taller."

Well, hell.

I was a measly five eight. My mother was six foot two. I'd never met my father, but I suspected he was a midget. My outspoken interviewee had to be pushing six four. He had over half a foot on me. Strangely enough, it did not endear him to me.

"You have a height requirement for interviews?" Yeah, I was bitter. Yeah, it showed.

Busy studying the top of my Wisconsin Badger cap, it took him a while to answer. When he did, he seemed at least somewhat embarrassed by his prior declaration.

"No, it's just, what with . . ." He stopped, switching his attention to Mandy, who was eyeballing him like a cat that's just spied the last bowl of cream. I half expected her to lick her lips in anticipation.

This time I did yank off my cap and slapped it down

on the reception desk. "Mandy, why don't you order some more bandages? Janet said she was running low."

My office manager didn't seem in any big hurry to get back to work, so I picked my cap up and strode around the counter. "My office is back here. Might as well get on with it."

Mr. Six Four, Peter Arpada, according to his application, managed to tear himself away from the reception desk and followed.

By the time we reached my private space, I'd regained a sense of calm. It wasn't that I was sensitive about being short, for an Amazon anyway. It was just that not many people pointed it out. Which, come to think of it, brought a question to mind. He didn't know I was an Amazon.

"Why did you expect me to be tall?" I blurted the question out before he had a chance to sit in the chair recently deserted by bad candidate number two.

"Oh, I don't know." He unzipped his portfolio and began flipping through pages. "The name, I guess, and the tattoo thing. I just expected someone different."

He smiled, and I tried hard to keep my face stern. There was an insult in there somewhere, but it was hard to focus on it under the full power of his pearly whites. I decided to let the whole height thing go and just work on marking him off my list as fast as I could.

"Let's see what you got." I held out my hand.

I should have been warned by the confident tilt his head took as he slapped the leather case into my hand, but I wasn't. Nothing could have prepared me for what I saw inside.

"These are . . . nice," I murmured. Nice my ass, these were killer. Not to be completely egotistical, but I hadn't seen anything this good outside of my own shop, created by me. I flipped to a wolf head, done in portrait style, then quickly moved to the more abstract stuff. The colors were especially good choices; pausing on the image of a woman's arm with a Celtic dragon wrapped around it, I frowned.

"What's your story?" I asked.

He paused, his hands splayed over the tops of his denim-clad legs. I couldn't help but notice how strong and efficient his hands looked, with long fingers and neatly clipped nails.

"My story?"

The question brought my attention back to his face.

"Yeah, you know, your history." I pointed to the image in front of me. "This looks like you have graffiti in your past."

"Oh." He gifted me with another thousand-watt smile. "I learned the style the old-fashioned way, with a spray can and a blank wall. You know teenagers—too much energy and too little to do. Graffiti beat the other options."

I responded with a noncommittal grunt. I wasn't interested in discussing excess teenage energy and what it might cause right now.

"Portrait and graffiti. Don't see an artist who can do

both too often." I couldn't help it. I was impressed. And not only could he do both, he rocked at both. I closed my eyes for a few beats, then reopened them. He was still there, and he was still male. He reached up to rub the back of his neck, causing his U2 concert tee to pull tight across his chest—very male.

"You have any problem working with women?" I blurted out.

"No, not at all." His lips tilted into another dangerous smile. "I like women."

My heart slammed against my chest. Not good. I so didn't need this right now—not ever.

Doing my best to pretend every inch of my body wasn't tingling with awareness, I stood up and held out his portfolio. "Very nice, but I have a few more candidates to consider. I have your number. I'll be in touch either way."

He leveled an assessing stare in my direction before accepting the portfolio. "Let me give you my cell-phone number. I'm out a lot." Reaching inside the leather case, he pulled out the sheet with the wolf portrait on it, then, before I could object, scribbled a number along the bottom.

"I have notepaper," I replied, staring at the sample of his work. I knew it was only a copy, that he had to keep an original somewhere else, but the depiction of the wolf was so accurate, the eyes so piercing, it seemed criminal to use it casually for scrap. It didn't help that the wolf was the traditional symbol for my clan. In fact, on the small of my back was a tattoo eerily similar to the one resting on the desk in front of me.

"But this is more memorable. I don't want you to forget me. Besides, I can see you like wolves." His gaze dropped to the wolf fetish nestled between my breasts, then flicked back to my face.

I stiffened in response. With a grin, he slid the paper across my desk toward me.

My eyes jumped from the image of the wolf to his tan face. Brown eyes filled with shrewd assessment stared back at me—like he expected something more, a reaction of some sort. A flutter of disquiet passed through me.

Without pausing to think, I placed my hand palm down onto the image, then held my breath, waiting. I'm not sure what I expected. It was silly, really. He was a man, and men just didn't have the power needed to convert ink into something more. And even a priestess couldn't create an image on paper capable of containing energy. Tattoos could only contain energy when attached to a living, breathing being, making it all the stranger that the dead girls' tattoos had been removed. Realizing I was back to thinking about the teens and making assumptions about what the killer knew, I frowned, then knocked the thoughts aside. Back to the problem at hand.

Under my palm, the paper felt cool and smooth—not even an indentation where the drawing was. *Because it's just a copy, dimwit.* Feeling silly, I jerked my palm up and balled my hand at my side.

"Well, thanks. Like I said, I'll be in touch."

He hesitated, long enough I thought he might argue, but he just slid his portfolio under his arm, flicked one long piece of unruly hair out of his eyes, and stood to leave.

I glanced at the wolf. Its gray eyes gleamed back at me, urging me to stop this man from going. I shoved the paper under a folder and plastered an efficient smile on my face. "Should know by the end of the week." The sentence sounded false even to my ears, but my applicant just smiled and turned to leave.

"Wait." The word passed my lips before my common sense could stop it.

He paused, his expression unreadable.

"The dragon. Do you think I could have a copy of that too? I'd like to show these"—I gestured to the folder that now hid the wolf from view—"to my partner, my mother. In case it's a close decision." Technically, my mother was my business partner, but I ran the place. I had no more intention of showing her his work than I did of giving Harmony a tattoo. But it was a good excuse, and I really wanted another look at that dragon.

If he thought my request odd, he didn't show it. Just pulled out the Celtic dragon image and held it out toward my desk. I reached for it, but he dropped it too quickly. In a graceful zigzag motion it floated like a feather caught on a breeze before landing faceup in front of me.

I refused to look at it again until he left. So, I stood there waiting while he nodded a last good-bye and wandered from my office. When I was sure he was gone, I strode to the door and pushed it closed with a click.

Back behind my desk, I pulled out the wolf and stared down at both pictures. They were fantastic—no doubt about that—but mystical? I ran one finger over the surface of the dragon. Nothing. Just ink and paper. I let out a breath in a relieved puff; obviously, the tension of the past few weeks was getting to me.

Nothing like letting your imagination run wild.

Rubbing the bridge of my nose, I held the dragon up to the window. Still, there was something about his work that was familiar. The thought nagged at me, knocking around in my head like a discarded soda can in the back of a pickup truck.

Try as I might, I couldn't shake anything solid loose. Not that it mattered. I wasn't hiring him no matter how talented he was.

Forcing myself not to give either piece another look, I balled up the images and tossed them in the trash.

Chapter Four

Candidate number four dressed like she was trying out for some rock-chick reality show. Unfortunately, she was over forty and the black eyeliner didn't do her crow's feet any favors. However, she was also prompt and female. What more could I ask for?

"I don't do feet," she announced, plopping down into a chair. "And I don't do cover-ups. Not my job to be fixing someone else's mistake."

Okay. Feet didn't tend to be anyone's favorite part of the body to tattoo, and I could understand her stance on trying to cover up someone else's work—kind of.

"Maybe we should talk about what you *do* do." I riffled through her file, searching for her résumé. I pulled it out and scanned it. "You have a very impressive list of experience here."

"I know my stuff." She crossed her arms over her chest and leaned back against the wooden office chair. Her slashed tee slipped off one shoulder.

"So, what you do . . ." I prompted.

" 'Bout anything. I'm not picky. If they can pay, I'll tattoo 'em." She reached up to pat the shell of hair spray that kept her streaked hair in its high-rise ponytail. "Oh, except memorials. Can't stand memorials. Had a guy a few years ago who was blubbering before I even had the stencil on him. It was embarrassing."

Okay. No feet, no cover-ups, and no memorials. She had just described 40 percent of our business.

"Well, let's look at what you brought with you." I held out my hand for the manila envelope she had shoved into the chair beside her.

As she pried it out from beneath a leather-covered thigh, I tried to maintain a positive outlook. I just needed an extra set of hands. So, she had a few self-imposed limits. I could work around that.

Ignoring the coffee stains on the outside of the envelope, I pulled out a stack of papers. On the top was a giant red rose with a feather dangling from one leaf.

"Nice," I commented and flipped to the next page. A group of yellow roses designed to fit onto the lower back. I smiled and turned to the next one. A rose wrapped around a heart. I was beginning to see a theme. Giving my guest a weak smile, I spread the remaining pages across my desktop. Nothing but roses in the entire bunch.

"You like roses."

She gave me a surprised look. "Of course; it's my thing."

At my blank stare, she continued, "Rose." She pointed to herself.

Oh yeah, her name—Rose. "But you do other things, right?" I tried to keep the statement positive.

"Sure, sure. I told you. I do it all."

"Except feet, cover-ups, and memorials," I couldn't help but add.

"That's right." She nodded her head, a look of complete sincerity on her face.

While I was trying to decide if Rose was worth her numerous thorns, Bubbe appeared by the open door. When she saw I was inside the office, she disappeared. She was quick, but not quick enough. There was no missing the ancient bone knife she grasped in one hand, or the squirming rabbit dangling from the other.

Uh-oh. My chair screeched across the wood floor as I shoved it away from my desk. My gaze shot back to Rose. "Well, thanks for stopping by. I have a few more interviews today, then you'll hear back from us."

She frowned. "Hey, but what's the pay? My last job, I rented. Gave the shop twenty percent for the space. You work out a deal like that?"

"Hard to say." I grabbed her by her fuchsia fingertips and jerked her out of her seat. "My office manager will give you a call."

Checking her manicure, she cast a suspicious look

over her shoulder at me and stomped out. I waited until the door to the shop closed behind her before spinning on my heel and going in search of Bubbe.

The door to her basement office was closed.

I didn't knock.

"Bubbe, what exactly do you think—" I stopped mid-tirade. A suburban mom dressed in yoga pants and pink cami top glanced up at me. In her hands was the stone knife, which shook violently above the quivering body of the rabbit. Bubbe held the rabbit by feet and ears.

"Bubbe!" I shrieked.

The soccer mom jumped backward, letting the knife clatter onto the cement floor. Bubbe barely cocked an eyebrow.

"Yes, *devochka moya*," she replied.

Bubbe liked to speak in Russian, especially in front of her clients. Her childhood was spent roaming the steppes in what is now called Russia, and everything from her clothing to her accent was calculated to remind you of that. Never mind that she had lived in America for around a hundred and fifty years.

"Drop the rabbit," I ordered. I wasn't completely sure what Bubbe had in mind for the little cottontail, but I didn't need locals thinking we practiced animal sacrifice.

"Pfft." She turned her back on me and gestured to the wide-eyed woman who had pressed her back so tightly against the wall I was afraid she'd leave a perfect size-six impression in the concrete. "Pick up the knife," Bubbe told her.

The woman glanced from me to Bubbe, obviously weighing which one of us was more dangerous. It was times like this I wished I'd inherited my mother's six-foot-two-inch frame. Unfortunately, without it, I just didn't look intimidating. And, thanks to Bubbe's high priestess status, she didn't need it.

My grandmother murmured a few words, and the air around her seemed to shift, making her look larger and darker. Cool air nipped at my ankles. The old reprobate was actually casting a spell to strengthen her position. I could have countercast but, number one, I didn't want to alert her to my newly found powers and, number two, me taking on Bubbe magically would have been like a field mouse taking on a cougar.

I still could have stopped her, but it would have meant throwing myself across the room and knocking her to the ground. Not exactly a tale I wanted Bubbe's client to be sharing with her friends over lattes. I couldn't give up completely, though. So, drawing myself up as tall as I could, I took a step forward and did my best to look threatening.

The soccer mom's gaze danced from me to Bubbe to the knife. Her hands quivered, and a thin sheen of sweat appeared over her upper lip.

I stared her down, willing her to stay safely against her wall and away from my grandmother's bunny-killing plans.

Bubbe murmured something else and flicked one finger toward the other woman's midsection. Her lower lip clamped between her teeth; the suburban mom folded her hands over her lower stomach, then with a breath that made her entire body shiver, squatted and slid her hand toward the knife.

I hated when my bluff was called.

"Bubbe," I warned.

My grandmother ignored me. "Remember what I told you. Just run it down his body."

I couldn't let this go on. Annoyed with Bubbe for giving me no more notice than she would a snot-nosed youngster, I took a step forward, right into the soccer mom's path.

"I said to stop." I faced Bubbe, fairly confident the other woman wouldn't decide to use the knife on me instead of the rabbit.

Still holding the bunny tight, Bubbe sighed, her lined face tired and sad. "What are you so afraid of, *devochka*?"

"Nothing, but you can't do this"—I motioned around the room—"here."

"This?" She shook her head. "You don't even know what 'this' is. If you did, you wouldn't have your—what you call it?—panties in such a wad."

I flushed. This was not a conversation I wanted to have in front of a customer—even if she was Bubbe's customer.

"She will not hurt the little bunny. Just give him a shave. Hair, that is all. No blood." She looked back at the woman. "You want a baby? Come. Let's finish this."

I blinked. Hair? That was it? I'd embarrassed myself

to save a rabbit from a close shave—literally? Even more embarrassed, I mumbled an apology under my breath and stumbled from the room.

"Amazons gave up paying a blood price, even rabbit blood, four hundred years ago." Mother stood in the doorway of her gym, dabbing her chest with a damp towel. Wet with sweat, her light brown hair looked almost as dark as mine. "You know that."

My mind stuttered. Blood price—could that be what the dead teens were? An arrow in my head began to whirl. Was this the killer's motivation?

"All Amazons?" I asked, my mind wrestling with the suspicion.

"We're talking about Bubbe." She gave the towel an impatient snap and stalked back into her gym.

I glanced toward my grandmother's workroom, guilt causing my gaze to fall short. I loved Bubbe, but still . . . I thought of the rabbit, his ears clutched in Bubbe's fingers. How could Mother expect me not to think she was going to kill the little carrot snatcher?

Feeling somewhat justified, I turned and followed Mother. Her gym was cool and quiet, as if the stacks of iron weights soaked up any stray noise that dared attempt to enter the room. Usually I found the place relaxing, but today tension streamed from Mother. My sense of vindication quickly dissipated, and I had to resist the urge to twist with discomfort like a guilty two-year-old. I covered with attitude.

"I never know what Bubbe may do," I said, defensiveness raising my voice.

She snorted. "You know what she won't do. She never supported the blood price or the mutilation. None of it. None of her children ever suffered—not even her sons."

"Not even her sons," I repeated, my fingernails jabbing into palms. Yet another sore spot. In the last few days it seemed like every scab I had had been picked to bleeding.

I'd first learned about my grandmother's sons when I was pregnant with my own. When they were only hours old, she'd left them on a doctor's doorstep—helpless little bundles, discarded, forgotten. I hadn't understood it then, and I didn't understand it now.

Mother picked up a fifty-pound dumbbell and began doing curls. I'd have thought she hadn't noticed the effect this topic still had on me, except for her next words. "Just because you didn't want to give up the boy you carried, doesn't mean Bubbe did anything wrong. You need to let it go."

Harsh as her words sounded, she didn't say them in a bad way—more resolved and a tad morose—like she had let me down. Which she had. Pretty much everyone had.

I'd never considered the abortion that many pregnant Amazons chose when they carried a male child. And at first I'd even agreed to give my son up for a human adoption, thinking in the long run it would be for his best, but then, as he grew inside me, as I'd felt him move, seen his foot shoving against my stomach, I'd lost my resolve.

It was almost the twenty-first century at the time. Amazons had all but disappeared from history, most people thinking us nothing more than legend, made up. Wasn't it time for us to give up the old ways we still clung to? To blend with humans rather than live on the outskirts, stealing and cheating while telling ourselves it was okay because we were superior—descended from gods?

I'd told everyone my plan, knowing it would be rough at first, but trusting that the women around me would understand, that those I'd grown up with, especially, would support me. I'd been wrong.

And then the unthinkable had happened. An otherwise problem-free pregnancy had ended—but my child didn't survive. I didn't even get to hold him. His body was carted off while I was still passed out, buried in an unmarked grave somewhere in the northern Illinois woods.

Amazons were strong. They didn't die in childbirth, and neither did their children.

Try as they might, no one could convince me my child had been the first. I even knew who had been responsible, but no one wanted to listen. The loss of a son? Not worth stirring up trouble in the tribe—if my accusations were true, the Amazon in question had just done what she thought was right. And as current high priestess of the safe camp, she'd had that right.

I had taken my daughter and left.

Bubbe and Mother had followed. They had never

asked forgiveness for not standing by my side, but they had left the tribe, and that was huge. For Harmony's sake, I'd found it within myself to forgive them, but not the rest. Nothing in the world could make me forgive them—just like nothing in the world could make me encourage Harmony to become one of them.

Lost in unpleasant thoughts of the past, I walked over to spot Mother as she slid under a barbell loaded with weights.

She pushed the heavy load up and held it for a count of ten before lowering it again to her chest. She completed eight more reps before continuing.

"You need to let it go."

"What happened? Where are they?" I couldn't help but ask, my anger melting into something close to melancholy. I'd wanted to keep my child so badly; how had Bubbe turned her back on not one son, but three?

My mother jumped up, took two more ten-pound weights from the nearby rack, and slid one on each end of the bar. "I don't know. It was long before me. She gave them away. You know that."

Something flickered in Mother's eyes, making me wonder if there was more she didn't want to tell me—didn't want to risk opening my only partially closed wounds even further. Or maybe she actually experienced regret for not knowing her brothers.

I picked up the towel Mother had dropped and ran the rough material through my hands.

"You think they're still alive?" I asked, my gaze drifting to the corner of the room. Somehow I couldn't bear to look at Mother when she answered.

"Who?" Mother had slid back under the bar.

I let my gaze flit back. She knew what I was talking about—it was just her way of telling me she'd had enough. Well, I hadn't.

"Your brothers," I replied.

Hands tight around the bar, she stared up at me. "Half brothers."

I made a *whatever* motion with my hand. To ensure secrecy and survival, Amazons didn't go for long-term relationships. Most likely all of Bubbe's children were from different fathers.

Mother huffed out an impatient breath. "Alive? I doubt it. Men can't be Amazons. They would have had mortal life spans."

I hadn't thought of that. It made it all sadder somehow. "How about their kids?" I asked.

"More like great-great-grandkids, if anything. Too many greats to matter." She started to lift the bar but stopped, letting it settle back onto the stand. "You're forgetting the point. Bubbe never went along with tradition for tradition's sake and she never sanctioned harming a living creature without cause. You need to trust her—trust us. Trust that being an Amazon is a good thing—something you should share with Harmony."

Like that was ever going to happen, especially now, when my suspicions were growing that the person who had deposited the dead teens on my doorstep was an Amazon sending me some ugly message. Disgusted with the whole topic, I dropped the towel onto her bare midriff and turned to leave.

"Melanippe," she called after me. I was tempted to keep walking, but catching a glimpse of her expression, I waited. The flicker I'd noticed earlier was back in her eyes. "The people you can count on most are those like you—start trusting them."

Then she plopped back down on her back, gritted her teeth, and bench-pressed more weight than a pair of NFL linebackers hyped up on two thousand dollars' worth of illegal steroids could.

I shook my head. People like me? If they were out there, they weren't Amazons. That I knew for sure.

Swallowing the dry lump in my throat, I left.

I took the front steps, the ones that led to the main entrance of the school and a small landing, then continued on to the first floor and my shop. Mandy had left the doors open, and a crisp fall breeze tossed a few early leaves onto the parquet.

My chat with Mother had left me disturbed, again. It added to the angst I'd been barely keeping reined in since discovering the first dead teen and being forced to get back in touch with my Amazon skills.

I had spent the last ten years trying not to think about the whole Amazon thing. And although living with Mother and Bubbe had made that difficult, if I tried really hard, I could go weeks, months, without dwelling on what the Amazons took from me—how my life would be different if I had been born something other than an Amazon.

Thinking about Bubbe's sons out there, somewhere—or at least their descendents—brought it all screaming back at me. What an insane tradition. Cutting off half the population, your own sons, brothers, and fathers, because they were male. Not that humans hadn't done it too, didn't still do it some places. The irony being they tended to dispose of their females, leave them out in the cold or drop them down a well. However, human wrongdoings didn't lessen those of the Amazons.

And . . . I paused on the landing and placed a shaking hand against the wall . . . I wasn't guilt-free. The realization rocked me to my core. I couldn't do something as simple as hire a man to work for me.

How could I expect to get past what had happened to me and to raise Harmony as a modern, accepting human when I refused to even consider a highly qualified male as a tattoo artist? I was a total hypocrite.

The realization lowered my already dipping self-image to something barely above complete waste of water and carbon.

I leaned my forehead against the cool plaster and closed my eyes. I'd spent the last ten years feeling all high and mighty, superior for lowering myself to mingle with humans, but when you boiled it down, I was as biased as any Amazon.

The only thing I had done differently since my son

had died was hide—from other Amazons, our past, and the truth of who I was.

I lifted my forehead and stared out into the front yard at the crumbling base of the old flagpole and the sign propped against it stating our hours.

I might not be able to undo thousands of years of wrongs. I might not even be able to lead the dead teens' souls to their loved ones, at least right now, but I could change a few hard-held prejudices. I thumped my fist against my chest.

I turned and ran up the steps to my office and my phone.

My unpleasant self-realization and my decision to break the chain of old prejudices made me feel better for the rest of my workday. But as I puttered around, getting ready for bed, the glow wore off and the faces of the two dead teens floated back to the forefront of my brain. I brushed my teeth seeing their images instead of my own in the bathroom mirror. After forcing myself to return to my room and bed, I managed to get to sleep, but awakened less than an hour later, still thinking of them. I waited another hour to do something about it.

I crept out the front and walked around to our small side yard. The way the school was angled on the lot protected the area from street view, and a row of eight-foot-tall holly bushes cut us off from our neighbor's house. Someone *could* look down from the windows above; Mother's bedroom was on this side, but it was toward the back. I picked a spot close to the front, under the kitchen window.

After a quick glance around, I squatted back on my heels and placed the flashlight I'd covered with cloth to dim the beam onto the dirt next to me. It was one A.M., a time of morning I'd come to dread—waking tense, alert for any sound. This time no outside force had awakened me—just my own nagging guilt. I had to know if the Amazons had gotten my message, and the middle of the night was really the only time I could be somewhat confident my family would be occupied and not stumble over me casting spells. Any of them discovering I even *could* cast spells was not something I wanted to deal with.

So one A.M. and here I was, squatting in the dirt, ready to call on Artemis and find out if the Amazons had gotten my message. Artemis might not be able to direct me to the girls' killer, but she could certainly help me plug into the tribe.

I flattened my bare palms into the soil, connecting, letting my body soak in the power that pulsed from deep in the earth's core. I needed all the strength I could get to do this. Linking myself spiritually to the Amazons again, after all these years . . . it was something I'd thought I'd never do.

Shaking off a renewed swell of anger—this one completely selfish, angry that the killer had chosen me to suck into her twisted world, leaving me with no choice but to face my heritage, at least to a degree—I carefully plucked acorns from the leather pouch I'd stolen from Bubbe's workroom and piled them in front of me. Next, I unwrapped two tiny stone figures: a bear and a leopard, not too different from the ones I'd left at the safe camp. The fetishes would help me link to the girls' families. If my message had been received, the totems would tell me; their clans' mourning would tell me.

I built the fire, a tiny one, but big enough, I hoped. I couldn't risk anything larger; performing the ceremony in my side yard was risky enough. I certainly didn't need the neighbors calling the fire department on me.

As the fire crackled, I tossed one of the acorns onto the blaze and murmured a prayer to Artemis.

"Artemis, huntress of the moon, guide me along the path to truth. Grant me the strength to see through the mist, to feel what those of this totem feel, to know what otherwise they might hide from me."

Smoke snaked from the fire: twisting, turning, morphing.

The world shifted beneath me and my nails gouged into the damp earth. The musky scent of decayed leaves filled my nostrils, then the smoke shifted again, this time taking on the round shape of a bear ambling through the woods. My breath caught in my chest. I reached out and grasped the bear totem in my hand.

Sorrow pierced me like a spear. The pain was so sudden and intense that I almost dropped the tiny stone figure. Gasping in a breath, I clutched the fetish tighter, pushed past the sorrow, and felt for what I knew would follow.

Anger pulsed against me. Revenge, retribution, the need was tangible. Flashes of steel, women flipping across a grassy clearing, fighting, training . . . my heart beat faster, as if I shared their exertion. Then the mood switched—darker, faces I couldn't make out gathered around a fire, a big fire, a council fire.

My own anger leapt at the sight. My hate for the council that had cost me so much was interfering with the vision.

Nostrils flaring, I tried to separate myself from the vision, to keep my past and emotion from intruding. I gripped the bear figure tighter in my hand and rubbed my thumb over its head, apologizing for my weakness, begging Artemis to forgive my digression. I squeezed my eyes shut until tears leaked out, but the effort was fruitless. The connection was lost.

I opened my eyes and, with a sinking feeling in the pit of my stomach, watched as the smoke thinned, spiraling down back into the fire, until I stared at nothing but a few smoldering embers.

I still held the tiny bear. Unclenching my fist, I let it drop onto the dirt. My palms pressed into the earth again; I hung my head and struggled to breathe.

My message had been received—at least for the first girl, and since I'd left the fetishes together, reason said for the second too. I waited for the guilt to diminish. I'd done my part. I'd warned the Amazons. But my wait was futile. There was no relief, no feeling of completion—just a hollow sickness deep in the pit of my stomach.

The girls were still dead, and I was still involved.

After hiding all signs of my clandestine spell-casting, I stumbled back to bed. I didn't expect to sleep, but somehow I did. Then around three, the sound of crying woke me. I clutched the wool blanket, my thoughts first rushing to Harmony—my mommy instincts in full force even though she hadn't suffered from night terrors since she'd been four. But the door to my bedroom was closed, no towheaded preschooler gazing up at me from the side of the bed.

Now, sitting upright, I touched my fingers to my fevered cheeks. They came back wet. The sobs had been coming from me.

A nightmare. I must have been having a nightmare. Not surprising, considering my life lately.

Scrubbing the moisture off my face with the wool blanket, I tried to settle back down, to brush aside the anxiety that still clung to me.

Then I felt them. The dead girls. Their presence weighed on me, then flitted away, only to return an instant later to tug at me like the impatient child I'd imagined when I first awoke.

They wanted me to help them, were becoming more restless as their fruitless wandering went on.

I tried to shake the feeling off and told myself it was

just the remnants of my nightmare—the heightened sense that came with waking deep in the night.

But it was a lie. As my mind wakened more fully and became less hazy, their presence grew stronger, not weaker.

Something had them trapped, and the little piece of my soul that had gone with them when I'd performed the death rites wasn't enough to keep them calm much longer. Their panic was growing, was big enough to be a tangible force in the small space of my bedroom, clawing over my skin, making me want to curl into a ball to protect myself.

Why is this my problem? Why did their killer choose me?

I picked up my pillow and flung it across the room, knocking a lamp to the ground with an earth-shattering crash.

The noise seemed to settle them. I waited for them to reappear or one of my family, awakened by the noise, to knock on my door, but all was quiet. I breathed in, my chin dropping to my chest, and my fingers crimped the blanket.

Damn it all. I didn't want to be involved, didn't want to face my past. Didn't want to be responsible for the souls of two dead teenagers.

Something flickered past me then, just a whisper of a touch, as if the girls were waiting, watching.

I refused to look up, as if staring at the navy blue wool of my blanket would make the nightmare I'd been thrown into disappear. I sat there the rest of the night, until dawn turned the sky outside my window a peachy pink and the morning sun broke the link between spirit and mortal.

No dead girls' spirits around to plead with me for help, to make me question who was more barbarous—the Amazons I'd left behind or me.

Chapter Five

I rose early that morning, unrested and edgy. Not only was my visit from the night before lurking in my mind, but today, for the first time ever, a man was joining the Amazons—or at least our little group of Amazons. I had called Peter right after leaving my conversation with Mother. He'd agreed to start today.

Short notice for everyone. Which meant no time to prepare my family—all in all, the best solution.

Fresh from a night of hauntings, I was ready to beard the lion of two millennia in my den.

After a quick look at my bedraggled reflection in the bathroom mirror, I dragged myself out to the main living area. Harmony was in her room polishing her nails while Bubbe stomped around the kitchen muttering something in Russian I didn't care to translate, and Mother had already disappeared into the basement. A peaceful, if early, morning in the Saka household.

Not up for conversation, I skipped breakfast and sneaked down the steps to the shop. I was rearranging the stations, trying to decide who would be best suited to pair with our new addition, when there was a rap on the front door. The metal pan of needles I was holding fell to the ground with a loud clatter. Dropping to my knees, I muttered a curse and began rounding up the once-sterile tools.

"We don't open till eleven," I yelled, my voice loud in the small cubicle.

The door rattled in response.

My hands shook as they hovered over the spilled needles. Jumpy. I was too damn jumpy. Lost spirits didn't knock on your front door and, bold as the killer might seem, so far all her gifts had been left in the dead of night. My palm sank onto the sharp end of a needle; the sudden pain brought me back to myself. I stared at the red bubble of blood forming on my hand and folded my fingers closed over it.

A fist hammered against the wood.

Blowing out a breath, I rubbed my palm against my jeans, leaving a red, angry stain, and started toward the steps. Let it be the killer. I was ready to end this.

I was halfway down the stairs when the rattling stopped. Frowning, I stomped down the last few steps anyway.

Only empty concrete stairs and an old chip bag shoved

against the building by a biting fall wind greeted me. I crumpled the trash in my hand and glanced around one more time—nothing. A familiar fragrance I couldn't quite peg drifted around me. My anger dissipated, replaced by a rush of unease.

My gaze darted around the yard, looking for any sign of my early-morning visitor, but there was nothing more suspicious than a squirrel busily hoarding nuts for the coming winter.

Unable to shake the unsettling impression off, I considered storming around the side of the building in hopes of catching whoever had made the earlier racket, just to prove to myself it was nothing more ominous than a bored neighborhood kid pulling a prank, but thought better of it.

I had stepped back inside, feeling as useless as the crumpled chip bag in my hand, and had started the trek up to the shop level when I heard voices coming from the basement.

Someone was visiting Mother.

This was unusual. Bubbe loved mingling with the locals—or more accurately, rooking them out of their cash—but Mother kept to herself. She did the odd tattoo for me, basic stuff, but that was it. I'd never known her to encourage company.

I paused, one hand on the wooden railing, the other still holding the chip bag, and considered going down to see who rated high enough to be invited into her world. Then, unbidden, a rough laugh escaped my lips. Secrets.

Mother wasn't the only one who had them. Maybe if I let her keep hers awhile longer, the cosmos would look kindly on me and return the favor by helping me to hide my own.

Besides, my latest secret, Peter, was due in at ten. I needed the time left until his arrival to work out how I was going to present him to my family. I tapped my fingers a couple of times on the banister, then went back to stocking Peter's station with bandages and other necessities of tattooing life.

The next couple of hours passed uneventfully. Harmony flounced off to school and Bubbe stomped directly from the second floor to the basement without stopping in the shop to harass me—another unusual occurrence. On a different day this might have raised some notice from me, but today I was too busy battling my warring emotions—still anxious thanks to my nocturnal visitors and their killer, proud I was doing my part to break old prejudices, and nervous that Bubbe, Mother, and centuries of other Amazons who had banned men from all but one aspect of their lives were right and I was on the brink of making a fatal error.

The third emotion was beginning to edge out the others when I glanced up at the clock and realized it was almost ten. Squaring my shoulders, I tromped down the stairs and unlocked the door.

Peter Arpada in all his brown-eyed, six-foot-plus-tall glory was waiting for me. He had a new, bigger portfolio under one arm and two steaming cups of premium coffee in his hands. My heart jumped a beat—for the coffee, I told myself. I don't splurge for the good stuff too often.

He followed me up the stairs.

"Interesting setup," he commented, once we were on the main/shop level. He was staring up the stairs that led to our living area.

"Uh, yeah. It works for us." I gestured for him to follow me through the glass doors that separated the tattoo cubicles from the waiting room. Wisconsin regulations required tattoo areas be separated from living areas by a full wall. Putting one on this level was easier than trying to close off the stairs some way. In other words, anyone who walked into our shop could just stroll up the stairs, past the PRIVATE: DO NOT ENTER sign and be in our living area. Assuming they made it past Mother, Bubbe, and me, that is. Until now, it had never occurred to me to worry about the possibility. Funny how a couple of dead bodies and having a man around could twist your view of things.

He gave the stairs one last glance, then followed.

"I thought I'd set you up here." I pointed to an empty cubicle in the front. "It's next to Cheryl. She'll be in at eleven. So she can show you around." Cheryl, a forty-something divorced mom of three, was one of the artists at my shop. The other, Janet, a fifty-year-old lesbian who had never bothered to tell her husband of twenty years her sexual preference, had the day off. I'd called Cheryl last night after I talked to Peter. She was the only one in on our new team addition.

"Won't you be showing me around?" He arched an eyebrow, and I would have sworn his eyes twinkled.

Despite my sleepless night and internal emotional battles, something inside me went all soft and girly. I obviously needed to get out more.

Trying to act casual, I grabbed one of the two rolling chairs in the space and, positioning it between us, pointed toward the back room. "Back there you'll find extra supplies and the autoclave. You're responsible for keeping your own equipment sterile, but Mandy, our office manager, will usually help out if she can." Spinning so the chair was against my back, I gestured past the reception area. "Over there's the little boys' room. That's it. You got the tour." Shoving the chair away, I took a step toward the reception area and freedom.

I hated to admit it, but he made me nervous—or my reaction to him made me nervous. No matter which, I needed to leave.

"What about these?"

Cursing my short legs for costing me the three seconds it took him to ask the question, I stopped and looked back. He was holding up his portfolio.

"And paperwork. Isn't there paperwork I need to fill out?"

"Mandy will help you with that—the paperwork, I mean." Remembering how Mandy had looked him over a few days earlier, I barely suppressed an eye roll. Yeah, she would help him out.

"And?" He shook the portfolio.

"If you have something you want added to the shop flash, give me a copy and I'll look it over. Each artist has a private flash too. Give those to Mandy, and she'll get them displayed." I waited to see if he had any other questions, but he just nodded and picked up the iron. As I left, I could tell he was doing a mental inventory of ink and supplies. I knew, because it's the first thing I'd do too.

Lucky for me, I had a cover-up scheduled for ten thirty, a long-time client I'd agreed to work on before the shop officially opened. It kept me busy and away from Peter. By the time I was done wrapping a bandage around my client's arm, I could hear low voices peppered by the occasional giggle coming from reception. *Guess Mandy is helping Peter with his paperwork.* I escorted the client out, giving her a last few care instructions on the way.

As I suspected, Mandy was pressed against the reception desk and Peter. What surprised me were the other two women—Cheryl and Janet—also as close as they could get to our new employee. Cheryl, maybe, but *Janet?*

"Slow morning?" I asked, my tone dry.

Four heads popped up to stare at me, only Janet had the grace to look embarrassed.

"What? You can't stay away, Janet?"

Her hand went up to rub her close-cropped head. "I remembered I left my . . . pen here last night."

Uh-huh. I shot a look at Cheryl. I'd thought she was the only one who'd known about Peter—wonder who else she had told? Anger swelled momentarily, but I forced the emotional uprising down. What did I care? It saved me from making the announcement. I turned to the gossip queen.

"How about you, Cheryl? You searching for a paper clip or something?"

Never one to be intimidated by me, Cheryl grinned. "We were just helping Peter pick what to put in his flash."

Mandy reached across the chest-high desk to slide a sheet of paper toward her. Her upper arm brushed Peter's chest in the process. A simple accident, I was sure.

"I love this one," Mandy gushed.

"There's a lot of nice work there." Eyes twinkling, Cheryl looked at me behind Peter's bowed head, her hand pointing to his muscled backside. "What about you, Mel? You see anything you like?"

At that moment, a forty-something man dressed in a suit and wearing a no-nonsense expression stepped out of the men's restroom. His hair matched the suit, short and conservative, but his face was too rugged for a complete fit. He didn't look like my typical client. I frowned and looked for another clue that would tell me his purpose here. His stance said he was physically fit and used to being in charge. And while his hands hung casually at his side, there was nothing casual about the expression in his blue eyes or the way his gaze worked its way around the room.

Glancing from the group clustered around the desk to me, he took a step forward. "Are you Mel Saka?"

I looked over my shoulder at my office manager. Mandy had the sense to look sheepish. "Sorry. There's somebody here to see you. I told him you were with a client and he said he'd—"

"Yeah, I can figure out the rest." I waved a hand at her and turned back to the man. "I'm Mel."

He stared at me, checking me over as if he could learn some secret I held simply by looking. I shook off a shiver of disquiet and squared my shoulders. "May I help you?"

He stood there another beat or two, then reached into his jacket. He brought out a leather wallet, flipping it open to display his ID.

"Detective Reynolds. Milwaukee Police Department. I was wondering if I could speak with you for a few moments."

I could feel the curious eyes of the group behind me pressing into my back. I resisted the urge to glance back at them. The bodies. Could he have traced them to me? I'd been careful—leaving the corpses in unpopulated areas, making sure nothing of mine touched them. I was confident no one had seen me anywhere near the bodies and any evidence left on them was from the killer, not me.

But if not that, what?

My mind flicked to Bubbe, the squirming rabbit grasped in her fist, the soccer mom's wide eyes on me when I stormed in on them. I glanced from his badge to him. "Milwaukee?"

"Yes." His gaze shot to the cluster of employees behind me. A frown lowering his brow, he shoved his ID back into his pocket. "Is there somewhere we can talk?"

Some ancient part of me reacted to his discomfort, made me want to refuse and force him to state his purpose there in the open. But the more modern, smart me realized there was no benefit to that track. Besides, careful as I had been, there was still the chance someone had reported something "odd" about me or my family to the police. If so, I didn't really want it broadcast to the entire staff. With a nod, I turned and led him into my office.

Once the door was closed, he straightened, walking around the room with a relaxed nonchalance that told me he was cataloging the contents. Back to being the confident cop, a man in charge. I bit back a flare of annoyance. "So what brings you to Madison, Detective?" With my arms folded over my chest, I slid into my chair.

"Strange place for a tattoo shop." He placed a finger into the metal blinds that covered the window overlooking the old school grounds and separate gym/lunchroom.

"It serves our purposes."

"Tattooing . . . and . . . ? " He turned until he faced me.

I smiled and leaned back against the hard wood of my chair. "Why are you here, Detective? Not to get a tattoo, I'm guessing."

"How long have you been tattooing, Ms. Saka?"

"Long enough."

"Ever tattoo someone under eighteen?"

I arched a brow. "That's illegal in Wisconsin."

"And you'd never break the law?" He strolled closer to my desk, slipping into a chair with misleading disinterest.

"If you're looking to bust me for tattooing someone underage, you wasted a lot of gas, Detective."

He gave me a look that was hard to read, then slipped his hand back into his jacket. This time to retrieve a stack of photos. He slid one across the desk to me. "This look familiar?"

Something in my gut tightened. Keeping my face blank, I looked down.

My worst fear rushed up and smacked me in the face. The photo showed the tattoo on the small of a woman's back—a bear, paws outstretched and teeth flashing.

My first early morning gift.

"Nice work," I commented, my throat dry, but my tone noncommittal.

He slid a second photo toward me.

I didn't really have to look, but I did—the leopard. I picked it up, stared at it for a second. Anxiety sliced through me. I lowered my hand to rest on my desktop, the photo still pinched between my fingers.

Keeping my eyes cast down until I was sure I was under control, I dropped the picture, then looked up. "Also nice. Is there a point here? You going to tell me why you're bringing these pictures to me?"

He made no move to pick up the photos, just snapped the ones still in his hand against the edge of my desk. "We took them to some artists in Milwaukee. Consensus was, they look like your work."

That startled me. Every artist has a signature style, something that even when they are copying another's work shines through. But to me, neither of the tattoos looked anything like mine. I picked up the second one, the leopard, and tried to look at it dispassionately, as just a tattoo, not a piece of a once-living girl.

"Are there more?" I nodded to the pictures still in his hand. There were twelve main tribes, each with a totem. He'd only shown me two. I'd only found and deposited two bodies. Were there more? Had the killer left bodies on someone else's doorstep?

He gave his head an almost imperceptible shake. "Just dupes."

I accepted his words with solemn resolve—not that I wanted there to be more dead girls, but if there had been others, not left on my doorstep . . . I shook the thought from my head. There hadn't been. I was the target.

I could feel his gaze on me. I looked up, meeting his eyes. "Where'd you say you got these?" I asked, not that I didn't know, but it seemed like the logical question.

He tapped the photos in his hand another time. "Is it your work?"

"I already said it wasn't."

"Did you?" An emotion glimmered in his eyes, determined, dangerous. Like the glint of steel before you see the actual knife slicing toward you.

"If it were my work, I'd tell you."

"Would you?" His expression said he didn't believe me. Smart guy.

I shrugged. "Okay, maybe I wouldn't, if I had a reason not to, but I didn't lie. The work isn't mine."

This time he nodded in quiet acceptance. "There's something, though. You know who did it?"

"No idea."

A short laugh escaped his lips. "And just when I thought we were becoming friends." Leaning forward, he placed both palms flat on the top of my desk. He was so close I could smell his toothpaste—cinnamon.

"This is serious. This isn't about slapping a fine on someone for underage tattooing. Whoever did these"— he glanced down at the photos—"knows something. Something *I* need to know."

I could feel the intensity rolling off him like heat off pavement. I wanted to help him. Wanted him to find the killer. But what could I tell him that wouldn't lead back to me?

"They're the same," I blurted.

He blinked, maybe startled that I replied—I know I was. "What?"

"These tattoos." I regretted the words as soon as they were spoken. None of this mattered, wouldn't help him find his killer because I wasn't going to tell him what else I knew about these tattoos—that they were done by an Amazon. However, my mind committed, I continued on, let myself get lost in discussing something I loved. I flipped the pictures back up to face us. "They're done by the same person. Look at the bear. See the thinness here." I pointed to the delicate stroking around the animal's muzzle. "The slight upward curve at the end of each line? Now, look at the leopard. The shading, the variation in line width? It's the same. Whoever did these tats wasn't just cranking them out. He—" I chose the pronoun carefully, wondering briefly if Detective Reynolds noticed— "put time and dedication into them, blood, sweat, and tears. Good tattooing is more than simple art. More than a drunken lark. It's ritual, beauty, strength, and power. That's what you have here—mixed into ink and sketched into some girl's skin. Whoever did this is good." All Amazons entrusted with the art were.

His blue eyes grew hard. "A girl? How'd you know these were both girls?"

I pulled back, startled out of my reverie. How'd I know the pictures were of girls? Because I'd seen them firsthand, held their lifeless bodies in my arms. But I couldn't exactly tell him that, now could I?

"The position. The lower back. Only women get tattoos there, and you already said it was someone underage—has to be a girl." I tilted my chin upward, daring him to call me on the statement. It was true, lower back was a female-preferred spot. There was no way he could prove there was any other reason for me to know the pictures were of girls.

I watched as he rolled this around for a few seconds. Something battled within him, but eventually he seemed to accept what I said, kind of.

"That's all you can give me?" He suddenly looked tired, like he'd used up his energy on his last explosion.

I nodded, guilt gnawing at my gut. He was one of the good guys, abrasive as I found him. But I couldn't tell him what he wanted to know.

He started to turn, then stopped. His hand going again into his jacket, he pulled out a business card. "You call me if you decide you can tell me more."

His way of letting me know he didn't believe my story completely.

My fingers reached for the card, but he didn't quite release it. "How about the breast? That a popular place for girls to get tattoos?"

This time I couldn't stop the slight tremble in my fingers any more than I could stop the lurch of my heart. "The breast?" I repeated.

"Yes, the breast. A lot of young girls get tattoos there?" He lay his hand over his right pectoral muscle. "Right here. Not big. Probably under a few inches in diameter."

Breathing through my nose, I slowed my heart rate, willed my mind not to think about the patch of missing skin, the raw flesh underneath. "More women than men. Why?"

"No reason," he replied. "No reason at all."

Chapter Six

I couldn't leave it alone. I'd thought about it all day, tried to convince myself that the police seeking me out was a good thing—that it showed they were seriously working the case. I'd tried reminding myself they were also more qualified to find a killer. *Who was I?* I was a mother. I owned a tattoo shop. Sure I was an Amazon—but so what? How would that help me to find the killer?

But I couldn't let it go. The girls, the police, my own guilt—they all ganged up on me and forced my hand.

I had to do something to stop this killer. Another midnight trek. This time to my basement . . . and Bubbe's shop. I'd stolen the bear and leopard totems from Bubbe's workspace when she'd been only a few feet away—out in the main basement area talking with a client.

But now I needed the others, and Bubbe's shop was locked up tight. I had a key. But my grandmother didn't just lock up her office. Right after she claimed the space as her own, she'd set a ward on the door.

I'd made fun of her at the time. What, she thought one of her suburban housewife clients or maybe a New Age college student was going to discover an undying need for a bag of bark or a stone carving?

Of course, she'd basically ignored me and wove the spell anyway.

Now, I had to get past it and any other little booby traps my wily grandmother had decided to put in place since then.

I laced my fingers together and pushed my hands out, palms forward in front of me, in my best knuckle-popping, let's-get-down-to-work safecracker mode. Warmed up, I closed my eyes and let my mind drift, opened myself to feel the hum of magic, to hear the buzz only a destructive ward can emit.

First pass there was nothing—no hum, no buzz, nothing. I gritted my teeth. There was a ward there. I'd seen Bubbe work on it and there was no way she didn't activate it every night.

Why she'd taken the time to build one so subtle I was having trouble detecting it was beyond me. If she was worried about only stopping a petty thief, she could have slapped any protective spell on here. But this . . . I opened my eyes, narrowed them as I studied the closed door . . . this was drawn to deceive, to keep another practitioner from realizing the door was even warded.

Which meant that after I got past the first ward, I'd find something else inside—something scary.

A prickle of unease crept up the back of my neck. Scary for Bubbe? Artemis only knew what that meant.

But I didn't turn away. If anything, the increased challenge spurred me forward. I needed the totems tucked away inside Bubbe's workspace, and I wanted to prove I could get to them, could beat my unbeatable grandmother.

This time I didn't close my eyes; instead, I concentrated on losing focus—on seeing past reality into the magic realm my grandmother had created. Tears began to stream down my cheeks. I resisted the urge to rub away the tired burn that was growing in my eyes. Lines began to weave in front of me, twist and turn. At first I thought it was just exhaustion taking over, but slowly the curving slices of color began to meld, forming a solid, clearly visible shape—a serpent, its tail wrapped around the doorknob, its head hovering a foot above mine as if resting on some invisible branch, stared down at me.

A serpent can bring with it many powers. It can kill silently or warn its victim off with a hiss or rattle. This one just hung there against the door, watching, waiting.

Of the twelve Amazon totems, the serpent was the one I trusted the least.

I bit back a hiss of my own.

In a different circumstance I might have tried to battle my way past the serpent, cut through the ward with brute force, but my grandmother wove this spell. The odds I could shove my way past it were slim, and with her sleeping only two stories above me, I'd have zero chance for escape.

I didn't want to battle my grandmother's magic tonight, but I wanted to battle her even less.

I really had no choice. If you can't kill the serpent outright, you either let it devour you, or you play mongoose—charm it.

I settled onto my heels and forced away all thoughts of how what I was about to do would look, how idiotic I would look weaving back and forth making eye contact with a serpent no one but me could see. And how likely it was that I'd goof the whole thing, set off the ward, and bring my grandmother and whatever host of surprises she had waiting behind the door down on my head.

Then I stared the serpent in the eyes and let my body begin to shift side to side. As I did, I made up my own chant and tried to channel every meerkat I'd seen perform the dance, compliments of Animal Planet.

Spells compliments of cable. Definitely something my grandmother wouldn't plan a defense against—or so I hoped.

The serpent's slitted gaze held mine. A shiver danced over my skin, but I kept up the movement, continued my chant encouraging the snake to give up his vigil, slither off to a dark corner of my basement and snack on a mouse.

My back began to ache and my mouth to dry. The snake didn't waver.

I heard a noise outside, a rattle. I ignored it, just like I ignored the now relentless need to blink, to drop my gaze. I'd never tried to outstare a snake before. In retrospect, a stupid thing to try with a creature that couldn't blink.

As my mind whirled, grasping for another solution, the snake suddenly lifted his head and opened his mouth wide, revealing fangs and a chasm of a throat that seemed to grow and grow until I was sure I'd figured out my grandmother's plan—for the ward to gulp me down whole. He loomed large above me, cutting off all light, until all I could see was his open mouth about to snap down on top of me, swallow me like he thought I was the promised field mouse. I raised my hands, forced my lips to move to sputter out a spell for a shield—weak and ineffectual as I knew it would be. I hadn't been prepared, hadn't realized how much unwinding Bubbe's ward would take out of me. Then, just as I thought his jaws were about to slip over my head and down my body, the snake snapped his mouth shut and slithered off the door.

My hands were shaking and a cold sweat covered my body. I could feel the snake undulating between my feet as he went in search of some prey. How I'd get him back on the door, spiraled precisely as my grandmother had left him, I had no idea.

A small problem I hadn't considered before taking on her ward. But I couldn't undo what was done. Might as well move on with my plan. I waited for the sensation of the snake's weight traveling past my ankle to cease, then moved forward.

My hand was on the knob when I heard the second rattle. I glanced at my watch. One A.M. Dead girl delivery time.

My shoulders squared at the morose thought, but I twisted toward the door that led outside anyway. Maybe I didn't need to call on Artemis tonight. Maybe she'd delivered the killer to me.

I grabbed one of Mother's training staffs—a six-foot-long pole of hardwood, and headed outside. I left behind whatever other traps Bubbe had laid in her office, and moved toward something that might prove to be even more horrifying.

It was lighter tonight. The full moon was almost upon us. I could see the outline of the banister that surrounded the basement stairwell. Running perpendicular to the steps was a sidewalk. On the other side of it was the old clapboard cafeteria and gym.

I could hear footsteps now, light and pacing back and forth, like someone was waiting for someone or something.

Me?

Only one way to find out. I crept to the top of the steps and peered out. A figure, six feet or so and female, stood with her back to me. In her hand was a staff much like the one I carried.

An Amazon. A blonde, not my mother and certainly not Bubbe or Harmony.

Adrenaline pumped through me. I leapt onto the sidewalk, bent to the side, and swung the staff, aiming it at the Amazon encroacher's head.

She spun, her staff meeting mine, and for the space of two heartbeats I stared directly into her golden eyes. It was too dark to see their color, but I knew it, knew the face. Zery. My once best friend. The Amazon Queen. The queen who stood by her tribe instead of me.

She must have seen the shock on my face. There was no way for me to hide it. No matter how angry I was with her for supporting my son's killer over me, I would never have believed her capable of killing an innocent Amazon girl.

"Why?" I murmured.

"Were you expecting me?" she asked at the same time, then laughed. Not the rippling, happy sound I remembered, but a hard, cold noise that curled inside me, made me want to strike out, knock some of my frustration with her betrayal out of my system for good.

We were at a standoff. Each pushing against her staff with all her strength, mine increased by my ten-year-old anger. Otherwise, I wouldn't have stood two seconds against her, never mind the minutes that seemed to have ticked by.

"Been keeping in shape, Mel? What else have you been doing?" Her foot moved toward my knee. An old trick—one I used to use on her, when tricks were my only defense against her superior strength.

I hopped to the side, managing to keep my staff up and shoved against hers as I did. But my advantage of surprise and personal rage was lost; I could feel her pushing forward, knew she'd soon have the upper hand. My body angled awkwardly. A muscle in my back screamed. The grain of the wooden staff dug into the skin on my unconditioned palms and fingers. Mother could have held onto that staff for hours, her calloused hands never tiring. And Zery could too. Not that she would have to; depending solely on warrior skills, I'd fall before Zery even got winded.

A memory of the snake jumping from the door, slithering off, gave me strength. I had other skills to call on.

Not wanting Zery to realize what I was doing, I mumbled under my breath, called on Artemis to calm me while I searched for a plan. I was drained from battling Bubbe's serpent, and even if I weren't, I didn't know whether my powers were developed enough to conjure something truly impressive. Better to go for something small, something I could explain away if needed—perform and still keep the true range of my powers hidden.

Ten feet behind Zery, shoved between the sidewalk and the main brick building, was an ancient oak. The thing was a hazard—its roots cracking the concrete walkway, its branches stretching from the windows of my office to Harmony's bedroom, scratching against glass and brick. Only a few weeks earlier a late summer storm had hit the tree hard. The winds had broken several smaller limbs and cracked one particularly large one. I'd been meaning to call a tree guy, have him finish the job the storm started before another wind came along and brought two hundred pounds of oak branch down on someone's head.

Now I was glad I hadn't.

Chapter Seven

I focused on the branch, then pulled in a breath through rounded lips. The air stirred, leaves rustled.

The noise registered with Zery. Her eyes flickered.

I drew on physical resources I didn't know I had and shoved harder against the staff. A rough grunt left my lips as I did. The leaves stilled, but Zery refocused—back on me.

She twisted, her staff spinning. I dropped to a squat, let the wooden pole whiz over my head. As I did, I looked back at the branch and blew every liter of air I could spare out of my lungs.

The limb shook, cracked.

Zery didn't hear the sound, or if she did, she ignored it. She finished her turn, landing in front of me, her staff ready to swing again. Her biceps bulged and her brows lowered. Something close to regret darkened her eyes as she pulled back the staff. This time she meant to kill me. I could read her intent in the tense lines running down her neck and the way her foot dug into the dirt as she braced herself for the impact of her staff colliding with my skull.

The realization comforted me, made what I was about to do easier. I focused on the branch and blew out again. This time Zery couldn't miss what I was doing. My breath left my body with such force my body shot backward. I fell to the ground. My jeans burning from the friction of being shoved across concrete and packed dirt.

The end of Zery's staff whizzed through empty space—where I had been seconds earlier. My back collided with the cafeteria's wall, my head jerking back to smack against the wooden—but plenty solid—wall as well.

And the branch fell, or started to.

There was a crack like lightning as the tree let loose of its damaged limb. Zery stood frozen, staring at me, processing what I had done, what she should do next, and completely missing what was about to happen.

I opened my mouth, a lifelong friendship bringing a warning to my lips, but there was no air left in me, no voice—only a squeak came out.

I tried to stand—couldn't. Reality, dark and ugly, settled around me.

Zery looked up, saw the branch, and started to move, but I knew she wouldn't make it, that it would crush her, maim her at least.

There was a whoosh—the branch falling, I thought at

first. Then I saw my mother. She leapt from the bathroom window, and kicked the branch as it fell. The limb hit the ground with a crash. I felt the impact through the soles of my boots. Zery stood beside it, untouched.

Then Mother hit, rolling from her shoulder to her opposite hip to her feet. Her gaze zipped to me, pinned me against the wall.

My fingers tightened around her staff, reminding me I still held it. I loosened my grip, let it fall to the ground.

Zery took a step forward, her own staff held low, ready to ram against my throat.

Mother whirled. "You're not queen here."

Zery shifted her attention to Mother, shifted her staff too, a casual change in grip, but one that fooled no one. She was ready to fight. "I'm queen everywhere."

I scrambled to a stand. I'd have liked to have leapt up with the same grace as Zery and Mother, but my back and head ached and I was still struggling not to gasp for breath. As it was, I only managed a half stand, my hands pressed into my thighs and my head hanging between my shoulders. "Don't let her leave," I rasped out.

"I'm here on Amazon business. You know that." Zery glanced at me, then back at Mother.

"Today you were. Not tonight. You didn't tell me you were coming tonight." Mother's stance was casual, her arms loose at her sides, but she moved slightly as she spoke, positioning herself between my old friend and me.

"The council decided the evidence was enough. If not Mel, who?"

At my name I stood. My back and head screamed, but air seemed to be flowing through my lungs again.

Zery took a step around Mother, toward me. Mother sidestepped, blocking her. At the same time I moved too— until Mother was sandwiched between Zery and me.

"Grab her," I said.

Zery laughed. "Are you planning to kill me too? Next time the entire tribe will show up." Her weight shifted to the side.

Mother held out a hand.

"You can't protect her any longer, Cleo. Not this time. Leaving the tribe, taking up residence with humans, that's one thing, but killing her own? You know what has to be done. You agreed to it."

A chill passed over me.

"I agreed to bringing her to council and I would have. *You* agreed to that."

Zery looked to the side. "The council didn't."

Mother's shoulders tensed. "They don't trust me? When have I not done what they asked? I've kept them informed of every move we've made. Mel pees—I see it, and they know about it."

My head lifted. Shock caused me to step backward. Mother had been spying on me for the council? How long? The entire ten years? Zery and Mother's exchange when I'd still been catching my breath . . . the visitor this morning—it all clicked now. It had been Zery telling

Mother the council wanted me brought back. Had I missed other visits? Or had Mother sneaked off to them . . . how often?

As if sensing my distress, Mother added, "It beat the alternative, Mel. You locked up, Harmony taken from you. Don't judge me for saving you both from that."

I tightened my jaw, fisted my hands. Betrayed again. Would I never learn?

"I have to take her." Zery had her gaze back on Mother.

Tired of them both talking about me like I had no vote and posed no threat, I stepped around Mother, got into Zery's face. "Try it."

She looked at me, surprise lifting one brow, then reached out. Her hand moved toward me. I waited. I was angry. As angry as I'd allowed myself to be since I'd learned to control the dark emotion a decade ago. And a decade ago I didn't have priestess powers, couldn't convert that rage into fire or a blue-hot charge.

But now, I could. Fire/electricity wasn't my preferred element, but I could use it and I did, let it vibrate inside me. Waited for her skin to touch mine, to release the charge, send us both flying.

Mother got in the way—shoved Zery against the shoulder, knocking her to the ground. I started to move, barely a flinch forward, and Mother held out one hand, her back still to me. "Don't."

That was it. One word and I froze, the power I'd coiled inside me, unwinding, dissipating like steam in a dry room. Zery's staff swung toward Mother. Mother grabbed it with both hands, ripped it from Zery's grip, then slammed the wooden pole into the dirt inches from Zery's head.

"No one is taking my daughter—not until *I* believe she's a killer."

Zery's eyes were dark, angry, but her voice was calm. "And if we convince you?"

Mother tensed, paused. I thought for an instant she wouldn't answer, then, "I'll bring her in myself."

On a normal night the words might have hit me, hurt, but in the middle of the insanity unfolding around me, they barely grazed the hard shell quickly forming around my heart.

I cursed, walked over to the staff I'd dropped, smashed it into a trash can, and then let it drop on the ground. They looked at me then.

"You both can go to hell." I rotated on my heel with every intention of waking my sleeping daughter and leaving. Leaving the shop, Mother, Bubbe, everything. I owed the Amazons nothing, wanted nothing *from* them or *to do* with them. How dare Mother pretend to leave them, pretend to support me—and actually be spying on me.

My life here was a lie.

I took four steps down the sidewalk. Overhead the tree rustled; a battery of acorns fell to the ground, peppering the area around me. I glared upward, ready to take my ire out on anyone and anything that dared disagree with my plan.

My gaze landed on my daughter's window. Fingernail-polish bottles lined the sill. Above them, attached with a suction cup to the glass, hung a unicorn-shaped sun catcher.

She'd gotten the thing at a birthday party four years earlier—had been so proud when she'd finished painting it.

And I'd been proud too, of how secure she was . . . happy.

How would jerking her out of her bed in the middle of the night affect her? And what would I tell her? The Amazons have found us? Your grandmother is a spy?

How could I explain any of this, and even if I could, how could I yank her from the only world she'd ever known, really remembered? Ask her to leave it all behind again?

My jaw clenched. I turned, crushing an acorn under my heel. I'd run away once. I wouldn't do it again.

I retrieved the staff. With it held in front of me, I approached the two Amazons—not Mother, not Zery, two Amazons I couldn't trust.

I expected Mother to tell me to put it down but, her mouth a grim line, she just nodded, muttered, "Should have let me teach you how to use it."

Zery folded her arms over her chest and angled her body so her back was to me—letting me know she didn't see me as a threat, *the bitch*. Addressing Mother, she said, "Bring her to council. We'll convince you."

"Of what?" I used the staff to poke Zery in the back— a nice sharp poke. Not hard enough to do her any damage, just tick her off.

Her body stiffened.

I grinned, dropped the end of the pole onto the ground next to my foot, then held onto it with one hand. The other hand I kept at my side, my thumb strumming my fingers.

My poke resulted in the desired results. Zery turned on me. Mother stuck out her arm, blocking Zery with her own staff.

"That you're a killer."

"Me?" I started to move forward.

Mother held out a hand to stop me. "Mel, those girls we've seen on TV, the dead ones. They're Amazons." Her eyes concentrated on my face, steady, trusting. She believed she was telling me something I didn't know. I dropped my eyelids, just for a second.

"She knows." Zery rushed forward. Mother held her back, but there was doubt on her face now.

I raised my chin, took a step toward them. "I had nothing to do with those girls' deaths." I glanced to the side—couldn't look at my old friend, couldn't believe she would think such a thing of me. Yes, I'd thought it of her . . . but I had reason.

Anger wrapped back around me, I glared back. "Why me?" It was an open question, more so than Mother could guess, but if Zery was the killer, she'd understand.

Zery took a step back, seemed to settle. "Amazons don't have enemies. No one outside the tribe even knows Amazons are real—except you."

"And you're sure the killer does?"

Zery pulled back. "What do you mean? She had to."

I'd pretty much assumed the same, but hearing the assumptions from Zery's lips put a new perspective on things—or maybe it was from being accused of the killings myself.

"These girls. Are they both from the Illinois safe camp?" I figured they had to be, or to have spent time there recently, but I wasn't revealing any of my assumptions to Zery—didn't want her to think I'd been spending time analyzing the deaths. There was no reason I would have been—if I hadn't already known they were Amazons.

Zery nodded, but her expression was grim, not giving me an inch.

"They about the same age? Go places together?" Sneaking out with other teens was just as popular an activity for Amazon teens as human. Probably more so. No boys in an Amazon camp. About the time puberty hit and hormones went wild, I'd spent more time out of camp at night than in.

"They wouldn't go off with a stranger."

I cocked a brow. Zery and I had hitched plenty of rides into human towns with random truckers and local boys.

She glanced at Mother, then pursed her lips. "It would be easier for someone who knew the camp."

Mother let out a sigh. "That's your proof?" She shoved

the staff back into Zery's hand and moved toward the basement stairwell. "Go home."

Zery hesitated. That's when I realized she didn't want me to be the killer—that maybe there was still some of my old friend inside the queen's body.

But she did want to find the killer, and so did I.

"What can we do?" I asked.

Mother's feet ground to a halt. Her hand already on the railing, she turned back and stared at me.

"Confess?" Zery asked, but as quickly as the question came, she shook her head, then pinned me with a stare. "Believe it or not, I hope you're not involved, Mel. But you know that if you are, I'll kill you myself."

I shrugged. I wouldn't expect anything less.

Seeing our uneasy truce, Mother crossed back to where we stood, came to a halt beside me, so close her bicep brushed my shoulder. A small show of support, but for Mother, huge.

"What else is being done?" she asked.

With the initial powder keg dampened, Mother and Zery settled into a conversation that I could tell they'd had before. More Zery filling Mother in on recent discussions than delivering plans previously unknown.

I listened, but definitely felt I was missing big chunks of information. I'd corner Mother later, force her to fill me in too. My mind had drifted somewhat, to what Zery's arrival and the knowledge that Mother and most likely Bubbe still had contact with the Amazons meant, when a turn in the conversation jerked me back.

"There are showers and a kitchen, but you'll have to clean it. Maybe do some repairs."

My ears perked and my shoulders pulled back. "Clean what?"

Back in warrior mode, they both ignored me. Together they began striding down the walkway. I expected them to turn toward the front entrance of my shop, but instead they hung a left. Strolled to the old gym door.

My eyes rounded and I quickened my pace—almost to a jog to catch them. Before I reached them, Mother had already opened the doors.

My eyes narrowed. I kept the gymnasium locked. We didn't use the place. It was expensive to heat, and I didn't want news of its unused state to get out to the local beer-drinking teen crowd. I'd found an untapped pony keg hidden in the aspen grove at the far corner of our property last spring. Bad enough my trees were being used as an alcohol hand-off locale—I didn't want my building to be usurped too.

The gym was only a few feet away from the main building, but the aspens where I'd found the keg hadn't been that much farther away. *Kids.*

Point being, Mother had to have had a key on her. And there was no reason for her to—not that I knew of.

I followed her and Zery into the dark gym. None of us reached for the lights. They worked, but I didn't want the place blazing if Bubbe or Harmony awoke. I figured Mother was thinking the same thing.

Mother bent and pulled a couple of flashlights from behind an overturned table.

Yeah, she'd been planning this.

She handed one to Zery and kept the other. I muttered under my breath.

Zery ran the beam over the interior. Things had been moved since I'd last been in the place. Nothing major, just broken furniture piled to the side, and what appeared to be new cleaning materials leaned against one wall. Based on her mention of showers and the kitchen, I guessed she'd turned the water back on too.

"This would work." Zery walked to the center of the room and tapped her fingers against her leg.

I stepped forward. "Work for what?"

Two beams of light turned on me, blinding me. I kept my regard steady and didn't blink.

"The Amazons need to be closer." Mother's voice was low, sure—just stating facts, not leaving an opening for input.

"Closer to what?" I did not like where this was headed. When I'd asked what we could do, I'd imagined sending Mother or Bubbe back to the camp for a while. Maybe even me doing some tattoo work to help strengthen those engaged in the hunt.

I did not envision Amazons here. No way.

"The bodies were found forty miles away," I added.

"How do you know that?" Zery asked.

I huffed out a breath. "The news?"

"Forty miles seems pretty exact." Suspicion was back in her voice, but Mother stepped in.

"The tribe thinks both girls had made trips to Madison."

That stopped me. I'd convinced myself the girls were killed in Illinois and just brought to Madison—to me.

Zery lowered her flashlight. I could almost feel the defeat in her voice. "We found coasters from a bar in their stuff—one near campus." The round circle of light from her flashlight began moving again, dancing over the space. "This will work," she said.

"No." I shook my head.

Mother's beam, which had dropped from my face too, rose again. "The tribe needs our help. This"—she moved her hand, sending the light bouncing up onto the ceiling and back down—"is what we have to offer. You've been to the camp. The house only sleeps twelve to fourteen, tops. More Amazons are coming from other states, Canada even. They need somewhere to stay and train. And we're here—near where the bodies were discovered and the bar."

I stood firm. "Why? What are they going to do while they are here?" Visions of Amazons canvassing Madison, accosting legislators, college students, and soccer moms ripped through my mind.

Zery clicked off her flashlight. Her voice reached out to me in the dark. "By your choice you aren't one of us, Mel. Our plans aren't for you to know."

"If you want to use my property, they are." A tense silence followed. I flexed my fingers, wished I still held Mother's staff.

Zery sighed. "They're angry, Mel, and they don't trust you. I won't tell you what we're doing; I can't. But we won't break any human laws . . . Not until we find the killer. Then Amazon law will rule. Until then, we'll play whatever cover story you pick for us, conduct our business in a way that no one, not even you, will know what we're doing. It's the best deal you're going to get. You need to take it. If you refuse, they'll come anyway, but it will be to pull you back for trial. Work with the tribe, and maybe they'll be willing to consider that someone else is doing this. Don't, and they'll be convinced you're hiding something."

Her feet padded across the wood floor, almost too light to hear. When she stood parallel to me, only a few feet away, she continued, "Think of your daughter. You don't want to introduce her to her tribe like that."

Then she brushed past—she and I both knowing she'd just said the one thing to sway me to her side.

Chapter Eight

Two days later, on Saturday, the Amazons started arriving. I'd told my employees and Harmony that I'd rented the gym and cafeteria to a women's self-defense group for a retreat.

Even with this background, I saw a few raised eyebrows as the Amazons started arriving in beat-up trucks and thirty-year-old campers. Their average height hitting over six feet and the confident swagger that came with being a warrior didn't help. A family of hearthkeepers arrived also, but no high priestess or artisans. Bubbe and I could fill those needs.

As much as I didn't want to be involved with the tribe, I also couldn't have an unlicensed artisan tattooing women in my gym. If someone needed body art, they'd have to come to me or Bubbe. Mother was too busy being in her element to bother with tattooing; besides, while she could manage a decent human tattoo, her mystical powers were crap.

Bubbe would serve as priestess. High priestesses were a lot more rare than the other talents, and for good reason. Putting two high priestesses in the same camp was a lot like putting two cats in the same bag, then shaking it. The goddess must consider this personality glitch when handing out the talents.

The rarity of high priestesses made having Bubbe fill in even more important in my mind. There were only six active high priestesses at any time—one for each safe camp. One of those was the woman I held responsible for my son's death—the woman I'd accused of doing something that caused his stillbirth.

If she showed up on my property, I wasn't sure what I would do, wasn't sure I could control the anger that still threatened to consume me. Mother, Bubbe, and Zery realized this, and no one had mentioned any possibility other than Bubbe filling the role. This was good, I supposed, for now. But some day I was going to see her again, and when I did, I was going to get some answers one way or another.

"Self-defense group, you said?" Peter placed a hand against the side of a dented Jamboree RV. "Looks more like a bunch of carnies."

The weather had turned warm again—unusually so for October—and Peter had taken advantage of it, wearing nothing but a tight-fitting T-shirt tucked into worn jeans. I rubbed suddenly sweaty palms against my thighs.

"I wouldn't say that too loudly if I were you."

Zery walked by with five twenty-pound staffs propped over her shoulder. Her hair was pulled back in a ponytail, and her butt was encased in Lycra workout pants.

Peter grinned and shoved himself away from the RV. A cluster of Amazons flicked their eyes in his direction, one pulling her hair over her shoulder and angling her body to reveal exactly what bench pressing a few hundred pounds can do for a female chest.

Peter's grin widened.

I tapped my fingers against my leg. "Don't you have an appointment?" I'd been checking the book every day since Peter's arrival to see if he was pulling in clients of his own.

The teasing expression dropped from his face. "I do. That's why I came looking for you. Someone's going to have to clear a path through all of this. My client's in a wheelchair. He can't be navigating around weights and luggage." He stooped and picked up a fifty-pound dumbbell that had rolled away from a stack.

I half-expected him to curl the thing. A show of strength like that was such a male thing to do—not that it would have impressed any of the warriors milling around. Then again, based on the appraising glances they'd been casting his way, he didn't need to do anything more than bend over to impress them.

A retort sprang to mind, but I quickly swallowed it when a man in a self-propelled wheelchair rolled up to a stack of duffel bags and boxes that blocked the sidewalk. Without waiting for assistance, he reached down and began flinging duffel bags out of his way. That caught the attention of the Amazons—fast. Five of them hurried forward.

He cocked a bushy eyebrow at the one in the lead and cast the last duffel into her gut. "Yours, I'm guessing?"

She caught the bag with a glare.

Cursing, I shoved past Peter and marched to their sides. Pisto, or Pistol, as many of the tribe called her, was not known for her demure temperament—not that many Amazons were.

"I'm running a business here. You can't block the walkway."

She didn't move. I could tell she was weighing her choices. I wasn't sure how Peter's client's disability would play into her decision. Wouldn't gain him any sympathy— I was sure of that.

After casting him one last suspicious glance, she grabbed four of the duffels and nodded to the warriors waiting behind her. With each of them grabbing two boxes at a time, the sidewalk was soon cleared.

During the whole process, none of them said a word— to me, Peter, or his client.

I let their obvious disdain pass. They had reason to hate me. I was a troublemaker in their version of history.

Peter's client was old and handicapped. In other words, in an Amazon's way of thinking, not potential baby seed. Peter was just being punished by association.

"Mel, this is Makis Diakos. He just moved to Madison." Peter seemed unaffected by their reaction.

"Really?" I frowned. I wanted to turn and see what the Amazons were doing behind me, but that would look strange, and be rude. "What brought you to Madison?"

Peter answered, "Makis is an artist. He taught me."

The man was Peter's senior by about forty years. I was intrigued. "You taught Peter? Then you must be good." It wasn't a compliment, just a statement of fact. If Peter wasn't one of the best, he wouldn't be working for me.

"Has he tattooed you before?" I glanced at Makis's arms, but they were fully covered, as were his legs. Long sleeves and long pants—kind of a strange choice for such a warm day. But I didn't know what put him in the wheelchair. Perhaps he had scars he didn't like to show. Perhaps the tattoos helped him feel more whole. They did me.

"A few." Makis looked up at me, watched me as if he was expecting something, as if he didn't quite trust me not to jerk up the sleeves of his shirt and see for myself.

A quiet settled around us. The Amazons had disappeared from around the front of the gym, and the other tattoo artists were inside working, I hoped. But this wasn't just a run-of-the-mill quiet. It was the kind you can feel, the kind that made you want to walk away or say something just to end it.

I was too stubborn to do it myself. I was on my property, and had been nothing but polite. I didn't know what Makis's issue with me might be, but I wasn't stumbling over myself to find out and apologize.

Peter cleared his throat. "Guess we better get going."

I watched as they moved toward the front door. Right before they turned the corner, they paused and glanced to their left—toward the gym entrance. Peter leaned down to say something in Makis's ear, and the older man nodded.

If the Amazons got me fined for blocking handicapped accessibility, I was not going to be happy.

I waited to make sure Peter and Makis had turned toward the shop and not the gym, then placed my hands on my hips and surveyed the mess the Amazons had made of my life. The parking lot and nearby street were full of decrepit vehicles blocking the handicapped parking spot, a fire hydrant, and a neighbor's garage. There was even a fifth wheel creating furrows in my grass.

I'd agreed to let them stay here, but based on Zery's promise, I had thought they would be somewhat subtle. *Silly me.*

The door flew open to the fifth wheel and a four-foot-long trunk was hurled out, knocking against my neighbor's city-issued trash can and sending it rolling down the street.

I guess this was another reason why all the safe camps were located miles from other people.

Glaring at the clueless warrior who jumped out of the

RV, I trotted after the trash can, then went looking for Zery. Like it or not, she was going to have to control her tribe.

Twenty minutes with Zery gave me the undeniable urge to break something.

Needing distance, I started up the stairs to my shop and office. Peter's smooth voice and a responding giggle from Mandy drifted down. I ground to a halt. I did not need to witness whatever love fest was going on up there right now.

I stomped back down the stairs, grabbed a wheelbarrow from a small shed tucked against the holly bushes, and headed out to clean up tree limbs. It wasn't an absolutely necessary task, but it would give me the chance to think—and I needed it.

The school sat on a full acre. A huge amount of land in this overpriced part of Madison. The place had been cheap when I saved the previous owner from foreclosure, but my property taxes weren't. For some reason, the high taxes made me feel guilty if I didn't keep up the curb appeal. Or maybe it was the constant thought that someday I might want to sell the place, move on again.

The biggest piece of land was in front of the school, a rolling grassy area that stood between my business and Monroe Street. Lilacs and a few shrubs lined the front two corners, leaving an open area in the middle that gave anyone tooling down Monroe a clear view of my shop. Because of that, I started in the middle of the lot and worked my way down the hill. By the time I'd gotten to the street, my wheelbarrow was half full, but mainly with discarded cans and other trash that had found its way onto my property. The worst of the storm debris was along the edges, next to the bigger trees that formed a living, if somewhat porous, barrier between my neighbors and my shop here in the front.

I pulled work gloves from my pocket and headed to one corner. From there the going was slower. Many of the limbs were too long to fit in the barrow. I picked up a particularly long one and placed one foot on its center with the idea of snapping the limb in half. As I did, something small and red caught my eye.

I bent closer. The triangular stub of a much-used piece of chalk lay partially hidden under a sheaf of leaves. I plucked it up and changed my first impression—not chalk, but a hard pastel. Perfect for doing rough sketches. I glanced up the hill at the redbrick facade of my shop. It was picturesque—if you didn't look too hard.

For some reason, the thought of someone appreciating its beauty enough to commit it to paper made me happy. With a smile, I pocketed the nub and went back to work.

I'd successfully snapped the limb into two somewhat manageable pieces when I had that eerie sense of being watched. I automatically gripped the three-inch-diameter piece of wood with the same hold I'd used with the staff and looked up.

A black and tan, short-haired dog peered at me from

behind a shrub. I let the creature stare at me before cautiously lowering to a kneel. My gaze steady but unthreatening, I held out one hand.

Dogs, especially hunting dogs like this one appeared to be, were sacred to Artemis, and Amazons honored that tradition. A few of the Amazons moving into my cafeteria had arrived with dogs. As a child, I'd spent hours playing with safe-camp dogs. I'd wanted one of my own until I'd had to watch Mother end one's life after it was hit by a car on a nearby highway. She had acted as if she had taken it in stride, but I'd seen the shake in her hands and heard the tremor in her voice when she pulled my tear-streaked face to her chest.

I'd decided right then that having a dog, loving something that much, wasn't for me.

Then I'd had Harmony.

Lost in thought, I dropped my gaze. Something stirred the air around me. The dog had emerged from the brush and stood an arm's reach away. His brown eyes were wary, but curiosity seemed to be pulling him out of his shell. Curiosity and maybe something else. I rooted around in the wheelbarrow and pulled a half-eaten bag of Doritos from the bottom.

I balanced one chip on my flat palm. "Hungry?"

At first I thought I'd misjudged him. He glanced from the chip to my face. I sat still.

Patience counts when dealing with suspicious canines. Finally, he edged forward, snagged the chip, and gulped it down. When he stepped back this time, it wasn't quite so far. If he'd worn a collar, I could have grabbed it—not that I would have. I had no desire to be bitten by a stray. I didn't know how rabies reacted with Amazon blood, but I didn't want to find out.

I did want to get him away from the street, though. Leaving the wheelbarrow where it was, I pulled another chip from the bag and with it held out behind me, slowly began walking back to the shop.

Step by step, chip by chip, he followed me.

Chapter Nine

Back at the shop, things had returned to chaos. Obviously, my talk with Zery had had the expected results—none. I crushed the now-empty chip bag in my hand.

Luckily, Harmony had had to spend most of the morning in her room finishing homework—a requirement on my part before she could move on to what she really wanted to do, visit a local corn maze with a group of friends. Generous mother that I was, I'd agreed to her going early to one of the girl's houses and spending the night there later. She was gone by the time I got back with the dog. And eager as I knew she would have been to get away before I could question her on the completeness of her homework, I was pretty confident she hadn't wasted time poking around the gym—today, anyway.

That said, I knew I couldn't keep her away forever. I hoped things would be settled down at least somewhat before she arrived home tomorrow—preferably with all Amazons locked out of sight inside the gym.

With her safely away, I debated whether my time alone had calmed me enough to battle with Zery again. Doubtful, but I made my way toward the open gym doors anyway. My new companion trotted at my side. His ears were up and his eyes alert. At least the chips had done him some good.

Two Amazon dogs flanked the doorway, like statues guarding the entrance to some ancient Buddhist temple. I expected them to stand as we walked closer to check out the new canine interloper, but neither did.

I looked down at the hound at my side. "You putting off some major alpha dog vibes or are they just lazy?"

His attention locked on the Amazons milling inside the gym, the dog didn't even glance my way.

The twang of metal on metal jerked my attention upward—into the gym where four Amazons faced off—all with swords. Real swords, thirty-six inches of steel flashing across the gym floor. To my right another group was sorting through a pile of ash wood and iron spears.

I jerked the gym doors closed.

Before I could twist back around, Mother was by my side. "Calm down," she said.

"What self-defense group do you know that practices sword fighting?" I spat out. "And spears? Seriously?"

"They're hurt, lost. Zery has told them they can only go out into Madison in pairs. The rest . . . they want to do something."

"And this is it?" I gestured to a warrior unpacking a box filled with maces and axes. "Do they think they can walk around Madison with broadaxes attached to their belts? We aren't going to war here."

Mother tilted her head. "We?"

I flicked my attention to the dog. His body was rigid, the hair on his back raised. Smart dog.

"*They. They* aren't going to war. They can't seriously be planning on using any of this."

Mother stared at the dog, with a question in her eyes, then looked back at me. "Probably not, but these weapons represent our past and roles . . . who gets to help with the investigation, who gets to punish the killer . . . those things have to be decided on some way. This is what Zery chose."

"So, whoever doesn't get her head chopped off gets first pick of the jobs?"

To my surprise, Mother grinned. "It would work."

Staring at her, I realized she was enjoying herself, coming back to herself. She loved the tribe, loved battling with other warriors. And the weapons shouldn't have been such a huge shock for me. I'd seen them before. Once a year, during the festival of Charisteria, Amazons staged battles with prizes awarded for the best performance in all traditional skills. I'd even competed myself.

"Charisteria is coming up," I murmured.

Mother nodded. "Zery is using that. All of these warriors were planning on competing. Zery decided to use that training to keep them busy and to decide who can handle the most responsibility."

I pressed the pads of my fingers against my eyes. The fact that what Mother said actually made some sense scared me more than the swords clanging around me. Still, I took her candidness as an opportunity. "What kind of 'investigating' does Zery have them doing?" My earlier visions of warriors going door to door in Madison returned.

Mother angled a brow. "You know I won't answer that."

Bubbe entered the gym from the cafeteria, pulling my attention away from Zery's plan and Mother's refusal to tell me about it. My grandmother was dressed in a traditional Russian *sarafan* complete with intricate embroidery. The long red jumper was worn over a white long-sleeved *rubakha*. A matching red-and-gold crescent-shaped *kokoshnik* was perched on her head.

Just like Mother, she was fully back in her element.

Behind me, the dog scratched at the door.

I drew myself up to my full height and squared my shoulders. "Only in the gym—with the doors closed."

"The spears—" Mother started.

"Are not being tossed around in full view of Monroe Street. Zery will have to figure something else out. She can use javelins or something. Same goes for anything they do outside this building—it has to be modern and one-hundred-percent explainable."

Mother placed her hands on her hips. I steeled myself for a fight, but she nodded. "That's reasonable."

Relief flowing over me, I jerked open the door. The dog bolted out into the growing dusk.

Mother's voice stopped me from dashing after him. "You know there will need to be trials—outside. You might want to think of something to tell the neighbors."

I didn't slam the door when I left the building. My life was a mess, but I knew who to blame: me. For whatever reason, the dead girls had been brought to me. I'd tried to deny my responsibility, but I couldn't any longer.

The girls, the police, and now the Amazons. All swirling around me. I couldn't stand back and wait for someone else to fix this. I especially couldn't wait for Zery's plan to become apparent. I was going to have to do it myself. Somehow.

I took a deep breath and watched cars speed down Monroe. A calm settled over me. I was going to do this. I was going to stop the killer. But where to start?

I didn't have to go search for a starting place. It came to me at one in the morning.

I woke to shouts and dogs barking. I jerked open the window closest to my bed and looked out. This gave an unobstructed view of the side of the cafeteria and not much more, but the voices were clear and angry. Leaning out further, I could see flames shooting up from in front of the shop. Dressed in the cotton shorts and T-shirt I'd slept in and not bothering with shoes, I shoved open my back window—the one attached to the old fire escape—and scurried down the cold metal stairs.

All the Amazons were out of the gym and moving toward the fire. I followed.

At the bottom of the hill, about twenty yards from Monroe Street, a huge bonfire crackled and spat. A ring of Amazons stood around it. In the center of their circle, next to the fire, stood Zery, Bubbe, and Mother.

Soaring anger carried me down the hill and into their midst.

"What do you think you are doing? We can't set a fire in the middle of the city like this." I glanced around, frantic for something to douse the flames, but in my rush outside I hadn't thought to grab a fire extinguisher. I yelled at a nearby warrior to go back to the shop and get the one mounted on the brick wall next to the front door.

"And shovels, get shovels." I babbled out instructions for finding those, only to have the warriors stare at Zery as if I'd said nothing at all.

I bit back a curse, ready to turn on the queen, but she gave a nod and five warriors took up the hill in a run.

Before I could vent my full thoughts on their late-night fire, Zery held up a hand. "We didn't do this."

My mouth snapped shut as I glanced at Mother and Bubbe for confirmation.

Bubbe gestured toward the fire. "*Devochka moya*, the killer has found us."

Then I focused, really focused, on the scene surrounding the fire. Ten spears protruded from the ground forming a semicircle around the flames.

I frowned. Ten. The number had no significance I could think of. Bubbe stepped toward the first spear and nodded to where the iron head stuck out of the soil.

Traced in the dirt with some kind of powder was an esoteric drawing of a deer. The design was classic Amazon, simple, but elegant, showing just enough of the animal's definitive characteristics to leave no doubt of what it was—the kind of design preferred for *givnomai* tattoos because of their smaller size.

I swallowed hard and kept my eyes cast down, away from Bubbe's prying eyes. I moved to the next spear and the next. In front of each was a drawing: lion, bull, hawk. I listed off the totems one by one—all present and accounted for except for two, the bear and the leopard.

"Two are missing." Bubbe stared into the fire.

It was an obvious statement, not one I thought needed a reply.

"Do you wonder why?" she asked. The flames crackled, laughing at us.

"I—"

"The dead girls' totems are missing, but they are not far, I don't think." She stepped toward the fire, stuck her hand into the roaring flames and pulled out a glowing metal spearhead. She dropped it on the ground at my feet and reached into the fire again—a second spearhead landed next to my bare toes. "He's mocking us."

The warriors arrived then and under Zery's command began dousing the flames. Within seconds nothing but a smoldering pile of wood remained. Not having the same level of control my grandmother had over fire, I was forced to wait, to contain my nervous energy. As soon as the heat had died down enough that I could stand next to it without gaining a permanent sunburn, I grabbed the closest spear and began shoving ash to the side.

The white outlines of two beasts slowly emerged—a leopard and a bear. I plunged the spear back into the ground. Cursed and walked away.

Another message. Saying what? That the killer *was* targeting all of the clans?

"Did you do this?" Zery's voice was low, controlled, barely hiding an anger that rivaled my own.

I turned on her. I was tired of her accusations and angry enough to challenge her to a fight right there. I held her gaze. What I saw in hers calmed me. She was as filled with rage as I was, but it wasn't directed at me. She didn't really believe I was the killer, probably never had.

"This is personal," I said. The dead girls were tied to me now and their deaths, this fire, all of it was meant as some kind of message . . . for me.

"Has been since the beginning," she replied. "There's nothing more personal than killing someone."

Unless it was violating them by stealing a patch of their skin, a piece of who they had been in life. I bit the inside of my cheek, reminded myself Zery didn't know this piece of information.

"I want to help," I said.

Zery raised a brow, then turned and walked back to the fire.

Hating every step, I followed her like a puppy. If I was going to find the killer, I needed to know more about the girls who had been killed. To do that I needed access to the Amazons who knew them. I needed access to the safe camp.

I was on her heels when she turned. "Why? You don't even want us here. Why say you want to help now?" She waved at the smoldering mess. "Because of this? Why would this change your mind? Make you want to come back to the tribe?"

"I didn't say I wanted back in."

She grunted and shook her head, then ignored me again to start shouting orders to her warriors.

I grabbed her by the arm—a bold, probably stupid move. She froze and stared down at my hand.

I didn't let go. "You made it clear the Amazons want me to be the killer. Wanted you to bring me back for trial. I have twenty Amazons living in my gymnasium practicing with broadswords. And now, I wake to a bonfire in my front yard—a bonfire it looks like the killer set. Why wouldn't I want to help? It's the only way I'll get rid of all of you, and get my life back. Besides . . ." I dropped my hold on her arm, but she stayed put, twisted her mouth to the side.

I breathed in, then continued. "I'm not a monster. I don't want any more girls killed either. And I can help. You know I can. I'm the only Amazon who really understands the human world and Madison, who has lived here."

"That's not important. We won't let humans get in our way," she replied.

"Do you want to endanger the whole tribe? There are laws, Zery. The police are already involved. A detective came here. He showed me pictures of the girls' *telios* tattoos, wanted to know if I could identify them. You don't know how to talk with the police, but I can. I can get information for you." It was a big promise and not one I was sure I could deliver on, but I was desperate.

I'd interested her; I could see it on her face. "You think he'd talk to you?"

I nodded. "But I need something from you first. I need safe passage to the tribe's camp, need to know more about the girls."

Without warning, she grabbed my hand and squeezed. "Why ask for passage now? You didn't the other night."

My breath caught in my throat. The totems; they'd found them and sensed me.

She leaned closer, whispered in my ear. "I didn't want to believe Alcippe when she said you delivered those totems, but it was you, wasn't it?"

I licked my lips. Across the dampened fire, Mother and Bubbe watched us. I didn't trust that Bubbe couldn't hear every word.

Zery let go of my hand. I squeezed my fingers in and out of a fist, forced the blood back into the digits.

She stepped to the side, blocking my view of my family—and their view of our conversation. "How'd you get them?"

It was my chance to share, to lighten my load, but as I looked at her, the smoke from the now-dead fire still hanging in the air behind her, I realized I couldn't. At some point I was going to have to open up to someone, tell them what had happened, but I wasn't ready yet—not until I understood why the killer had brought the girls to me.

I realized some part of me wondered if something I had done had cost the girls their lives. The killer hadn't picked me at random. I needed to know more, do more, then I'd share.

I blew out a breath and stared my old friend in the eyes, prayed some of our lifelong bond still existed. "I didn't kill those girls and I don't know who did, but I want to find out—just as much as you do, more than you do."

There was doubt in Zery's eyes, indecision. I clasped her hand in mine. "Let me help."

The expression on her face was serious, deadly serious. I thought she was going to say no.

Instead, I got, "I'm sorry for the loss of your son. I never said that before, and I'm sorry for that too."

Damn her. My eyes began to leak. Tears hung on my lower lashes, threatening to fall.

She squeezed my hand, then dropped it and took a step back. "I'll let Alcippe know you're coming. You'll have to deal with her. She doesn't trust you, and she won't like you being there."

Alcippe, the high priestess who killed my son. The feeling was mutual.

Chapter Ten

I went to bed antsy and woke up feeling pretty much the same.

Sunday was my usual day off, when I took one. Today, Janet was scheduled to be in and in charge—making it a perfect time to head south to the safe camp. Unfortunately, in the early hours of the morning she'd left a message on voice mail saying she was sick. I alternated Sunday management between her and Cheryl. But Cheryl had her kids every other weekend, and this weekend was special. She'd taken them to the Dells, a city just north of Madison filled with water parks.

I wasn't ready to ditch my plans, though. After pressing the 3 on my phone to delete Janet's message, I scribbled out a short note and taped it to Mother's door. She wouldn't like being tied to the shop instead of being free to play Amazon warrior, but she'd do it. I just had to be out of the building before she got back upstairs from her morning workout.

One good thing . . . Harmony was still at her friend's and probably would be most of the day. I had purposely not given her a "must be home by" time. I figured I wouldn't see her until dark.

My business and home life were covered for today, but I was going to have to find some regularly scheduled activity to occupy my daughter soon. With the killer free and targeting Amazons—even if she didn't know she was an Amazon herself—I couldn't do the normal suburban thing and tell her to hang at the mall. I needed to know someone was watching her, would let me know if anyone approached her. And I couldn't continually send her to someone else's house. It broke the unspoken code of playdate etiquette that still applied, even though her playdate days were long behind us both.

I needed my girl watched, safe and away from warring Amazons. Something I'd have to work on when I got back from today's jaunt.

I walked out the front door at nine fifteen. The black mark the fire had left on my lawn was impossible to miss—as was the over-six-foot-tall male standing beside it.

With a sigh, I walked down the incline, curious as to what brought Peter here so early, but more occupied with rehearsing my feeble cover lie for the burnt disaster that was my front yard.

He was rooting around in the ashes with the toe of his boot when I arrived. I'd made sure to remove all signs of the totem animals last night before deserting the site for my bed.

"Bonfire? Are those allowed in Madison?" he asked.

I brushed hair from my face. "I don't know, and luckily no one showed up from the city to tell me." Luck had nothing to do with it. Bubbe had cast a spell, similar to the ones used to keep safe camps secret, over the space. It had been a quick and dirty piece of magic, but I guessed it had done the job. At least no police or neighbors had called to complain. Obviously, it hadn't been strong enough to keep Peter from noticing the mess, though.

"The new tenants got a little carried away." I picked up a piece of charred wood and tossed it in the air. Soot rubbed off on my palm. With a frown, I dropped the wood and rubbed my hand on my jeans.

"Weenie roast gone wrong?"

"Something like that." When he said it, it sounded even more lame than when I'd heard similar words come out of my own mouth.

"Listen, I've got some errands to run today. You want to keep an eye on things?" I asked.

His eyes widened. "Me?"

I flushed. I shouldn't have asked him. I had left the note on Mother's door, even unwilling she was a better choice than Peter. He'd only worked for me a few days. "Never mind."

"No, I'd love to." He wrapped his fingers around my biceps, but softly, then just as quickly he pulled his hand back. His fingers trailed over my skin. A shiver passed over my body.

"Anything I should be watching out for?" he added.

Lost in the sensation of his fingers drifting over my skin, I almost missed the question. "N-no . . . n-n-othing . . . special." The words came out in a stutter.

"What exactly were they doing last night?" He opened his fingers, lying flat on his palm was an iron spearhead.

I reached out to grab it. His fingers closed, cutting off my view of the weapon's head.

I laughed, tried to cover my stupid move. The spearhead told him nothing. "That's theirs. Some kind of initiation rite, I take it. I didn't ask too many questions—just told them not to do it again."

"Then I don't need to stand guard with an extinguisher?"

I hoped to hell not. I shook my head, laughed again. "No, Zery and I came to an understanding."

"Zery?" He angled his head, like a dog trying to pin down the source of some sound.

"The woman in charge; that's her name." I held out my hand, silently asking for the spearhead.

He tossed it in the air, let it settle back on his palm, then tucked it into the pocket of his pants. "No worries. I'll take it to her. You're in a hurry, right?"

I forced my lips into a smile. "Thanks." I hadn't gone

over my cover story with Zery, but I couldn't imagine her opening up to Peter. She'd probably do no more than grunt, no matter what he said to her.

I stood there a second longer than felt comfortable. Peter watched me, waiting.

"Uh-oh, and my daughter, Harmony. She's at a friend's. I should be back before she gets home."

"Good to know." His face wore a *what else?* expression.

"Guess I'll be going."

He nodded.

I glanced at my watch. He had hours before his shift started. I couldn't order him to work. I glanced at my watch again. "You're here early."

He shrugged and slipped his lips into one of those smiles that made my hormones smile with him and told my brain to agree to whatever he said, whatever he wanted to do. "Still getting settled. I have some paperwork to go through, some new designs to add to the flash. And, honestly, I've got nowhere else to be."

"Oh, sure." I searched for a reason to order him to the shop, away from the burnt circle of earth. The little gears that ran my brain were clacking so loudly I was surprised he didn't ask about the noise. "I left a note on Mother's door that she would be in charge. Maybe, since you're here, you could go up and let her know she's off the hook." If Mother had made her way up from her workout and found my note, she'd probably done no more than wad it into a ball. If she hadn't stopped working out, she wouldn't welcome an intrusion from Peter. But really, was that my problem?

"Walk me up?" I nodded toward the hill and tried a smile of my own. The flirtatious move felt about as natural as breathing under water.

His hand drifted to the pocket where he'd stashed the spearhead, but he just shoved the fingers of both hands into his front pockets and started moving with me up the hill.

"Speaking of Harmony . . ."

I jumped, my mind far from my daughter at that point.

"If you're looking for something for her to do after school, I might know something."

"Why would you think—?"

"I noticed since your new tenants moved in that she's not been around much—had a lot of 'friend time.' Then with—" He jerked his head back toward the charred spot we'd left behind. "If I'm wrong . . ."

"No." *Why deny it?* "I rented the space to them and I'm locked in now, but after last night . . . I'm thinking it might be better if she wasn't too influenced by them."

Peter bent at the waist to help propel himself up the hill.

The roar of a lawn mower and the scent of cut grass drifted from one of my neighbor's yards. A moment of normal in an insane world.

"My client, Makis, the man in the wheelchair?" Peter

held out a hand to help me up the incline. I stared at it, not getting for a second what he was doing. Then realizing what he was offering, I shook my head and plowed ahead, moved ahead of him.

You can take the Amazon out of the tribe . . .

Peter's long gait closed the small space I'd put between us. "He's starting an after-school art program. He used to teach high school. I told you I'd known him awhile."

A response didn't seem necessary. I concentrated on trying to regain the lead his longer legs had stolen from me.

"He has a shop not far from the school. He's starting a class next week. I think they've got permission to paint a mural for some business off Regent. They'll even get paid, but he's going to work with the kids a bit first."

"So, the classes . . . ?"

"Are cheap, might even be able to work out a trade. Makis wants me to do some touch-up work on one of his older tattoos."

Free class, some extra lip-gloss money for Harmony, and an opportunity to keep her away from spear-tossing Amazons who just might decide to enlighten her on her own heritage? *Yeah. I am interested.*

Peter told me he'd leave Makis's contact information on my desk. I bent to tie my shoe while he walked in the front door. I considered going back down the hill to make sure no signs of the sketches were left behind—if we'd missed a spearhead, who knew what else might have slipped our attention? It had been late and dark, and we had been far from relaxed.

As I was weighing the risk of Peter seeing me back at the scene of the crime and raising new questions in his mind, Bubbe stepped out of the basement, escorting yet another workout-attired suburban mom—this one dressed in matching baby blue hoodie and capris. What these women spent on clothing supposedly meant for sweat boggled my brain.

Bubbe tapped a finger on the railing. "Don't judge."

I yanked my attention from the blond ponytail bouncing toward the parking lot and frowned at my grandmother. "I wasn't."

"Ha." She pursed her lips, a light forming in her eyes I didn't care for.

I tried to cut her off. "Could you do another sweep of the front lawn? Peter was down there. He found a spearhead."

She lifted one shoulder in a *so what?* gesture. "You brought him here."

My eyes narrowed. "Don't judge."

She dropped her gaze to the hand still resting on the banister, but before she did, I would have sworn I saw a sparkle in her still-young eyes. "My snake is missing. Have you seen him?" She lifted her eyes and her brows—the challenge and her real question clear.

"You have a snake?" I let my lips pull down in a moue.

She shook her head. "Secrets. So many secrets. Why keep them from me?"

Or try, she meant.

I let my hand slip down the strap of my messenger bag to the keys clipped there. Pretending to struggle with the carabiner, I continued walking.

The old fraud. Like she didn't have plenty of secrets. My grandmother was a bundle of secrets. She probably knew the whereabouts of Jimmy Hoffa, Amelia Earhart, and Atlantis. Hell, she might have been responsible for the disappearance of all three.

Muttering under my breath, I climbed in my truck and headed south.

I pulled into the dirt driveway that led to the safe camp and flipped off the truck's motor. I'd been here only a few days before, but this was different—it was day and I was expected. What lovely greeting party would Alcippe have planned for me?

I'd thought Bubbe or Mother might have offered some advice for me—but neither had. Neither had even mentioned my trip, although I knew both were aware of it. My family . . . pretty much of the sink or swim on your own mindset.

I gripped the steering wheel for a few moments. The tendons of my hand shone white from the stress. I could do this. I could walk back into that house, even into the room where I'd lost my son. Maybe I'd gain something from this visit. If I could beard this lion, I could do anything.

The engine turned over so smoothly, I didn't even realize my hand had turned the key.

Determination a hard rock in my heart, I continued down the drive.

The Amazons were out, exercising the horses, working in the garden, and, of course, fighting. The big guns were back at my house, but what looked like a pair of younger Amazons faced off with staffs, performing moves that would easily qualify them for a role in a Jackie Chan movie.

When I pulled in, horses were reined to a stop, pruners stilled, and staffs slowed. All eyes watched me. Resisting the urge to place my hands on my head, I stepped from the truck.

Before both of my feet met gravel, Alcippe was out the front door, her hands held deceptively at her sides, palms facing me. With the theme song from *The Good, the Bad and the Ugly* scrolling through my head, I stepped onto the path that led to the front door.

Alcippe shared my grandmother's love of a flowing wardrobe, although hers didn't scream of any one culture— more just hippie-shop chic. Her gray hair was pulled back, making her jaw look more square, her eyes more piercing.

"Why are you here?" She looked like she wanted to spit.

"Not to see you."

She muttered something under her breath, and I was instantly on alert. A high priestess muttering was much like a gunslinger's finger flickering near his six-shooter—or worse, it could be the bullet. But nothing happened, nothing I could see or sense anyway.

"Zery wants to trust you. I don't," she said, then turned in a whirl of purple and red, heading back inside.

Ah, an insult. Telling the tribe she was so unafraid of me, she'd turn her back.

I picked up a rock and tossed it in my palm. I considered throwing it, just to get out some aggression, and for the satisfying feel of pelting it against her back. Instead, I forgot myself even more, allowed myself to use magic. Even though I'd been hiding my growing skills from my family, I couldn't resist pulling them out when faced with Alcippe. I murmured a tiny incantation, just something to get her attention—not show my true strength, not yet . . . unless I needed to.

I closed my other hand and blew into my balled fist.

As I'd guessed, Alcippe's turned back was a ruse. She hadn't lowered all her defenses. She immediately sensed the magic and froze.

A tornado whirled within my grip—innocent now, but if I released it, said the few words it would take to let it grow . . . could it reach the old woman, suck her up, and swirl her away before she had a chance to fight back?

Alcippe didn't give me an opportunity to find out. She whirled, her hands rising from her sides. Grass shot up at my feet, wrapping around my legs. A nearby tree lurched, the roots shifting beneath my feet, knocking me onto my knees.

Then three of the young warriors were beside me. Three staffs jammed against my throat. Alcippe appeared, her face upside-down from my present state of viewing.

"Be grateful Zery gave you safe passage . . . this time." Then she did spit, inches from my face.

The tornado spun in my fist, growing with my anger. My fingers loosened. I wanted to let it go as badly as I'd ever wanted anything, but I wasn't strong enough to control the magic, not yet. I could create it, but then it would feed on my emotions, uncontrolled by my head. I might get Alcippe, but I'd also get every Amazon in the camp. I'd be unable to do anything except watch as the entire place was flattened, then the remains swept up and away.

Gritting my jaw until I thought the bone would pop, I forced down my anger, smashed my palm into the dirt and ground the life out of my spell.

"You heard her. Zery gave me safe passage. Who do you follow, the queen or her?" I muttered.

Alcippe had started moving away; at my words she stopped, but she didn't say anything. She knew I'd called her hand.

The warrior most visible, the one whose staff was jabbed against my throat, licked her lips, but she didn't glance at the others. I kept my focus on her, steady and sure.

With no warning, she stepped back. The others quickly followed.

Rubbing my throat with one hand, I pushed myself

out of the gravel with the other. Bits of it clung to my jeans. I brushed off the backs of my legs, pretended not to feel Alcippe's glare on the top of my head.

How I wanted to rise up and attack, but this wasn't about me, and Zery had risked a lot by giving me passage. If I attacked Alcippe now, the priestess would win. She'd be proven right, her standing elevated—even if I killed her, she'd survive in martyrdom. I couldn't have that. I wanted to take from her what she'd taken from me— what we each valued most. For me, it had been one of my children; for her, it would be her standing in the tribe.

I wanted her to mess up, and I wanted to be the person to expose her. I wanted to take her down.

I stood, and captured Alcippe's gaze. "Another time?"

"Soon," she responded.

I smiled, then turned my back on her as she'd done to me earlier. The warriors parted, and I took a breath. Adrenaline pumped through me, but I needed calm to gain trust. Calm and strong, that was the persona that would enable me to get more. I squared my shoulders and grabbed the attention of the warrior I'd pegged as the leader.

"Anyone here know either of the girls who were killed?"

Her gaze flowed down my body, assessing me. I angled my head, showing I expected an answer but was confident enough to wait for it.

Finally . . . "All of us. At least somewhat."

"But some more than others?"

"Some."

Ah, the joys of conversing with a warrior. Knowing I wasn't going to get many clues from her, I surveyed the rest of the tribe, looking to see who seemed most interested and most nervous. One of the women working in the garden showed a sudden interest in removing a stubborn weed. She bent down and hid her face.

I stepped away from the warriors, on a straight path to the hearth-keeper now up to her neck in pumpkin leaves.

I bent down beside her and rolled over a pumpkin, checking for rot. She glanced up. "Are you a hearth-keeper?" she murmured. She was young and pretty, with a round face and caring eyes.

The pumpkin was solid, orange, and ready for picking. I gave it a thump for effect, then twisted it off the vine. "I'm not anything. I take care of what needs taking care of."

A line formed between her brows. She was having a hard time fitting my words into the tidily divided world of the Amazons.

"You know why I'm here."

She glanced up. One of the older hearth-keepers picked up a hoe and chopped at the ground. I moved to the side, blocking her view. "Zery sent me." It was a stretch, but close enough. "I heard some of the girls were sneaking off to Madison. You know anything about that?"

Her gaze danced around the clearing, but when it

landed back on me, I could see she'd made a decision. "A few of us. We've been doing it for a while."

Jackpot. I jerked another pumpkin from the vine and shoved it into her hands. "Don't we need to put these somewhere cool? So they don't rot?"

"Good idea." She rubbed dirt from her pumpkin with a rag she had tucked in her jeans, then stood. We walked past the glarer, neither of us sparing her a glance. I changed my walk, putting as much warrior swagger into it as I could muster. I could have tossed a little magic her way, but that would have just got Alcippe back on my ass. Besides, Bubbe always said the greatest strength was great restraint. Not something I usually practiced, but now seemed like a smart time to start.

We passed Alcippe on our way around the house. Her fingers twitched as I walked by. I smiled at the girl walking beside me and attempted chitchat, saying something nonsensical about which pumpkins made the best pies—*as if I knew*. The young Amazon played along, and we both passed the high priestess without darting a glance in her direction, but the hair on the back of my neck curled upward, and my eyes scanned the terrain ahead, watching for another attack. Earth was Alcippe's element of choice—not that she couldn't call on one of the other three—but since it seemed to be her steady fallback, like air was mine, I assumed it was her area of strength.

We made it to the root cellar intact, but as the girl started to descend the steps, I stopped her. Being under a pile of earth and stone with Alcippe so close did not seem like a good plan. "Is there somewhere else we could go?"

She adjusted the pumpkin, wedging it against her hip for a better grip, then glanced at the back of the farmhouse. "We could make pies. You were just talking about it."

I was? "How private . . . ?"

"Plenty. Everyone's outside. It'll be fun and get me out of cooking later." She laughed. "Not that I mind."

Yeah, who would mind standing over a hot stove, slaving away for a bunch of ungrateful warriors? I suppressed a grimace. Instead, I stepped back and held out one arm. "Lead on."

A bounce in her step, she headed toward the back door. I smacked my palm against the pumpkin pressed against my stomach. I was going to bake a pie. Mother would love this.

Chapter Eleven

Luckily, the back door led directly into the kitchen, not a room I'd spent much time in during any of my stays at this safe house. Future warriors, which had been my mother's plans for me, did not learn to cook; future priestesses, my grandmother's plans for me, were considered a threat to all things culinary. Their tendency to play with the elements, especially fire and wind, wreaked havoc with recipe outcomes.

By the time I'd settled into my own artisan plan as an adult, there had been no reason for me to enter the kitchen.

So, the room happily held no bad memories. I could almost pretend I wasn't in the house where I'd lost my son at all.

Almost.

"Is there a problem?" Dana, she'd told me her name a few minutes earlier, stopped in the process of pulling an apron over her head. Her face showing curiosity and a little concern, she watched me as I stared through the door that led from the kitchen into the rest of the house. The dining room I remembered. Things hadn't changed much in ten years—same battered oak table and chairs, same ugly 1970s gold chandelier. Memories started creeping back.

"No, nothing." I shoved the swinging door closed with my foot and turned my back on it.

Dana chattered merrily, pulling pie pans, spoons, butter, and other necessities from cupboards, drawers, and the refrigerator. In the kitchen, or maybe out from under the other Amazons' watchful glares, she was a different person—confident and content.

I grabbed a knife and did the only job I knew for sure I'd be able to master. I chopped the pumpkin in two and scooped out seeds, dumping the stringy stuff onto a cookie sheet Dana had set out for the purpose.

"The trips to Madison . . ." I prompted.

"They were fun. Maybe because we knew we weren't supposed to be going there." While Dana pulled out various ingredients, she watched as I cut the pumpkin into pieces. When I was done, she tossed them into a bowl with water, covered it with a lid, and put it into the microwave.

Pumpkin-cooking under way, she cut butter into a bowl of flour with a fork, sprinkled some ice water on top, and started kneading the mixture with her bare hands.

I watched, somewhat fascinated. It was like watching Bubbe perform a new spell. How this mess would work out to dessert was beyond my understanding.

After only a few seconds of kneading, she flipped the dough out of the bowl onto the flour-covered tabletop and held out a rolling pin. "Make it that size." She nodded toward a pie pan.

I wiped my hands on my pants. Horror shot through Dana's eyes. I spun, expecting Alcippe or a band of warriors to be standing behind me, but aside from Dana and me, the kitchen was still vacant.

With a shrug, I picked up the rolling pin and did my best to flatten the dough. "So, Madison. You went there to . . . ?" I prompted.

Dana edged around me and took the now-steaming bowl of pumpkin from the microwave. After dropping the pumpkin into a blender and pureeing it smooth, Dana replied, "Boys, of course."

Of course. "You find any?"

A tiny smile curved Dana's lips and her hand moved toward her middle. "We did."

"You're pregnant?" The rolling pin fell from my fingers with a thud.

"I'm twenty-two."

Well, then that was okay, another few years and her eggs would have been all dried up. I ground my teeth together to keep my sarcastic thoughts to myself. Thanks to the priestesses, Amazons had had control over their reproduction for centuries before female humans had. Because of our long lives, most of us waited into our eighties to have a child.

"Were the other girls . . . ?" The thought made my stomach lurch. I hadn't sensed spirits aside from the girls', but I was far from the most experienced in such deductions.

Dana poured the pumpkin back into its bowl along with a mixture of sugar and spices. Stirring, she replied, "I don't think so. None of the other girls who went with us are—just me." Again with the dreamy, too-stupid-to-know-better look.

I mean, I loved Harmony. But at twenty-two, I'd have no more been able to take care of her than—I glanced around—than bake this pie. And that, of course, was the difference. Dana was a hearth-keeper and obviously one content with her fate. The whole maternal thing was probably as natural to her as casting a spell was to Bubbe or tossing a spear was to Mother. I'd never been that natural at anything. I was good at art, but even that didn't come to me like breathing.

"So, boys. What kind did you meet?"

"College boys, mainly. Most of the girls were warriors. Tereis was. Aggie was an artisan."

No one had told me the dead girls' names, but it was easy to guess who she was talking about.

"They both wanted athletes."

Of course.

"The bar we went to. A lot of UW football players hang out there."

"And your guy?" It wasn't really a piece of information I needed to know, but I was interested.

"He worked there. Part-time. He wasn't as . . . you know." She mimicked broad shoulders with her hands. "But there was something about him. I don't think he was stronger than the guys the other girls went after. Just different."

She walked over to survey my work. It must have passed muster. She flopped it into the pie pan.

"Was there any one guy the other girls showed interest in, or that showed interest in them?"

Busy pressing perfect ridges into the crust, Dana sighed. "All the guys showed interest in the others, especially the warriors."

Some things never changed. "But no one in particular? Did Tereis and Aggie talk to the same boy?"

Dana poured the pumpkin into the crust, then tapped the spoon against the bowl's lip. "Not that I noticed. Tim"—she touched her stomach, an unconscious gesture that told me who she was referring to—"tried to be polite, but they brushed him off. Had bigger fish to fry, I guess." She carried the pie to the oven and jerked the door open. The rack inside rattled.

Then, as if remembering what had happened to the pair, she flushed. "Not that I blame them. I realize it's important to pick someone strong. I just . . ." She stared down at the unbaked pie.

"Want something different."

She looked up, her thumb gouging into the crimped edge of the crust. "Is that wrong?"

I took the pie from her and slid it into the oven, then ran a hand down her arm, just a light brush—my skin barely making contact with hers.

"Not at all."

I spent another hour and a half wandering around the compound trying to convince some of the other Amazons to talk to me. A few did, but none were as forthcoming as Dana. The girl had a much better sense of who she was than I'd ever had, probably than I did right now, but I could tell we shared one thing. Neither of us truly felt as if we fit. I'd had friends, as it appeared she did, but living as an Amazon never felt quite right to me—like wearing someone else's shoes. They might look right to the outside world, but you knew inside they weren't, could feel it with every step you took.

She'd sought me out again before I left, shoving a cardboard box with the pie in it into my hands. My first pie. Okay, she'd done most of the work, but, still, I was strangely proud. I placed the box in the coveted position of shotgun for the ride home.

It was after two. I'd be able to make it back to Madison probably before Harmony arrived home. I might even be able to drive by the bar and see if Tim was working. If he worked at the place, he'd be familiar with the football players who hung out there, and probably more cognizant of who the girls went off with.

I was hoping one name would crop up for both. That would really simplify things. Unfortunately, I didn't have pictures of either girl. Amazons weren't big on photography. But I suspected a healthy American boy wouldn't forget any of the Amazons too quickly.

I just hoped he didn't ask about Dana. I wasn't going to be sharing news of his upcoming daddyhood with him, but I didn't relish the idea of hiding it from him either.

As it turned out, traffic was a bugger getting out of Illinois—some kind of mystery backup where a toll booth used to sit on Highway 39 in Rockford. I pulled into my drive at five. I wanted to see my daughter and my shop, sink into the life I'd built for myself. Visiting the Amazon camp had more of an effect on me than I'd thought it would when I had left earlier today. I'd had an itchy need to get home as quickly as I could since passing the traffic snarl. I'd almost been glad of the excuse to skip the trip downtown to the bar.

Harmony and her best friend, Rachel, stood outside the gym. Next to them, Pisto, the blond warrior who had confronted Peter's client, demonstrated various stances with a staff. The pie box clenched in my arms, I walked up.

"I thought you spent the day at Rachel's."

Harmony glanced at me, her eyes wide, blue and innocent. "We did. She just walked me home."

"And then what? You going to walk *her* back home?" Rachel lived two streets behind us. The walking each other home game had become a favorite ploy as soon as they were old enough that both Rachel's mother and I felt secure to let them out of our sight for a few minutes. The "walk home" could take hours.

"No." Complete indignation on my daughter's part. "CleCle"—Harmony's name for my mother—"said the tribe was taking in students. Rachel and I thought it might be fun to take some."

"The tribe?" What had Mother done?

"Yeah. The self-defense group." She frowned at Pisto. "Isn't that what you called yourselves?"

Pisto tilted the staff back and forth in front of her. Her gaze caught mine. "We do."

"Anyway, CleCle suggested it, and Pisto"—she nodded at the warrior—"said she'd work us in for free. You can't beat that."

"I doubt Rachel's mother—" I started, but both girls cut me off, jabbering as only teenage girls can. Finally, Rachel's voice won out.

"My mom will be thrilled. She's been saying the school should offer some kind of self-defense class for girls. The killings really have her freaked out. Besides, in a few years we'll be going to college. Everyone should be able to defend herself before that." She pulled her body erect, speaking with all the authority of a middle-aged corporate executive—in other words, a perfect imitation of her mother. Her father owned a bead shop off Monroe. He was also head flapjack flipper at a local "pancakes for peace" event and had probably walked around the globe for various peace walks. I doubted the idea of his daughter learning to smash a man's skull with a twenty-pound staff would hold a lot of appeal for him.

"Self-defense is an important skill for women in today's world." Mother had sneaked up behind me, like the cat that was tattooed on her breast.

I curled my lip, revealing a hint of the snarl that threatened to spill out. After everything that had happened, I couldn't disagree with Mother. I could actually have been talked into letting Harmony train with her, but not with Pisto and the tribe. I couldn't trust what they might tell my daughter. When she found out about the Amazons, it damn well had to come from me.

"Too bad the 'tribe' only has evening classes." I glared at Pisto, daring her to disagree with my words. Her only response was a bored flutter of her eyelashes. I looked at my daughter, a *have I got good news for you* smile on my face. "I've already signed you up for classes after school. Your evenings are fully booked."

"What?" I could see my daughter getting ready to dig in her heels, to scream about the injustice of being signed up for something without her full and prior approval. It didn't stop me from sending her to gymnastics when she was five (something Mother had fully approved of), and it wasn't going to stop me now. I shoved the pie box against Mother's chest, trusting she wouldn't let it fall to the ground, and looped my arm through my daughter's. "Art class. A friend of Peter's is teaching it."

"Peter's?" Rachel nudged Harmony in the side. I ignored the gesture. So what if Peter's "friend" wasn't exactly what they might be expecting. Far be it from me to shatter their hormone-ridden dreams.

Harmony quickly moved from objection to negotiation. "Can Rachel take it too? What kind of art will we be learning? Will I need any supplies?"

Once she mentioned shopping, even if it was for dry art supplies, I knew I had her.

I stopped to toss a smile back at Mother. She had lifted the aluminum foil cover Dana had placed over the pie and was staring as if the box contained a two-headed lizard. "It's a pie," she said.

"I know. I baked it for you. I was thinking some hearth-keeping skills might be a good thing for Harmony to learn too."

The look on Mother's face made my entire day worthwhile.

We had the pie for dessert after dinner. I ate well more than my share, just to enjoy the expression on Mother's face every time I picked up the knife and sliced into the orange goodness. Bubbe seemed to be on to me, but Mother was as easy to provoke as a two-year-old who had missed her nap—at least when it came to hints of hearth-keeping. And honestly, I wasn't just prodding her. Working with Dana had made me realize yet another part of life I'd missed out on. Being taught how to cook, clean, and take care of babies wouldn't scar my daughter—it was one of Artemis's aspects, after all, and key to survival.

No, Harmony learning a few skills wouldn't be a bad idea. Me learning a few wouldn't either. And there were plenty of classes available in Madison. When everything settled down, I just might see about enrolling us—a nice mother/daughter treat. Maybe I'd ask Mother if she wanted to join us.

All in all, I went to bed happy. I felt like I'd started fulfilling my promise to the dead teens. I'd gotten Harmony to agree to the art class. And I had a full—if somewhat bloated—belly. Life was as good as it could be with a gymnasium full of Amazons and a serial killer on the loose.

The last fact was where my mind went first when I woke at one A.M., but there had been no stone cast against my window. It was the dead girls. They were back.

I sat up this time, my sheet pulled around me, my back against the headboard. A nervous energy danced around the room, like the girls' spirits wanted to tell me something but couldn't figure out how to get the thoughts across.

After their last visit, I'd made a few preparations in case they returned. I pulled a bag of dirt and a candle from my bedside table's drawer, along with the two totems I'd decided to keep. Not reinstating Bubbe's serpent ward had told her I'd been snooping around her space. As soon as she made that discovery, I knew she'd immediately cataloged all her possessions and discovered they were missing. Why return them now?

I kneeled on the floor, then carefully dumped the dirt and formed it into one small compact pile. With the candle shoved into the middle and the two totems lying on the soil, I was ready.

The girls brushed around me, breaths cool, then hot, stirring the hair on the back of my neck, causing my worn T-shirt to flutter against my skin. They were agitated, even more than they had been on their last visit. The sadness I'd sensed then was still present, but pressed down by something heavier, darker . . . angrier . . .

Praying their movement wouldn't make my job harder, I lit the candle with trembling fingers. The flame flickered but held.

If I'd known their *givnomais,* the process would have been easier. The combination of *telios* and *givnomai* was as unique as a fingerprint. No two living Amazons through history had shared the same matching combination. A priestess checked to assure this before she gave any girl her *givnomai.* This caused a lot of disappointment when a girl's first choice was taken, but since the magic would be weakened if shared, they all got over it. They didn't have a choice.

I could have drawn the *givnomais* in the dirt. It wouldn't have given them their voices, nothing as dramatic as that, but it would have guaranteed no interference and no listening in—a private call versus talking on a party line.

But I hadn't thought to ask while at the safe camp. Chances were, none there knew anyway. Because the combination was so personal, most Amazons kept their *telioses* hidden. A secret only their closest friends, relatives, and the artist who gave them the mark knew. I knew Mother's, but not Bubbe's. And I knew the fifty or so Amazons I'd tattooed before leaving the tribe. And I knew Zery's. That was it.

The flutters changed to a flap, whispers to murmurs. I could almost make out a word. A hiss like a snake. The serpent from Bubbe's ward? Were they warning me against it? Or against someone from the serpent clan?

Frustrated, I bent lower until my chin almost touched the candle's flame. I placed a hand on each totem, willed my brain to understand what they were trying to say.

The smell of wax filled my lungs. A breath, strong, like a slap, hit me from the side. The candle went out.

Alone in the darkness, I heard it . . . "Zery . . ." and the girls were gone.

Chapter Twelve

I didn't pause to think about what questions my bond with the dead girls might bring up. I didn't pause to pull on pants or shoes. I didn't pause for anything.

I leapt up and rushed from my room, ran straight down the fire escape. Once outside, I stared at the closed doors of my gymnasium. A few dozen Amazons slept inside. I couldn't rush in, screaming for Zery. To do so would pretty much guarantee I wouldn't leave with my head attached to my shoulders.

I took a breath, waited for my pounding heart to slow. I'd have to go in like a warrior: calm, controlled, and ready to fight whatever waited inside. I had my hand on the door handle when fingers wrapped around my upper arm.

"What are you doing?" Mother, fully dressed and armed for battle, squeezed my arm. Normally I would have flexed the muscle or pulled away, but honestly, I was just too darn glad to see her.

"Zery. Something's happened to her."

"How do you—?"

The expression on my face must have told her there wasn't time to ask.

She pushed me behind her and knocked on the door with her staff, a fast but complicated rhythm that I had no hope of memorizing.

The door was flung open. An Amazon, wide awake and obviously on guard duty, slammed her staff across the opening, barring our entrance.

"We need to talk to Zery." Mother had the art of body language down. Every inch of her said *don't question me.*

The guard flicked her gaze from my intimidating parent to me, then twisted her lips to the side. "Not her."

I moved forward, copying Mother's stance as best I could, but it was hard to look intimidating in a stained UW Badger tee and no pants—or bra, for that matter. "Yes—"

Mother cut me off, with an elbow to my side. "We need to see Zery." I couldn't see her face, but I could tell by the other warrior's that Mother's expression had to be somewhere between pissed-off mother bear and starved lioness. The warrior stepped aside.

Mother left her staff by the door. I started to object, but she gave a terse shake of her head. "Their house. If something goes wrong, I'll deal with it."

I didn't like it, but it wasn't my choice. Already ten

feet ahead of me, Mother cut to the right, weaving behind the sleeping Amazons who had tossed sleeping bags on the main gym floor. Zery, as queen, had taken an old office as a bedroom. It was in the basement, near the showers. I followed Mother down the steps. Behind me a warrior followed—not the guard. She must have awakened another to keep an eye on us while she stayed by her post at the door.

Mother waited for me by the closed office door. Her attention was behind me. "Pisto," she said, giving a slight nod of acknowledgment. I glanced at the taller woman—the daughter my mother never had. She, like Mother, was fully dressed. Did they sleep that way or was speed-changing part of the training?

"What's so urgent you have to wake the queen at this time of night?" she asked. Neither her body nor expression gave away any annoyance, at least to someone who hadn't lived with a cryptic warrior all her life. But I could feel tension rolling off her like heat off a summer sidewalk.

Mother opened her mouth, but I decided it was time to take charge. "I just need to see her. If she's angry because we woke her, she can take it out on me. You can all take it out on me." *Let her be in there.* An angry Zery I could deal with, a . . . I cut my own thoughts off. I didn't know why the spirits said her name. It didn't mean . . .

Tired of the games, I pushed past the larger women and shoved open the door. The original furniture consisted of a metal desk and a chair. Zery had added a wooden box full of weapons and a cot. The cot was empty.

Panic flooded over me. I groped for the electric switch, somehow thinking in the dark I'd missed my six-foot, one-hundred-and-eighty-pound friend. But the yellow glow only revealed that the cot had been slept in. The pillow bore the indentation of Zery's head, and the thin quilt lay bunched at the bottom of the cot, like she'd shoved it down before standing.

I started to move forward, to search for some clue, but a knife jabbed into my throat.

"Where is she?" The heat of Pisto's body released the woodsy smell of the homemade soap preferred by Amazons. She was shaken. I couldn't blame her. Her queen was missing.

My friend was missing. I was shaken too, and pissed.

I spun out of her reach and grabbed a weapon of my own, a flail, from Zery's box. I had no clue how to use the thing, but Pisto didn't know that. I held it above my head as if ready to give it a swing, but my action seemed unnecessary. Mother and Pisto both stood back, staring at me as if I'd just performed a miracle. Which perhaps I had. I'd escaped the clutch of a seasoned warrior. How had I done that?

I didn't have time to analyze the question. Instead I pressed my advantage—swung the flail until it twirled in a slow jerky arc. "You tell me. Where would Zery go? Is anything missing?"

Her brows lowered, Pisto stared at me. Her gaze

tracked the round-and-round movement of the studded metal ball. My shoulder began to ache, and I realized I'd screwed up royally. I had no idea how to make the thing stop, not without bashing my own brains out.

Mother cursed, an unprecedented act on her part, then jerked the flail from my hand. The head hit the wall, knocking a foot-wide chunk of plaster onto the floor. I grabbed my arm, began massaging my shoulder.

"Her sword. Does she keep it here?" Mother asked.

I glanced at the box. There was no sword.

Lips pursed, Pisto nodded. "But she prefers a staff."

Zery's staff stood angled against the wall.

"Well, she has a sword. That's something." I tried to take comfort in the words. I tried to tell myself Zery was too strong to be taken by the killer—the girls he had taken were just that, girls—inexperienced and too full of their own emerging talents to realize danger. But it didn't help.

Above our heads, the floors rattled—feet pounding as Amazons awoke and raced from the building.

"Pisto, it's Zery. Come now." The guard's voice.

I didn't wait for Mother or Pisto. I grabbed Zery's staff and flew up the stairs.

The Amazons were back in my front yard. This time there was no fire, but there was an Amazon queen staked out spread-eagle.

Zery lay unconscious on the ground. She was stomach up, and dressed in a T-shirt and shorts. Her arms and legs were spread, her body forming a five-pointed star. Shoved into the ground next to her was a sword—the one missing from her room, I guessed.

Bubbe had control of the scene, holding the Amazons back with one hand and a good dose of magic. She'd gathered air into a flat spinning disc that she held out like a shield. If an Amazon tried to approach, she knocked her aside like a gnat.

She had also, I hoped, done something to put a hush over the noise the group was creating. Yells, feet stamping, and unsheathed swords clattering drowned out anything I could hear, but I ignored it all and rushed as close to where Zery lay as Bubbe's air shield would let me. I tried to get past her, but the old miscreant pointed a finger at me, letting me know she wouldn't hesitate to send me soaring into the grass-covered hill behind me.

Then Mother and Pisto arrived. With a few smacks of their staffs against one another's, the raging Amazons quieted—not completely still, but still enough we could hear my grandmother speak.

"She's caught in a web. Not one easily broken. I've tried."

I frowned at my grandmother. I had never heard her say she couldn't do something.

"But she's just lying there," one of the warriors called out.

Pisto strode forward. Bubbe, her focus on the warrior who had spoken, missed her movement. The Amazon lieutenant got within three feet of Zery, before my grandmother noticed—telling me my grandmother was truly shaken. That fact scared me almost as much as what happened next.

Zery's body jerked. Her eyes, which had been closed, flew open. Her face flashed shock, then pain, then determination.

"Pisto, stop!" I yelled.

The Amazon froze, her gaze on her queen's face. She'd seen it too—the pain. But like me, she couldn't see what was causing it. Then, with no movement of her head, just her eyes, Zery glanced down toward her left breast, and I saw the source . . . a growing circle of blood, right where Zery's *givnomai* tattoo was—or should be.

My stomach lurched. Was it missing; had the killer already stolen it from her? Was she dying before our eyes?

"Zery." Her staff fell from my hands.

Ignoring my grandmother's glare, I stumbled to her side. "What can you do? What have you tried?" Accusations camouflaged as questions. I knew Bubbe wouldn't leave Zery there, pinned to the ground like a dead bug on a collector's Styrofoam pad.

She jerked a hand toward Mother, who grasped me from behind.

"Melanippe. What do you think? You think I leave Zery there for no good cause? The web. It's set. I take a step; she bleeds. I reach my hand to unravel the spell; she bleeds."

I took a breath. Tried to focus. "What's holding her there?"

The creases in Bubbe's forehead deepened. "The magic."

"No bonds?" I leaned forward, looking around my grandmother at Zery's wrists. There was a shadow on them—a design.

Bubbe pushed her lips against my ear. Her lips were dry as they brushed against my skin. "A drawing. An artisan's work, one skilled as priestess as well."

I turned my head. Our noses almost brushing, I stared her in the eyes. Questions, concern, fear—all three showed in her gaze.

Not me. I wouldn't . . . The objections must have shown on my face. She reached with a gnarled hand and stroked my face. "I know, *devochka moya*, but the others . . . ? I have no control of their minds."

"Any priestess could do this," I whispered, my mind rolling, thinking of Alcippe and her anger at Zery for sending me to the camp.

"Some, not all. And none would use an artisan skill when a priestess spell is quicker."

She was right, why take the time to draw something, murmuring over each line, pouring some of yourself into every bit of shading, when you could wave your hand, call up the wind or fire or one of the other elements to do your bidding? Only an artisan, someone who loved that connection, needed it, would go to that trouble, but still my mind couldn't shake an image of Alcippe . . . the anger in her eyes when she'd stepped out of the safe house's front door.

"Can art do that?" I nodded to Zery. "Hold someone down?"

"I would have said no . . ." My grandmother clucked her tongue. "And I would have been wrong."

"I have to get closer." I had to see what the design was, see if I recognized it.

Bubbe looked away, her lips disappearing into her mouth.

"I'm the only artisan here," I said, enunciating each word with precision.

Finally she stepped away, her hand going up as she did, ready to pummel back the warriors if needed. Mother's fingers squeezed my arm one last time before she stepped back. She motioned to another warrior, and a flashlight was pushed into my hand. I shined it first on Pisto. Her body was rigid, afraid to move forward and hurt Zery further, but forced by allegiance to not leave her queen.

I respected that, but I didn't want her getting in my way. As I waited, Mother circled around the group, placed a hand on Pisto from behind. The younger warrior ignored her at first, but Mother bit out something I couldn't hear, probably wouldn't have understood if I had. Something about loyalty and death, maybe with a dash of tradition thrown in to round it all out. In other words: Amazon propaganda.

I wasn't going to save Zery because she was an Amazon or my queen. I was going to save her because she was a living being and my friend—my best friend, no matter past differences.

With Pisto under Mother's control, I moved the beam of light onto Zery. She was still awake, her gaze glued to me. I couldn't tell what she was feeling. Her eyes just looked confused, like she didn't know where she was or what was happening to her. I wondered if she recognized any of us.

The thought was disturbing, but at least she wasn't jerking in pain. I shifted the beam again, this time only a little lower to a shadow I hadn't noticed before—across her mouth. Lines, like stitches. I almost dropped the flashlight.

Her mouth was sewn closed.

No wonder she hadn't called out—she couldn't. Something caught in my throat, the pie I'd gorged on earlier being heaved upward.

My body jerked, a hacking noise leaving my chest. Bubbe spun, her glare like a physical touch knocking me back upright. Show no weakness. Act strong even when you aren't—the key to dealing with animals and Amazons.

I stiffened my shoulders and forced the beam back on Zery's face—not stitches . . . lines. A drawing, like Bubbe had said held her down. Someone had drawn stitches on her mouth, closing it with ink and magic. I took a breath. Sick, but not the horror I'd first imagined. Unless Zery . . . how had the magic felt when her attacker drew those lines? Could it have been that different from the actual act?

A shiver danced up my spine, but I shook it off. Focus,

focus, focus. I had to break this spell, not let myself get lost in the hideous act itself.

I redirected the light to her wrists and bare feet. Chains were drawn around her wrists. Stakes of ink pierced her feet.

I knew how to free her.

I looked across at Mother. "Denatured alcohol. If you can't find it, bring Listerine." Without a question, Mother took off at a trot toward the shop.

Then I glanced back at Bubbe. "You said a web?"

She nodded. "A spider's work."

I wasn't sure what that meant. Hard to escape? I reached out, let my mind go like I had when I'd discovered Bubbe's serpent. This time it only took seconds. A complicated web of silver magic glowed before me. It covered the space between where Pisto and I stood and in the center of all the spirals, under the web, lay Zery. So, she'd been pinned down first, and the web spun on top of her. Made sense.

Now I could see the trap, but how did I navigate it? How did a fly?

The answer was easy. He didn't, but a spider could travel across his own web without getting stuck.

But I was no spider . . . or was I? I didn't like the direction my thoughts were taking me, but I had to follow them. The dead girls had been left for me. Had Zery too? Was it possible I could walk this web, when Bubbe couldn't? Was she simply a fly, while the killer saw me as a fellow spider?

I hated the thought, but prayed it was true too.

I closed my eyes, pulled in another breath, and dug my bare toes into the grass until I felt the soil beneath. I needed contact with the earth for this, needed all the strength I could call on. Then I opened my eyes.

The web still shone, as silver and perfect as before, one concentric circle around another with lines intersecting their core over Zery's heart. But that was it, no secret entry, no key to the path to my friend.

Disappointment, failure. I lowered the flashlight, dropping my gaze as I did. And there, right where the web started to go out of focus, I saw them—tiny bronze spots speckled throughout the web. A path leading from the outside of the web, curving around, then back, jutting out on a straight line, then following the curve again, until stopping next to Zery's sword, not the Amazon queen herself.

The sword. It wasn't there because Zery had brought it. It was there so I could kill her.

The realization hit me hard. What kind of sick bastard did this killer think I was?

It didn't matter. What did matter was that I could see the path. I could save her.

Mother arrived, a plastic bottle of denatured alcohol in her hand. I grabbed it like the desperate alcoholics you hear of, who supposedly drink the stuff for a cheap—if potentially deadly—buzz. Then, with the bottle held against my heart, I sidestepped around the edge of the web, careful not to step on even a sliver of magical silk.

I took my first step, and Pisto jumped in front of me, her staff lifted, ready to jab into my throat. The web quivered, like it was coming to life. Surprise rounded Pisto's eyes. Her feet slipped beneath her or, more accurately, the web now stuck to her feet moved beneath her. Her knees buckled. She flailed the staff overhead, then jammed it into the ground in an effort to keep from falling, but the web began to grow around her, around her legs, like an invisible spider was wrapping her, his prey, with silk. The whole process took only seconds.

I clutched the alcohol to my chest, determined not to drop it, and stared at the mummified Amazon. She was coated in silver threads, nothing but the top of her blond head visible.

"What—?" I could feel the group behind me move forward, felt Bubbe's shield click into place too. She was holding them off, but it was harder now. They'd seen one of their own fall.

"Melanippe?" Bubbe, her voice more unsure than I'd ever heard it. "What happened?"

I glanced at my grandmother. Her back was to me, but when I glanced at Mother, saw the confusion in her eyes, I realized having her back turned wasn't the issue. They were flies. Bubbe might sense the design, but she couldn't see it, not like I could, not like the spider.

"Is she breathing?" I asked my mother.

She gave a short nod. "Barely."

Barely was enough. I had no idea how to save Pisto from the web. I hoped if I saved Zery, somehow the rest of the spell would disintegrate. Besides, I had no time to waste. While Pisto lay quietly in her bundle, Zery had come to life—bucking against her bonds, her lips pulling against the stitches. If she made contact with the web, what would happen? I didn't want to find out.

"Zery, lay still." It was an order, plain and simple—a tone no one had probably used with the queen since she was fourteen and her destiny had been discovered.

To my surprise, she quieted. Everyone did. A group of twenty-plus Amazon warriors stood completely silent, watching me. Every hair on my body would have been standing at attention if I wasn't already slipping back into the zone, channeling every nature show I'd ever seen—becoming the spider.

My sight dimmed, almost to the point of blindness, but it didn't matter, didn't disturb me in the least. I didn't need it, knew deep inside I could feel my way along the web. I picked up my foot and held it out in front of me, the silk path vibrated as my weight shifted, but only slightly, not enough to alert my prey—not that it mattered. She was caught . . . waiting for me. I turned away from the victim already subdued and moved toward the one still waiting in the center of my web. My foot hovered over the thread, but I didn't set it down. Magic—cold, cloying—tickled my sole. I shifted so my foot would land six inches farther down the path—nothing. I lowered my foot, picked up the other, and continued on my way.

Somewhere along the way, my speed increased. I scurried along the silk, hopping from one safe section of thread to another—never doubting where I was going or that I wouldn't arrive there safely.

At the center I stalled. My path stopped at the sword, not my prey. I scuttled around the weapon, unsure what to do next. I reached out and realized I already had something grasped in my hands—a bottle.

A bottle. I looked up. Forms surrounded the web, spots of light—one shone on me. I held my arm up to block the glare and liquid poured down my chest—cold. And the smell . . . medicinal . . . familiar. I shuddered and turned my head to save my lungs.

With the movement, the spell I'd sunk into snapped. My sight returned, but suddenly I had no idea where to place my feet. I could feel myself swaying as if I were trying to stay on a tightrope.

The bottle fell from my grasp. I watched it fall, end over end, alcohol pouring out of it, splattering me, Zery, and the ground. Seconds before it was going to hit, I dove for the sword, jerked it from the ground just as the thread began to weave around me.

Chapter Thirteen

The thread whipped around my legs, jerking my entire body off the ground with the intensity of its movements, then slamming me back down as it swerved around again. It took a second for my brain to focus, a second I didn't have. Mother and Bubbe yelled, Bubbe at the Amazons, warning them to stay back, Mother at me, telling me to use the sword.

The sword. It had been put here for a purpose. I thought it was there to kill Zery, but maybe . . . I hacked with all the precision and patience of Freddy Krueger—barely considering where my own limbs were before slashing down with the blade. My position was awkward, on my back, the thread halfway up my body now. My arms screamed and my back ached, but I lifted the sword over and over, brought it down again and again.

Then Bubbe was beside me; I could feel her casting as she ran, dropping a spell like a net over me. I tried to lift the sword again, but it had tripled in weight. Tears escaped my eyes. I jerked on the handle—could still feel the spider's threads sticking to me, had to get them loose, was willing to cut off my own leg to accomplish it.

"Melanippe! Stop." Mother barked out the command—a tone I recognized, the same tone I'd used on Zery. I looked down. Strands of silver thread still clung to me, but slowly they melted away, turning back into what the caster had used to form them—water, simple, safe water. I brushed the beads from my skin, unable to get them off myself fast enough.

Behind me, Pisto heaved for breath. Two Amazons, the guard who had let us into the gym and another woman I didn't know, helped her to sit. The lieutenant sucked in noisy gasps. The others turned their heads and tried to pretend they didn't notice the signs of her weakness.

Then two women approached, and helped her to stand. Both hearth-keepers, I realized—the only Amazons allowed to show concern or weakness.

"Zery?" The guard kneeled next to the queen, murmured some words, then stood and headed toward the sword that had fallen from my fingers.

I reached it before her, grabbed the hilt, and pointed the tip at her breast.

"What are you doing?" I asked.

Her expression said she didn't have to answer. I drove

the tip against her shirt, felt the material give and the metal find flesh. My arms were still shrieking, but I'd moved past the pain. Too much adrenaline had surged through my body. If I had managed to cut off my own leg, I doubted I would have felt it.

"Talk," I ordered. The *I'm in charge* voice was coming easily to me at this point.

"She deserves better than this. I won't let her die at the hands of a cowardly killer—one who won't face us in battle."

I almost skewered her. The sight of Mother pointing a dagger at her throat stopped me.

"Do what you came for," Mother said. Her gaze never left the guard, but I knew she was talking to me. Dragging the sword behind me, I stumbled to Zery's side, then dropped to my knees beside her.

"Never thought I'd want to hear your voice bossing me around again," I muttered to her.

"You'll only bring her more pain and humiliation. I tried to touch her. Just a brush of my fingers, and her body jerked beneath my hand," the guard called.

I didn't turn, and the guard said no more. I assumed Mother's dagger did something to silence her; at that moment I didn't care what.

"Warriors. Such a pain in the ass. Have I said that to you recently? No, guess not. Haven't been talking a whole lot, have we?" I babbled to Zery, my eyes scanning the ground, looking for the bottle of alcohol. I had more in the shop, but I didn't dare leave Zery's side, couldn't trust that one of her fervent followers wouldn't impale her with her own sword. And I couldn't send Mother either. Bubbe had held the group off earlier, but I didn't know if that had drained her—I didn't want to find out with Zery's death, or mine.

Because I knew the Amazons well enough to realize that whatever happened in the next few minutes, somehow in the tribe's mind the fault would be mine. But the praise, if I saved Zery? That wouldn't exist.

I didn't care. I'd face the group later, worry about saving my own skin after I'd saved my friend's.

My gaze lit on the bottle. I dove for it, praying some liquid remained inside. I held it up, prayed again—but for nothing. The bottle was empty.

I flung the useless plastic trash away from me. A speckle of liquid flew from it, dotting Zery's shirt. I stared at the spots, wondering if I could have somehow stretched those tiny drops. My hand dropped to my own shirt, not speckled, but drenched.

Stupid. Stupid me.

I knee-walked to Zery's face, pulled my shirt out, and began to scrub the area around her lips harder than I'd ever scrubbed Harmony—even when she'd coated herself in Sharpie.

Zery flinched when I first touched her, but then relaxed. I watched her shirt for any increase in blood but there wasn't any. As I'd guessed, she was meant for me—I was the only one who could choose what to do with this gift, the only one who could save her. But I was also the reason she was staked out like a cowboy on an anthill.

I couldn't congratulate myself for saving my friend, not without accepting that I was the reason she was targeted to start with.

Slowly the ink disappeared. As it did, Zery's lips began to part. With them still halfway sewn together, she mumbled, "Feet."

That answered my question about the pain. The drawn-on stakes hurt more than the chains. How much did they hurt? I didn't want to know or, at least, didn't want to think about it right now.

"I need you to tell your crazy warriors you're going to live—not to skewer you like Sunday's chicken." I rubbed harder, partially to get the ink off faster, partially to get out my frustration.

"Sunday's chicken?" she mumbled, and half her mouth, the half I'd freed, lifted in a smile.

I loved her right then. As much as I'd loved her before the whole ugly blowup. And my anger fled. So, she'd chosen Alcippe and the tribe over me. It didn't matter. I'd never had a friend like Zery, someone who understood me and accepted me as well.

I needed to accept her too. She'd made her choice. It was part of who she was. She wouldn't be Zery if she hadn't.

Her mouth clean of ink, I knee-walked to her feet, rubbed the heel of my hand over my eyes as I did. Then, while she barked out orders like the queen she was, I scrubbed away the killer's marks and planned how I'd scrub him or her away too.

I tried to stay with Zery after that, but the Amazons moved in, and the looks they shot me were far from thankful or trusting. I could have stayed anyway, had enough rage simmering inside me to challenge the lot of them, but Zery was tired. I could see it in the dark circles that had formed under her eyes and the way her lower lip seemed to pull downward when she spoke.

She was using every ounce of her reserves to reassure her troops she was the titanium-clad superwoman they'd always known. She didn't need me mucking everything up by acting all concerned and caring—or by letting my pent-up aggression run free. So, I finished my job, clamped my mouth shut, and pointed my body toward my shop.

Tonight I'd go back to bed, stare at the ceiling, and think about how I was going to find the bastard who was doing all this. I already knew what I'd do to him when I did.

The next morning my resolve was just as strong, but the strain of balancing my Amazon espionage with regular life was taking its toll too. My soul was ablaze, but my body and mind were tired. Two pieces of pumpkin pie helped perk up the body, and knowing Harmony would be starting art class that afternoon eased some tension in my overtaxed brain.

I'd sorted out the details of Harmony's enrollment last night before all the excitement. I had talked with Makis on the phone after discovering he had no Web site or email address, was apparently as much of a Luddite as my grandmother. Harmony was a little distressed that Rachel's parents hadn't yet agreed for her to attend too—they valued things like time for homework on school nights. But in ever-confident teenage fashion, my daughter and her friend had worked out a plan to wear them down.

As long as Harmony was accounted for, I didn't care. Rachel's parents could worry about battling their own determined teen. May Artemis bless them all.

With Harmony off to school and my belly full of starch and sugar, I headed to the gym. I needed to hear Zery's version of her attack. I hoped the warriors were giving her some distance today.

The day was colder—one of the freaky pleasures of living in southern Wisconsin. Day-to-day temperature ranges of thirty degrees were not unheard of. I wrapped a ratty hoodie around my body and bulldozed my way through the wind.

Zery was in the gym, pummeling a weight bag with her staff. When I entered, the temperature in the room dropped another thirty degrees, at least. And I had thought it was an outdoors thing.

Shrugging off the warriors' icy stares, I pulled back my hood and strutted across the battered wood floor.

"I could never decide if you were the bravest person I know or the dumbest." Zery spun and whacked the bag with her foot.

I waited for it to slow its erratic jumping, then grabbed hold. "Cliché," I said, trying to look nonchalant, like seeing her there so healthy and strong didn't affect me, didn't make me want to pull her in for a hug.

She stopped, her chest moving up and down from her exertion. "Don't you mean touché?"

"Nope." I grinned at her, my way of apologizing for the horrible things I'd thought of her in the past.

She grunted. But the corner of her lip edged up a little.

She dropped the staff and slammed a fist into the bag. I held on.

"So, you going to tell me what happened?" I asked.

"I could ask you the same thing. I've heard some pretty crazy allegations already. And I haven't seen Pisto yet. She went on a run, but I hear she's pissed."

"Pisto pissed? I can't imagine."

Zery slammed the bag with another kick, knocking me back a few steps. I tightened my grip and grounded my stance.

"You're a smart-ass too. I'd forgotten that." Another kick, then a laugh. She shook her head. "I take that back. I hadn't. How could I?"

"Someone had to keep your big old 'I am queen' head in line."

She took a step back and folded her arms over her chest. The laughter left her face. "But then you left, and I had to fend for myself."

"Yeah. Bad times." I patted the bag, pretended to take extra time slowing it to a complete stop.

She heaved out a breath and stared at me like she could see inside me. Which wasn't far-fetched. There had been a time I'd thought Zery knew what I was thinking before I did. "Okay, Mel. Let's talk. I'll tell you what happened to me, but you have to give something too. I need to know what you're hiding—all of it."

I curled my fingers against the bag and scratched the surface of the ancient leather.

Tell Zery what I am hiding. I wished I could—I did. But if I told her I'd known about the girls for weeks, had hauled both of them off without coming to the tribe . . . She was queen. I'd gotten angry at her before for being who and what she was. I wouldn't again, but just like I wouldn't blame a bull for goring me, I wouldn't stand in front of it with a red cape either. Not unless I had a pretty fancy dance worked out, which I didn't, not yet.

I stared at my hand. Tiny flecks of red were embedded under my short-cropped nails.

I met her gaze. "I'll tell you what I did last night."

"That's not what I asked for."

I shrugged. "It's all I've got."

She dropped to a squat, picked up her staff, and swung it toward my feet, all in one graceful motion. Without thinking, I somersaulted forward in a tiny leap that propelled my body over the staff and back on my feet.

Also on her feet, Zery placed the end of her staff on the floor. "It's not all you've got—not by a long shot, but it's all you'll give me. Fair enough—for now."

Chapter Fourteen

We went to the cafeteria to talk. It was the closest thing we had to neutral ground. And since it was almost nine by this point, the place was empty. I made myself at home, grabbing us coffee and cream.

"You thinking of adding hearth-keeping to your list of skills?" Zery took a sip of her coffee, black, of course.

In the process of adding cream to mine, I smiled. "I might. Just to annoy Mother, if for no other reason."

She tilted her head. "When are you going to stop competing with your family?" The question was light, but it hit home. Still, I decided to keep my answer equally light in tone.

"Have you met my family? I have no hope of ever beating them. I might as well get some fun out of annoying them."

"You don't fool me."

I looked at her, surprised and a little frightened, but she kept talking.

"Believing you were in your family's shadow is the only thing that ever stopped you. You could have been queen. Maybe should have."

I laughed, spewing coffee across the tabletop. That was a good one. I looked up, thinking to share the joke with Zery, but her expression was set. She was serious.

"Yeah, so what happened yesterday . . ." I prompted.

She flicked her gaze from her coffee to me and back. For a second I thought she was going to push the whole "living in the shadow of your family" thing, but she didn't.

"It was a pretty normal day. I went for a run. Spent a few hours practicing. Took a shower. Went to bed. Woke up staked to your front yard."

That was helpful. "Any details in there you'd like to add?"

She twisted her lips. "I had some drink called wheatgrass for lunch. One of your grandmother's clients made it. You think there was something in it?"

Besides the green gunk most people cleaned off their lawn mowers?

"How'd you get to the yard?" I asked, ignoring the wheatgrass. For now I had to assume anything approved by Bubbe was safe—magically speaking.

"I walked, I think. It's pretty fuzzy. I remember feeling like someone was calling me, though. Part of me didn't want to listen, but it was like I had a thread tied around my heart . . . tugging me forward."

"Zery, how's your *givnomai*?" Last night blood had stained her shirt over the tattoo, but I couldn't see the bulge of a bandage through her tee.

She placed her fingers on the spot. "Fine. Why?"

My brows lowered. "It was bleeding. Don't you remember?"

She tapped the spot again. "Was it? I wondered why my shirt was bloody."

"You didn't feel it?"

A hollowness appeared in her eyes. "I was feeling so much. It was hard to sort one ache from another."

I dropped my gaze to my coffee. Gave her a minute to push past whatever was going on in her head.

"Anyway, when it was all said and done, I was fine. No cuts or bruises even. Pisto didn't have it as lucky."

Pisto hadn't had her lips sewn shut or her feet staked through. Although the magic hadn't done physical damage to Zery, I could tell there were emotional marks. She wasn't used to being helpless, to fighting a foe she couldn't see. It would be hard on anyone, but an Amazon queen?

She covered it well.

"Pisto had welts, but me?" She held up a wrist. Her skin was smooth and bruise-free. "Why is that?"

"Wrong Saka to ask. I'm not the priestess." I took a drink.

"Mel . . ."

I set the cup down and jerked up the leg of my jeans. Red, raised stripes marked where the silk had lashed around my bare skin when I'd slipped from spider and almost been caught in the web. "Different kind of magic. The web was priestess magic. It's elemental, but real. Real wind, real fire, water, or earth. But what was done to you . . . it was something different."

"What?"

I took another swallow. "Bubbe'd never seen it before."

She wrapped her hand around her mug, waited.

"Artisan. It was artisan."

Her hand moved, jostling her cup. Coffee slopped onto her fingers. She made no move to wipe it away. "Artisan magic can only enhance what already exists. This was something else. Those spikes—they weren't enhancing anything inside me. Or the stitches." Her fingers wandered to her lips. I wondered if she was even aware of the action.

"I know. I told you Bubbe'd never seen it before. I hadn't either."

She flattened both palms against the table and leaned forward. "Are you saying an artisan tied me out last night? Made me feel like metal was piercing my flesh, like a needle was tugging its way through my lips?"

"Someone with artisan skills, but they'd have to have priestess powers too. The web was pure priestess."

"No one is that strong in more than one area, except . . ." The anger in her eyes changed to suspicion. "You got me out when even your grandmother couldn't. You got past both spells. And in the gym, the way you leapt, and the other day when Pisto went for you . . . ?" She leaned closer; her next words were a low growl. "How many skills do you have, Mel? What have you been doing while hiding up here? Did you really leave because of your son, or did you have some other agenda all along?"

The distrust on her face hurt. It shouldn't have. We hadn't trusted each other for a long time, but just as I was ready to forgive her, admit I'd been wrong, she was accusing me of . . . what?

"I wouldn't hurt you, Zery." I expected her to laugh at the very idea. *Me* be able to hurt *her,* the Amazon queen? It was ridiculous. But she didn't. Instead, she stared at some spot beyond me.

"Why would I save you, if I had lured you out there?" I added.

She kept her face turned for another second, then covered it with one hand. When she looked back at me, the wear of everything she'd been through last night, with the dead girls, all of it showed on her face.

"If not you, who?"

I didn't let my relief that she was willing to let her suspicions go, at least for now, show. "I don't know. It could be a priestess. Bubbe doesn't think so, but it could be."

"Don't accuse Alcippe."

Her vehemence startled me.

"I didn't, but why—"

"If you even make a hint of accusing her, it will back-fire on you. I told you, the tribe already suspects you. If it looks like all of this is an opportunity for you to get Alcippe . . ." She drummed the table with her fingers. "Don't do it."

"Even if I think she's guilty?"

"If you think she's guilty and you get some real proof, come to me."

It was a fair answer, but not what I wanted to hear—not now or ten years ago, but this time I swallowed my ire.

"It did kind of ache yesterday." Zery rubbed her chest, where her *givnomai* lay hidden under her tee. "I hadn't thought about it a lot, but now that you mentioned it . . ."

"How about your back? Your *telios*? Did you feel any-thing there?"

A line formed between her eyes. "Maybe a twinge, in the afternoon, but I'd been working out pretty hard that morning."

I took a breath, pressed my hands flat on the table, and used my best coaxing voice. "Can you go through your day again . . . with a little more detail?"

"Really, nothing special happened. I told you: break-fast, exercise, spar, lunch, spar some more, then . . ." She looked at me sideways. "I've had a team watching the bar—the one the girls were going to. I had a meeting with them in the afternoon. I had to pull them off. They were . . . they weren't getting along with the locals. I needed a new plan. I was thinking of going myself or sending Pisto, but I don't know that either of us would pass for a twenty-year-old human."

Like it mattered. Zery could look sixty and college-age men would still flock to her.

"After that meeting, I needed air and went for a walk. That's where I was when you got back."

I'd wondered but hadn't asked. To be honest, I hadn't wanted to see Zery yesterday. I'd wanted time to sort out my day by myself. If I had searched her out, would I have stopped what happened later?

She interrupted my guilty thoughts by sliding her cup to the side and tacking on, "Oh, and there was the dog too. Maybe he did it."

I frowned. "Dog?"

"A hound, black and tan—kind of skinny. He followed me home from my walk. I offered him some of the mix we feed our dogs, but he wouldn't take it. He liked fries, though." She smiled.

Just a dog. Sounded like the stray I'd fed chips to earlier in the week. He'd run off that day. Curious what had happened to him, I asked, "How long did he stay?"

She held up one hand. "A while. He followed me into the shower. I thought he was going to stay for good, but after I toweled off, he asked to go out and he hasn't been back. Not that I know of."

I nodded. Probably out hunting for his next meal. Maybe he'd come back again—if someone didn't call the city on him.

"So, the dog saw your *givnomai*. Anyone else?"

She arched a brow. "What are you thinking?"

I explained my theory that the killer was using the power of the *givnomai* to control the victims. "Who else knows your *givnomai*, Zery?"

Her expression was guarded. "You."

I didn't bother protesting my innocence again. I'd said it. She was either going to accept it or she wasn't.

"No one else here," she added.

She was leaving someone out—Alcippe, I guessed.

"Anyone who knows priestess and artisan skills?" I asked.

She didn't answer, which was answer enough. I didn't think she was protecting Alcippe, just asserting her power as queen. Her next statement sealed that opinion.

"Let me worry about who has seen my *givnomai*, but thanks for the tip."

Sensing this line of discussion was going nowhere else, I turned the conversation to my day at the camp, filled her in on what Dana and the others had told me, which really wasn't anything Zery didn't already know. I could have been annoyed that she hadn't volunteered the information herself, but I was the one who had asked to go to the camp in exchange for talking with Reynolds. Zery had kept her deal with me without betraying any trusts. Plus, from her point of view, there was always the chance

I would learn something she didn't know. It just hadn't worked out that way.

What I didn't tell her was that I'd had a run-in with Alcippe. I could have told her the high priestess had questioned her authority, challenged it almost, but after Zery's warning, I knew anything else I said would just be seen as attacking the high priestess. If Alcippe was involved in any of this, I'd figure out a way to nail her myself.

We were pretty much done and just waiting for the other to realize it when the outside door opened—the one that led to the sidewalk between the gym/cafeteria and the school building.

Peter stepped inside. I knew instantly it was him, by the breadth of shoulders that blocked the outside light.

"Oh, hi." He smiled that high-watt smile, and my toes curled in my shoes. I needed to see Bubbe about something for my hormones. They seemed to be running rampant lately.

"I heard there was coffee." He held out a stainless-steel travel mug. "The pot in the shop's toast."

"That's a hundred-dollar coffeemaker." I pushed myself to a stand.

"Not anymore." He grinned and headed to the coffeepot. I'd only left about an inch in the carafe. I thought he'd see that and move on, but to my surprise he dumped out the grounds and began making fresh.

"Little hearth-keeper in that one," Zery murmured.

"Not a bad thing, if you're really going to do this human thing." She waggled her brows.

I rolled my eyes, but then turned them back toward Peter. He was wearing jeans and a sweater—a close-fitting sweater. And his back was turned to us—my favorite view.

"Looks like he has other assets too," Zery teased. I chose to ignore the interplay this time.

"He's a very good tattoo artist."

"There you go . . . hearth-keeper, artisan, and an ass to kill for. What more could an Amazon want?" She rapped the table with her knuckles, then shoved her cup toward me and stood. "I'll leave this with you. Give him a reason to come closer. Maybe he'll wash up for you too."

As she left, Peter turned. He should have watched Zery, any other Y-chromosome-carrying human would have, but he didn't. His chocolate gaze locked on me.

Zery's words came back to me. If I was really going to "do this human thing" it would make sense for me to date, at least some. I hadn't had anything more than passing contact with a man since my son's father. I angled my face, away from Peter.

Michael. I hadn't thought of him in years. In a way, he was as responsible for me leaving the tribe as the loss of our son and my subsequent betrayal by the Amazons. I'd made the mistake of knowing him, and not just in the biblical sense. He'd been a tattoo artist. We'd met at a rally—kind of a conference for artists. He'd had a gift. When I first saw pictures of his work, I thought another Amazon was at the event. I'd searched him out, sure Michael was some twist on an Amazon name I didn't recognize, but when I met him, there'd been no mistaking him for a woman—not even a warrior.

I'd been a goner on the spot.

I smiled, a sad twist of my lips. I had a folder with pictures of his work in it somewhere. I'd kept it, but had shoved it deep in a trunk that I never opened. Maybe it was time I dug it out and purged one more ghost from my past.

"Coffee?" Peter held out a fresh mug.

I reached up to take it, but as my fingers brushed his, realization hit me. I knew why Peter's art had tweaked at me so. Why I'd thought it was familiar.

It reminded me of Michael. Peter reminded me of Michael.

The coffee he'd released to my grip fell to the floor, splattering up both of our legs.

Neither of us jumped. We both just stood there, staring.

I didn't ask Peter if he knew Michael, didn't even apologize for the spill. Just turned and walked out of the cafeteria and hightailed it to my truck and then to the bar. He probably thought I'd lost my mind. I was beginning to suspect it myself.

Michael had been from somewhere in Tennessee and had the accent to prove it. From what Peter had told me, he'd spent most of his life in Chicago. Worlds apart. There was, of course, the possibility they were cousins or some other relation, but it was highly unlikely. Much more likely, there was a slight similarity in style and the biggest thing the pair had in common was the attraction I felt for both. After Michael, that was scary.

When I'd been with Michael, I'd come close to breaking a steadfast Amazon rule. I'd come close to giving him my heart. I'd barely walked away. Without his knowledge, I'd kept up with him through online bulletin boards and occasionally an email to mutual tattoo acquaintances. Two years after the rally, a year and three months after the birth and death of our son, Michael had died too. Some freak dog attack.

Still mourning the loss of my son and my tribe, his death had hit me hard—and the worst part was I couldn't show it to anyone, couldn't even admit I knew about it. Scandalized as Mother and Bubbe had been when I left the tribe, if I'd admitted to following what was happening with Michael . . . I smacked the steering wheel of my truck with the palm of my hand.

Liar. It wasn't Bubbe and Mother who had stopped me from publicly admitting my sorrow. It was me. I hadn't been ready to face that I had felt a connection to a man. It was just wrong—against everything I'd been brought up to believe.

I'd heard humans talk about Catholic guilt, but it had nothing on Amazon guilt. It was amazing how easily you could say things with your mouth, even believe them with your brain . . . but your heart, your gut . . . those two were a lot harder to convince.

I pulled onto Frances Street and found a rare parking spot off street. The bar, actually more of a tavern, opened at eleven for lunch. It was five after. My timing was perfect. I went in and sat at the counter. A bartender, female and somewhere in her fifties, took my order—fried cheese curds and a burger. Major benefit of being an Amazon, no need to watch calorie intake.

When she brought my water, I added a local microbrew they had on tap to my order. It would take a lot of alcohol to affect me, but maybe it would take the edge off my nerves. Besides, it gave me another chance to chat with the bartender.

When she came back, I already had a twenty lying on the bar in front of me. I motioned to the bill. "You can ring me out if you like."

She cocked a brow. "You in a hurry?"

I took a sip of the ale. "No, but I thought you might get busy. Might as well settle up now."

She shrugged and went to the cash register.

A few seconds later she was back, my change in hand. "You need anything else, just holler." She started to turn, but I held up a hand.

"Actually, I was hoping to run into someone here. A boy my niece used to date. Great kid."

She waited, a noncommittal look on her face. "What's his name?"

"Tim." It was all Dana had told me, because it was all she knew—I had asked for a last name. "Works part-time, I think, bartending?"

"Common name." The woman's eyes drifted to the door, then jerked back to me. "But we don't have anyone by it on the payroll."

"Really?" Dana hadn't lied to me. She'd had no reason to. "I was pretty sure she said he worked here."

"A lot of bars around here. She must have been confused."

"Could be." I held her gaze. She was lying to me. I didn't know why, but she was. I wasn't one to play polite and just let her walk away. "But I don't think so."

The door to the bar opened and a group of state workers, easily identifiable by badges and practical shoes, filed in. She made a move to grab a stack of menus. I placed my hand over hers to stop her.

"What gives?"

She sighed, the wrinkles around her eyes relaxing with the breath. "He comes in sometimes. Works a few hours when we're busy and he needs the cash. I'm a small business owner, trying to eke out a living. Someone's willing to work for tips—who am I to send him away? You know?"

I did know. I removed my hand and finished my beer.

A man willing to work for just tips—even a young man. That was odd—Amazon-like, even. Cash-only jobs were our mainstay. Anyone's mainstay who wanted to fly under the radar.

What was up with Dana's Tim? What was he hiding or hiding from?

He, just like this bar, was a common thread connecting the dead girls and life outside the Amazon camp. I thought of Dana, her hand on her belly and her face alight with joy. The burger I'd just eaten hardened to stone.

I slipped my messenger bag over my head and turned to leave.

"Enjoy your lunch?"

I spun. Detective Reynolds stared at me over crossed arms.

I adjusted my bag so it sat in the small of my back, then smiled. "Hit the spot. What about you? What brings you here? You aren't following me, are you?" I tried to sound flirty, but failed miserably.

"Should I be?"

Behind him a blond man watched us with interest. I could tell by the travel-worn suits they were together.

"Long drive to stalk one lone tattoo artist, but . . . whatever." I dug another five out of my bag and slipped it under my beer mug. I hoped the extra tip would convince the barkeep I was on her side and maybe keep her from telling Detective Reynolds too much about our conversation—in case he asked.

He raised a brow. "Big tipper."

Ignoring the jibe, I nodded to his partner and made for the door. I only got a few feet.

"You going to be around this afternoon?"

I stopped but didn't turn. "Should be."

"Try. I think we might need to have another chat."

Goody. I couldn't wait.

Chapter Fifteen

Once on the street I let out a breath. Just what I needed, Detective Reynolds poking around the shop while Zery and company were doing whatever the hell they would be doing today. Maybe if I were lucky, they'd have brought up a team of horses and be jousting or something.

That would be fun to explain.

Maybe I'd just go for the truth. *Detective Reynolds, meet my old friend Zery, the Amazon Queen. I know she looks thirty, but really she's pushed past ninety. And don't mind Bubbe over there in the corner—she's just calling up a serpent to guard her prized collections of animal parts and hunks of stone. And Mother? She wouldn't hurt anyone with that broadsword—at least not today. After all, it isn't that "time of the month" just yet.*

Yeah, good times.

Mumbling to myself, I looked for an excuse to hang

out—out of view—and see how long the detective stayed in the tavern and where he went next. A book/crystal shop across the street offered the best solution and, as a bonus, it doubled as a coffee shop.

I wandered in, bought a coffee, and plopped myself down at a table near the window. I had barely got my coffee to proper drinking temperature when Detective Reynolds and his companion stepped out onto the street. I pulled back, letting the purple gauze curtains disguise my presence, but my caution was unnecessary. Reynolds and his friend made a hard right, back toward Frances Street where they, like I, had most likely left their car.

I wandered out of the shop, keeping enough distance between myself and the pair that I could play at coincidence if caught. (Not that I thought the detective would buy that excuse, but he wouldn't be able to disprove it either.) One block down, they climbed into an unmarked car, did a U-turn, and left.

I walked over to a park bench and sat down. I'd said I'd be back at my shop today. I hadn't said when.

I took a sip of coffee and let the caffeine roll through me. It was lunch hour on a warm October Monday, and State Street was busy with state employees and university students resisting the work week by stretching their lunch break as much as possible. I tilted back my head and closed my eyes, let the sounds and smells of State Street encompass me.

The downtown area was one of the reasons I'd picked

Madison. Like Dana and her friends, Zery and I used to come here back in our younger days—the late 1960s, so not that young for me, but still a lot younger than I felt now. Our hangout of choice had been about a half mile southwest, off Mifflin, home of counterculture and all things anti-establishment. A dream for an Amazon looking for a no-commitment fling.

Zery and I had been friends before that too. Our families seemed to wind up at the same camps a lot. We'd first met in Texas when I was ten and Zery was seven. A hurricane had destroyed a safe camp there, and Bubbe was called in to help with cleanup. We had met off and on every decade since then, surviving everything from the Great Depression to disco. And we had always been friends, always found a place and a way to be ourselves, to have some fun no matter how horrid things were in the human world at the time. But here in Madison, those had been some of the best times—the last few years before Zery started her queen training in earnest.

When I closed my eyes, I could almost pretend I was there again, when things were simpler and no one but me was dependent on my actions.

"You spilled."

My eyelids flew open. A boy not much older than Harmony, and decidedly too clean-cut to have walked out of my daydreams even with the diamond stud he sported in the tip of one ear, pointed at the brown circle of coffee developing on my leg. "Crap." I grabbed the paper coffee cup that had lurched to one side and placed it on the ground under the bench.

"Here." He pulled a napkin from a white paper bag.

I started to wave it off, but realized most people probably objected to walking around with coaster-sized coffee stains on their clothing. Me? I was more disturbed by the loss of my brew.

"Thanks." I began dabbing at the spot in what I hoped was a convincing manner. When the damp denim was properly coated with paper fuzz, I wadded the napkin into a ball and retrieved what was left of my coffee.

The boy sat down beside me and began pulling lunch from his sack.

It seemed rude to immediately jump up and leave. I sat there, sipping my drink and wondering how long I needed to stay for pretense's sake.

After a few minutes he finished with his sandwich and flipped open a notebook. Without saying a word, he began sketching.

This was the obvious time to leave, but what he was drawing kept me in my seat. Tattoos. Or what would have made great ones.

"You're an artist?" I asked.

He looked up, his eyes rounded as if surprised I was still there. "I guess. I play at it."

I nodded at the stylized version of a badger. "That looks like a tattoo."

"Really?" He looked pleased with my observation. "A

buddy wanted a tat, but couldn't find one he liked. I said I'd draw something for him."

"Badgers are pretty popular around here. I wouldn't think he'd have a problem."

"Yeah, if you want a cartoon wearing a red sweater with a big W on the front. He didn't."

"Oh." I glanced at his drawing again. "You did a good job capturing the . . ." I searched for a word. If I'd been talking to an Amazon, it would have been easy. What he'd done was capture the essence of what a badger was: their wild aggressive nature that made the small animal formidable, made bigger creatures—including men—fear it. I reached out a hand, then pulled back, realizing what I'd been about to do.

I had to stop seeing powers everywhere. First with Peter, now this random boy.

"Are you into art?" He lowered his pencil and looked at me, genuine interest on his face.

"You could say that." I paused, feeling strange telling him too much about myself . . . old habits I needed to get over. "I own a tattoo shop. Mel's."

"Really? I've heard of you."

He looked impressed. My head swelled a little.

"Thanks." Lame response, but I wasn't used to compliments . . . at least his tone had made it sound like a compliment.

"You don't know . . ." He stopped, looked down at his drawing and twiddled his pencil, hitting it softly against the paper.

"What?" I took a sip of coffee and tried to look supportive and not nosy.

"It's just I've been trying to get on at one of the tat shops down here. Just cleaning up, working the desk, stuff like that. Eventually I'd like to apprentice, but I realize that could take awhile. I could do Web work, whatever they needed until they thought they could trust me." He added a line to the badger's snout—a small mark that somehow added another dimension to the creature, showing not just his aggression, but his determination.

All animals had multiple aspects. How the artist chose to depict them could make all the difference in the power the totem enhanced in its owner—in Amazon art, that is—but what I was looking at was just a drawing, a human drawing.

He looked up. "Anyway, I was wondering if you knew someone who might be willing to give me a shot—just sweeping up and stuff to start."

He was so damn eager. Made me think of the first time I realized I had a talent for art, finally had something of my own. I'd trailed every artisan I could find until one finally agreed to just let me watch her work. I'd just wanted a chance to learn.

That's all he was asking for too, and he'd do the grunt work to get that chance.

"I just might." I pulled a business card from my pocket. "Stop by and ask for Mandy. She'll have some paperwork for you to fill out."

He stared at the white rectangle like I'd handed him the key to the city. "Really?"

"Really." Then I picked up my cup and stood to leave. "Oh, what's your name?"

"Nick. Nick Johnson."

"See you tomorrow, Nick Johnson." I left feeling like I'd done something good, for him and for me. Another step away from my Amazon hang-ups; now not one but *two* men would be working at my shop. How free-minded was I?

The rest of Monday passed; I did some routine tattoos, worked with Mandy a little, and closed up. To my relief, Detective Reynolds didn't make an appearance. After work I went to the gym and told Zery what I'd learned at The Tavern, but I didn't mention seeing the detective there. Our deal had been that I'd talk with him, not that I'd tell her every time I did. Besides, she was already battling the pressure of the tribe's suspicions of me. If she learned the police shared the view . . . well, there was no reason to go there. My time with Zery cost me, though. I missed hearing what happened at Harmony's art class. She was in bed by the time I returned, but with my daughter I knew the "no news is good news" adage held true. If she hadn't liked the class, she would have sought me out and made sure I knew.

I didn't get a chance to talk with her the next morning either. Before Harmony had even rousted herself from bed, a muffler-less compact chugged into the parking lot.

I knew without looking it was another Amazon arriving. You just didn't see a lot of vehicles two door-dings from a life on blocks rolling around Madison. You did see them at Amazon safe camps. It was about all you saw there.

Wondering who the newest arrival might be, and not wanting her to wander into the shop by mistake, I jogged down the fire escape and waited for the vehicle's motor to slow to blessed silence.

Dana unfolded from the driver's seat. She stopped to jerk a very large duffel out of the seat beside her, then another. I could see more duffels and bags filling the back.

Crap. Now what?

I marched toward her.

She took one look at me and burst into tears.

Double crap.

"The baby. It's a boy."

I stopped. She stopped too, both hands at her sides, her arm muscles straining from the weight of the duffels. Her face was streaked with tears, and her eyes brimmed with uncertainty.

I did the only thing I could. I opened my arms. She dropped the bags and fell against me, sobbing.

Upstairs in the kitchen I drank coffee and watched as Dana went about slicing apples and mixing them with sugar for, yes, a pie. The whole baking thing seemed to calm her.

"Where's the flour?" She scrubbed at tearstained eyes with the back of her hand.

I vaguely motioned to a cupboard. Harmony had bought some last year when she and Rachel decided to make a piñata as their part of a Spanish class Cinco de Mayo celebration.

Dana found the bag of flour and returned to the table. "Alcippe told me last night. I didn't know what to do, don't know what I will do." She sniffed loudly. "What would you do?"

That was a loaded question and not one I thought I needed to answer—I'd already answered it ten years ago, quite visibly.

"What would Mel do about what?" Mother strode into the room, wearing Lycra and a thin sheen of sweat. She grabbed a dish towel from near the sink and rubbed it over her face. Then she looked at me.

I set down my cup. "This is Dana. We met the other day on my trip"—I glanced at Harmony's door—"to Illinois."

"Oh."

"Dana's expecting . . ."

Mother's eyes started to glaze. Baby talk was not her thing. "A boy," I finished.

"Oh!" She dropped the towel on the floor, and pinned me with a look. "You didn't?"

"I didn't do anything. Dana just . . ." I switched my gaze to the pregnant girl who was busy bending to retrieve the towel. She hadn't exactly told me why she was here. I could guess . . . already had, but with Mother staring me down, I wasn't placing words in Dana's mouth.

Mother turned to watch the girl too. Apparently unaware of our surveillance, Dana turned in a circle, the towel held out in front of her. Finally she stopped.

"Is there . . . do you have . . . ?" She held out the towel.

Realizing she was looking for a place to deposit the soiled cloth, I nodded to a small pile of dishrags and towels that had accumulated in a corner near the door. "In the basement. Just throw it over there."

Looking unsure and slightly disapproving, Dana tossed the towel on the pile, then went to wash her hands.

"Dana," I said, giving Mother a *give me a chance* look. "Why are you here?"

She turned, surprised. "Where else could I go? I knew you'd know what to do. What my options are."

"Options for what?" Harmony bumped into the table, her pink backpack slung over one shoulder and a fresh coat of lip gloss on her lips.

I was going to have to start belling my family.

"Hi." Dana smiled as if she'd just baked a perfect soufflé—at least I imagined that was what would produce such a euphoric expression. I didn't have much insight into the mind of a hearth-keeper. "You must be Harmony. I've heard so much about you."

She had? From who?

"You have? From who?" my daughter parroted my thoughts.

I was curious, but I didn't want to hear her answer in

front of my still innocent-to-the-existence-of-Amazons daughter.

"Dana's your cousin," I blurted out.

"Really?" Shock, then joy flowed over Harmony's teenage body. "I didn't know we had family outside of . . ." She graced Mother and me with a grudging look. I assumed Bubbe was included in the less than enthusiastic pronouncement.

"Distant cousin," I added. "Dana found us on one of those genealogy sites online." I flapped my hand randomly. "She's just traveling through."

"Oh." My daughter's face fell.

I hadn't realized not having other family had left such a hole in her existence. Unfortunately for her, Dana was not going to be the answer to this apparent lack. Just as soon as I could get Dana settled down and thinking straight, she was heading back to northern Illinois or one of the other safe camps. Maybe realizing she didn't have to go back to Alcippe would be enough to get her on the road.

She said she was having a boy but, according to what everyone had told me, in the millennia since Ares and Otrera had hooked up and the first Amazon was born, I was the only one who'd had an unwavering need to raise a male child myself.

Why would Dana be the second? And if she was, it didn't really involve me or my family, did it?

"Actually, I'm moving to Madison," Dana announced,

her fingers wrapped around a mass of pie dough, like a bride holding a bouquet.

A squeal erupted from Harmony.

Apparently urged on by my daughter's enthusiastic response, Dana continued, "And I'm having a baby!"

"Oh." Harmony turned, eyes huge in her face, and stared at me. I grabbed a granola bar from a drawer and shoved it into her hand.

"Better get to school."

"But the bus—"

"Walk slow." With a shove, I sent her on her way.

With Harmony safely on her way, I turned back to a confused-looking Dana.

"Did I . . . ?" Dana started.

"In the human world teens having babies, especially unmarried teens, is not reason to celebrate."

"But I'm . . ."

"I know—twenty-two." I shoved my fingers into my hair.

Dana dropped the pie dough and beat a fast retreat from the room, brushing past an intrigued-looking Bubbe on her way.

Crap, all over again.

Without pausing to explain, I rushed after the upset hearth-keeper. She'd swung left and disappeared inside the door to one of the many rooms we didn't actually use for anything besides storing dust.

I followed her.

She was standing next to the window, her palm pressed against the glass and loud sobs lifting her breasts.

"Dana." I took a step in.

She turned further toward the outside view, hiding her face.

"I didn't mean . . . it's just . . ." *I sucked at this.* "Harmony doesn't know we're Amazons," I finally blurted.

That got her attention. Her face jerked toward me. "She doesn't? How can't she know she's an Amazon? It's who she is."

A throb was beginning in the area of my left temple. I lay two fingers against the spot. "She's not an Amazon; she's Harmony."

Dana blinked, her blue eyes clouding with confusion. "But isn't she your—"

"I mean, she *is* an Amazon, but I didn't raise her as one and she doesn't know about the Amazons, and I want her to be *herself* first." Why did this all make a lot more sense when I said it to myself or my argumentative mother and grandmother? Saying it to Dana's sweet, bewildered stare made it all sound . . . idiotic.

"She doesn't know what she is? She hasn't trained? Or apprenticed?"

Horror now. Great.

"No. I mean, there isn't any reason . . . girls here . . ." I was blathering. Finally, I gave it up and grabbed Dana by the hand instead. "The point is, you can't just say things around Harmony that you might back at camp."

"But I *am* pregnant."

I sighed.

"And I'm not giving him up. Alcippe wants me to, but I'm not. You understand that, right? You know how I feel?" Her hand shook in mine, as if her entire body was shaking with barely contained emotion.

"Of course I do, but—"

"I know it's a lot to ask, and I just met you, but all the Amazons know who you are and what you did. A bunch of us always said if this"—she looked down at her stomach—"happened to us, we'd be brave like you. That we wouldn't let anyone take our baby from us—even if he was a boy.

"But I'm not strong. Not like you. If you send me back there, I'll give in. I know I will, and I'll hate myself for the rest of my life." Her shoulders heaved in a display more filled with drama than what I'd seen come out of Harmony in her entire fourteen years of life.

That was when I knew I was in trouble.

Chapter Sixteen

While Dana finished her pie, Mother agreed to help me carry her bags upstairs.

"Which room did you give her?" Mother asked.

"The one by yours." I jerked a bag out of the compact's rear seat and hurled it toward my loving parent.

"When's the baby due?"

"Eight months give or take, and before you ask, no, I'm not switching with you. We have thick walls. You'll be fine."

Mother grunted, and I didn't think it was from the weight of the duffel.

She looped her arm through the handles of three more bags. "Does Alcippe know?"

"That she's pregnant? Yes. That she's here?" I shrugged.

Mother shot me a look. "She isn't going to like it."

"See, a silver lining already." I stacked another duffel onto Mother's pile and started chugging up the sidewalk toward the front door. Mother passed me in two strides. I did a jog step to catch up, but only managed to drop two of the duffels I was attempting to warrior-handle onto the ground.

"What's up?" Peter scooped up the bags and tucked one under each arm.

I thought about going all Amazon and insisting he hand over the bags, but in the interest of being more broad-minded, thought better of it. "There are more in the car." I jerked my head back toward where the compact sat—the hatchback wide open.

As I did, my newest employee, Nick, wheeled into view on a skateboard. In a graphic T-shirt and torn jeans he looked a lot less like the clean-cut boy I remembered and a lot more like trouble.

I swallowed the thought. Same kid, different clothes.

He stopped by Dana's car, glanced from it to Peter and me and our loaded-down arms. I dropped my bags at Peter's feet, hoping he'd pick up my clue—and the bags.

"Nick, you're earlier than I thought you'd be."

He flipped the board up and grabbed it by the tip. "Sorry, I have somewhere I need to be."

"You aren't staying?"

He shook his head. His attention wandered past me. I turned, thinking Mother had reappeared, but there was no one there.

"You look busy," he said.

"We are." Again I looked at Peter, but he hadn't moved, and seemed fascinated by my conversation with Nick. "But you'll need to do some paperwork."

"Sure, not a problem. I'll stop by later." Nick's gaze was on Peter now.

Realizing I had committed some kind of etiquette faux pas, I introduced them. Neither jumped forward to greet the other. They just stood there, each sizing the other up, like two dogs whose paths had crossed in a neutral field. Neither declaring the territory, but neither backing off either.

I rolled my eyes and retrieved the bags I'd dropped. Nick wheeled off, and I didn't bother to turn around to watch him leave, or to see if Peter was following me as I continued down the sidewalk.

I didn't get far; Pisto in all her golden glory stepped out of the cafeteria door. Her gaze went first to Peter, then the car, then locked onto me. "Is that Dana's car?"

"Could be." I kept walking. There was something about Pisto's stance I didn't like. That was a lie. There was something about Pisto I didn't like.

She stepped in front of me. "Is it?"

I heaved out a breath. Why did this have to be so hard? "You're in my way."

She crossed her arms under her chest. "What's she doing here? And where are you going with those bags?"

I considered not answering again, because, seriously, she was getting on my last nerve, but again, in the interest of having a broader mind . . . "You'd need to ask her. And upstairs." This time I shoved my way past her. The shocked look on her face as I bumped her from the sidewalk was beyond rewarding.

Unfortunately, the feeling only lasted about two seconds—the time it took for her to drop her hand on my shoulder and pull me back.

I dropped the bags and turned. I didn't have a plan and I'm not sure what I would have done, but even in a flash of anger I couldn't miss Peter's six-foot-four frame looming up behind us or the unmarked police car pulling into the parking lot.

Pisto wasn't as preoccupied as I was. She grabbed my hand as I raised it from my side. "I'm not taken in by you," she murmured. "You may have Zery conned, but not me."

A fan. How nice.

I wanted more than anything to knee her in the groin . . . thigh . . . whatever I could reach, or suck in a big lungful of air and blow her back to northern Illinois, but with my growing audience, neither was an option.

"There a problem?" Detective Reynolds and friend stepped onto the sidewalk. His tone was casual, but I could see the tension in his body.

Pisto tensed, a small move that no one but I noticed. "You knew we had company, right? A well-trained warrior like you wouldn't slip like that . . ." I murmured the words, for her alone.

She pulled back her lip, showing her teeth. From a

distance, it might have looked like a smile. Up close there was no missing the threat.

I pulled my wrist from her grip. "No problem." I turned my back on the Amazon. I didn't want to introduce her to the detective and hoped she'd be too dense to realize that's what he was. Pretending she wasn't glowering at my back, I moved forward, as far as the basement steps. "We can go in this way." I motioned to the stairs. I wanted Detective and friend inside my shop, hidden from the Amazons as quickly as possible.

Reynolds arched a brow. "Aren't you in the middle of something?" He glanced behind me. I followed his line of sight, hoping he wasn't referring to Pisto. He wasn't. The Amazon was gone, and his gaze was only directed to the duffels I'd left on the sidewalk.

Peter stepped forward and scooped them up. "I'll get them."

I looked back at the detective. He wandered forward, but his partner hung back.

"You can both come," I prompted.

Reynolds looked behind him as if surprised to see someone there. "Blake's not feeling well. He needs some air." Then he glanced at Peter.

I was done with introductions. I turned on the ball of my foot and tramped down the stairs. I could hear Reynolds tap his hand against the metal railing a few times, as if deciding whether to follow—or maybe it was some secret police signal. Whatever, in a little while he stepped through the basement door behind me.

• • •

Bubbe's door was wide open. I tried sidling past, but Reynolds came to an immediate halt next to it.

"What's this?" he asked.

I stopped, turned, and immediately hoped Bubbe hadn't left any wild woodland critters tied to the table.

The detective had half his body in the room. I walked over and pulled the door closed. He had the good grace to step back before it whacked him in the nose. "My grandmother's business."

He raised both brows in question.

"She tells fortunes." I didn't wait for a reply, just started walking.

I lost him outside Mother's workout room.

"Some pretty heavy duty equipment you have there." This time he was all the way in. I'd have had to put him in a headlock to get him out gracefully.

I ground my teeth together at the sheer annoyance of having him control our progress, but then realized something. As long as Bubbe didn't stroll past, Mother's workspace was probably the safest place for our chat.

He glanced around, apparently realizing I didn't have a bowie knife tucked under a stack of weights, and turned to leave. I, however, had already plopped myself down on a weight bench.

"So, did you find another body?" The thought had just occurred to me. I didn't really think he had—he would have approached me differently, but a piece of me almost hoped he had. Not that I wished another girl dead, but I definitely wanted to believe the killer had severed whatever tie he or she felt to me.

"Should we have?"

I pulled back, too surprised to hide my reaction. "That was aggressive."

He took a step forward. "You haven't seen aggressive."

I almost laughed. I could say the same thing to him.

"Is something funny?".

I could see I'd tripped his trigger. I had to get better at hiding my expressions. I stood up. "No. Nothing about this is funny, especially the fact that you seem to suspect me of killing two girls. I told you before. I didn't do it."

"I never accused you of being the killer."

I made a *pfft* sound with my lips.

"If anything, I accused you of knowing something about the girls, of doing their tattoos."

"Well, I didn't." As far as I was concerned, our talk was over—or should have been. He wandered farther into the room, picked up a medicine ball, and tossed it in the air as if testing its weight.

"So, why were you at The Tavern?"

"Lunch? How about you?"

He smiled, a not-so-sweet *stop bullshitting me* turn of his lips. "It had nothing to do with the dead girls?"

"I like fried cheese curds."

He laughed. "And I like brats with mustard. You didn't answer my question."

I hated to lie, but I'd served my time as a teenager—I

knew how. "No. It had nothing to do with the dead girls."
I held his gaze, didn't let mine waver, even when he took
a step back toward me. Less than a foot away, he stopped
and smiled again.

"You're good."

He was in my space. My heart rate sped up a few beats.
Our verbal sparring was a strange turn-on. He smelled of
cinnamon again and some kind of soap. The mixture was
bizarrely alluring.

"I'd be happy to set you up with an appointment. I
should have time later today."

He blinked, obviously not following my response.

"A tattoo? You were complimenting my skill . . ."

He grinned, a real grin, and for a second I thought he
was going to reach out and touch me.

"Alan, you in there?" his partner's voice called from
the main part of the basement.

Reynolds didn't reply at first, just kept his gaze on me.
Then with a chuckle he said, "You are good." He moved
toward the door. "Here," he called.

I wasn't sure what had happened, if he suspected me
more or less, but I did know I was happy to see him go.
Somewhere along the way, I'd lost control of the conversation—not that he'd had it.

We were both walking away from this exchange unful-
filled.

I waited for Detective Reynolds to let himself out the
door we'd entered through, then took the front steps to-

ward the main entrance—the steps to my shop. I got as far as the landing before the sound of shouting stopped me.

Outside, I had to go around the far side of my shop, the side away from the gym/cafeteria, to see what was going on.

Dana and Pisto stood a few feet away from each other, both of their faces taut with anger.

"It's my life." Dana reached for one of many duffel bags that lay scattered over the leaf-strewn ground. Pisto grabbed her by the arm, jerking her back to a stand.

I moved forward, but the two were too caught up in their argument to notice me. There was a growl, and the dog I'd befriended a few days earlier shot from behind me. He launched himself at Pisto, knocking into her side. Without missing a beat, the warrior swung, but the animal's teeth were sunk into the loose-fitting sweatshirt she wore.

He hit the ground, but Pisto did too, or almost did. She landed in a semicrouch; one hand kept her from falling completely. All four legs firmly placed on the dirt, the dog pressed his advantage, began pulling at the shirt, snarling as he did.

With her free hand, Pisto grabbed a duffel and flung it at the animal. He dropped lower. The bag sailed over his back.

Dana stood to the side, her hands shaking and her eyes dancing in her face.

I looked around for a weapon. I didn't care for the warrior and certainly didn't like the way she'd been treating Dana, but I couldn't stand by and see her bitten. My gaze lit on the water spigot that jutted out of the side of the building. I'd unhooked the hose weeks earlier, but I could work with the water.

I ran over and twisted the knob until water poured out. Then, forming a tunnel with my hand, I channeled the water through the opening and imagined it shooting forward. The water came together into a steady stream. I concentrated harder and envisioned footage of firemen battling a flame. The stream hardened and became stronger, so much so that my arms began to shake with the effort to control the seemingly solid, vibrating line of water.

Gritting my teeth, I dug my heels into the now-soft dirt and directed the make-believe hose at the dog. The first shot hit him in the snout. His jaws snapped open. As his body slid backward, pushed by the water, he stared at me with what could only be called surprise.

Pisto sprang to her feet and pulled a knife from her boot. In two long strides she was next to the disoriented hound. Without pausing to think, I turned the hose on her. The knife, caught in the flow, flew backward into the holly bushes.

Pisto, her face twisted in outrage, turned toward me. Faced with a raging warrior, I did the only thing I could: I sprayed her right in the gut. She bent forward, cradling the spray, and stumbled backward in the same instant. Behind her, the dog stood and she fell over his back, onto her seat in the muddy leaf-covered ground.

I un-tunneled my hands, let the water flow normally again, and prepared for what I knew was coming. With a cry of outrage, Pisto jumped to her feet, this time with a broken tree limb in her hands. I pulled in a breath, not sure what I was going to do, but knowing with Pisto's state of mind I was going to have to think fast.

As options swirled through my brain—tornado, dust cloud, running—Dana came to life and sprang in front of the storming warrior. Her hands held out in front of her, her body angled and tense, she yelled, "Pisto! Stop! Think!"

Pisto was thinking; I could see that. And what she was thinking didn't bode well.

"This isn't about Mel," Dana added. Her shirt was splattered with debris and her feet slid in the mud, but she didn't move, didn't back down from the obviously enraged warrior, not even when Pisto took another step closer.

Again the dog shot forward, but this time I stopped him—body-checking him before he could reach the pair.

Been there. Done that. Didn't feel like repeating it—at least not now.

He sat, but his body trembled, and I didn't think it was from fear or his recent dousing. With his attention locked on Pisto, his lip edged upward.

I had to say I shared the sentiment.

Pisto jerked off her sodden sweatshirt and tossed it on the ground. Underneath, her skin and jog bra were damp. She ran her hands over her arms, flicking off moisture as she did. "It is about her." She turned to look at me. As she did, I realized she wasn't wearing the high-necked sports tops warriors wore when working out. In this thing, her *givnomai* was clearly visible—the rough outline of a horse caught midstride as it dashed across her breast.

I was shocked she trusted me enough to bare her *givnomai* in front of me, but then again, she hadn't planned to. She'd been wearing the sweatshirt. When she pulled it off, she was caught up in anger. Still, it was a slip. It made me wonder if all the Amazons were this lax. If so, my idea that the killer was using *givnomais* to prey on the Amazons fit. I filed the thought for later and went back to studying her tattoo.

A horse. It made sense. I could guess why she chose it: strength and the ability to get many things done at once. I might not like Pisto, but she took her role as Zery's right hand seriously.

"It's about you and your little hearth-keeper buddies idolizing her, thinking you can throw off thousands of years of tradition because it doesn't suit you. Well, you can't." She picked up an armful of duffels and started moving toward the back—I assumed with the intention of cutting around behind the shop to the parking lot and Dana's car.

"I'm putting these back in your car. You need to follow."

As Pisto stormed off, loaded down with Dana's possessions, Dana turned in the opposite direction—moving toward the front.

I stepped in front of her. "What's happening?"

In my experience warriors were bossy but never proprietorial. That is, unless . . . "Who is Pisto to you?"

Dana sighed. "My sister-half, of course. But our mother died when I was still young. Pisto raised me. I've been a disappointment to her."

A pregnant hearth-keeping sister who chose to live with the tribe's only exile—a disappointment to the queen's second-in-command? Surely not.

I wasn't sure if it was to show my support for feeling like you're a disappointment or for the pain of having to put up with Pisto as a sister, but in an uncharacteristic showing of physical emotion, I pulled Dana into a hug.

She collapsed against me. "I'm not going back. Even if you won't let me stay here, I'll go somewhere else. You blended. I can do it too."

I didn't say anything, just stroked her hair and wished I could make everything simple for her—remove the old biases, have the world accept her, whatever would make the next sure-to-be-hard months of her life easier. But I couldn't. I could, however, continue doing what I'd been doing for ten years—pissing off the Amazons.

"You don't have to go somewhere else. You and your baby can stay here, as long as you want."

There I'd said it, sealed my fate a little more. I just hoped Dana's appearance didn't signal an influx of whoever her "hearth-keeper buddies" were—the ones who, according to Pisto, idolized me. I'd never been idolized before. Even my own daughter had skipped that phase. I knew mothers whose four-year-olds worshipped them, mine just asked me to get out of her light while she scribbled out her Crayola masterpieces.

But while being appreciated was certainly appealing, becoming housemother to a group of pregnant hearth-keepers wasn't.

As I ushered her into the school, I had to ask, "None of your friends are pregnant, are they?"

My confrontation with Pisto used up all of my energy for dealing with Amazons. Which was just as well, as I had a full day and night scheduled at the shop. We stayed open till ten. I usually didn't work that late, but my Amazon side activities had cost me. I had clients to work in and with Janet still sick, not enough staff to pick up the load.

By the time I got the shop closed and myself up to our living area, Harmony was in bed and Mother and Bubbe were in their own rooms doing Artemis knew what. I grabbed some cold chicken from the refrigerator and went to bed.

Chapter Seventeen

The next morning over a breakfast of apple pie, I got to hear about Harmony's first two art classes—how utterly "crush" (I assumed that meant great) the project they were working on was going to be, how "down" (nice?) her teacher was, and most important, how "hot" (that one I understood way better than I wanted to) one particular boy was. The last part wasn't directed at me. Actually, none of it was. Dana and Harmony had been giggling over the details for the past twenty minutes.

At the moment my daughter was acting a little too "average American teen" even for my liking. I picked up her backpack and shoved it onto her lap. "Time for school. Dana will be here when you get back."

With an eye roll, she took my implied advice and trotted down the stairs.

I left for my office, where I barricaded myself in until lunch. Paperwork was stacked to my shoulders, and if I didn't sign some checks, the Amazons wouldn't be the only ones coming after me with sticks.

I'd signed my last John Hancock of the morning when there was a knock on my door. Expecting Mandy, I shouted for the person to enter.

Peter, again with the premium coffee, wandered through the door. The coffee and the cautious look on his face both warned me I wasn't going to like the reason for his visit.

He shut the door behind him, but graciously waited for me to take my first sip to jerk the rug out from under me—not that I'd been feeling that secure on it anyway.

"How well do you know this Dana?"

I took another sip.

"It's just . . . she's been spending a lot of time with Harmony, and the other day I found something I thought you might want to see."

I waited for him to hand me something, but instead he pointed to my computer. "It's on there."

Feeling more confused by the second, I rolled my chair backward to allow him space beside me. With a few clicks, he'd navigated his way to one of those social-networking sites where pseudomodels and dreaming-big bands posted pictures and music.

"Here." He stepped back.

"You have got to be— What is this?" What I saw on the screen shocked me—pictures of obviously drunk girls hanging on boys and revealing more skin than an elephant in a bikini.

"Not here." He clicked some more. "Here." This page was a little less shocking, but only marginally. It seemed to be focused on body art—female body art. Again, it was obvious that wherever the photos had been taken, alcohol aplenty had been flowing.

The first row was butt shots—just generic run-of-the-mill angels and flowers, typical stuff for girls, if in a slightly tantalizing position. His finger pointed to the next row, three pictures over.

Dana hanging on a boy whose face wasn't visible, but while little of the boy had made it into the shot, plenty of Dana had. Both of her breasts spilled from her bra. And clearly visible on top of the right one—her *givnomai*, a bee.

Answered my question about the Amazons getting lax.

"Damn it." Stupid, stupid girl, didn't she know . . . My eyes wandered to the row below and my brain froze.

The next row, not a single face was visible, but I didn't need faces. From the growling bear and snarling leopard tattoos, I could identify the first two girls as easily as if they'd walked up and introduced themselves. The dead girls—their *telioses* immortalized for all to see.

"Whose page is this?" I asked.

Peter propped his butt onto my desk beside me. "Screen name is 'tatluvr.' That's all I know."

I blinked in frustration, then switched my concentration back to the screen. If the dead girls' *telioses* were on here, were their *givnomais* too? Sure enough, a few pictures down from Dana's, I spotted them. I couldn't know for sure which image went with which girl—these pictures were much more focused on their breasts than Dana's had been, but I knew without a doubt the tiger and even the octopus I was looking at were Amazon *givnomais*.

I wanted to investigate the site more, but not with Peter lounging next to me. I had to get rid of him, but first there was something I needed to know. "How'd you find this?"

He stared at the wall.

"You aren't going to tell me you were just surfing and found this, because if you do . . ." I let the obvious say itself.

"You wouldn't believe a client sent it to me?"

"No. I wouldn't."

He tapped his finger against my mouse pad. "Harmony. She was complaining that you wouldn't let her get a tattoo, and telling me 'everyone' had tattoos, even Dana. Then she showed me this. I guess Dana showed her the site, thinking some boy Dana liked would be pictured there."

"Her baby's father."

"Yeah." Peter looked at me, and I felt like the worst mother ever.

He held up both hands. "No judgments."

No, of course not. I let it go, followed up on another point of interest instead.

"I didn't realize you and Harmony talked." First Dana,

now Peter. Did my daughter confide in everyone except me?

His reply consisted of a sympathetic stare.

I picked up the mouse. Unable to resist, I clicked through the next few pages. There were at least three more photos easily identifiable as Amazon—one *telios*, a hare; and two *givnomais*, a salmon and a deer.

"We have to find out who set up this page."

Peter didn't ask why, just replied in a low tone, "You could call your detective friend."

I glanced up at him, surprised by the mention of Reynolds, but even more so by the tone—as if the detective and I had, well, something going.

Alone in the basement with Reynolds, I'd felt an awareness. I couldn't deny that, but in front of Peter I was confident we'd been nothing but professional, distant, even.

"I wouldn't call him a friend." Whatever had happened in Mother's workout space didn't make us friends.

"Really? He seemed kind of friendly." Peter twiddled with the cord on my mouse. I stifled the urge to jerk the wire out of his fingers.

"Well, he isn't. We aren't."

Peter shrugged. "None of my business." But his expression said it was.

Feast or famine. I hadn't had a man interested in me for a decade and suddenly I had two . . . kind of . . .

maybe . . . I looked at Peter, tried to figure out what was going on in his head. Was he attracted to me? Was I attracted to him? Or was something about all the stress I'd been under doing weird things to my libido?

He leaned down. "Of course, it could be my business." And he kissed me.

I think my heart stopped from shock—but it started back up again, double time.

His fingers cradled the nape of my neck, tipping my face to his. He tasted of premium coffee, hazelnut. Had to love a man secure enough to buy a flavored brew.

My hands somehow found their way to his knees and then I was standing, my legs between his, my fingers resting lightly on his hips. He didn't change his grip, didn't pull me closer, and I was afraid to move further myself, like any overt action on my part would cause him to pull away. As surprised as I had been when the kiss started, as his lips moved over mine and parts of me constricted that I'd forgotten could constrict, I knew I didn't want the kiss to end.

But it did, and in as confusing a manner as it had started.

He pulled his mouth free, placed his hands over mine, and gave them a light squeeze. "So, you'll talk to Harmony?"

My mind was foggy and my eyes were half closed. I fluttered my eyelids, trying to make sense of what he was saying. *Talk to Harmony about our kiss? Was that necessary?*

"She seems pretty taken with Dana, and after seeing this . . . well, you don't want her to think flashing tattoos to get on some Web site is a good idea."

Things were back in focus now, and embarrassment at how lost in the moment I'd become while Peter had clearly moved on settled in. I pulled my hands from his legs and stepped back. "Not too big of a worry. At least for a few years. Harmony doesn't have any tattoos and won't till she's legal."

"Still, it wouldn't hurt . . ." Peter slid away from my desk. I turned—picked up a piece of paper and shoved it into a random file.

Fingers trailed down my spine, stopping right at the spot where my shirt separated from my jeans. Every muscle in my body locked up, while my heart jumped back into beating overtime.

"And let me know about that detective. I'm hoping he *is* my business."

Before I could think of how to reply, he'd spun back around my desk and sauntered from the room.

I plopped into my chair with enough force it rolled backward two feet. After heel-walking back to my start point I stared at my computer screen, but I wasn't seeing teenage girls exposing themselves for the camera, or even dead Amazons at the moment—my mind was in too big of a whirl.

I sat there another few minutes, then shook myself. One kiss and I lost track of everything else going on. Just showed humans had nothing on Amazons as far as being ruled by basic urges.

I forced my eyes and mind to focus. There were a lot of thoughts pinging around in my brain—Peter's kiss and the idea that Reynolds was attracted to me. I wasn't sure how I felt about either; my body was sure how it felt, but my mind, not so much. That Harmony was confiding in not only Dana, but also Peter—a man she had only met a little over a week ago—rather than me. The disturbing fact that Dana thought it was an okay idea to show my daughter a Web site with girls, Dana being one of them, obviously drunk and flashing skin. And finally, the biggie, that on said Web site there were pictures of both dead Amazon girls, not to mention the other girls who I knew from their art were also Amazons. *Givnomais* displayed for the world to see on the Internet . . . Someone in the tribe wasn't doing her job educating these girls. It pissed me off.

I put my anger aside, for now.

I had to find out who took these pictures and posted them on the Web. I had to stop this leak, and in the process most likely I'd find the killer.

And while not a total technophobe, I had clue zero on how to do that. Except asking Dana. If she didn't know, I might have to do something crazy, like be responsible and call the police.

Dana was back upstairs. I realized this as soon as I opened my office door—the smell of melting chocolate was a dead giveaway. As was the plate of freshly baked cookies sitting next to the group flash on the reception counter. They were still warm and gooey when I sank my teeth into one.

I followed my nose up the stairs. For all the smells filling the building, the kitchen was frighteningly clean. I stood there, trying to think where a pregnant woman who had just baked six-dozen cookies (neatly resting on wire racks I didn't know I owned) and scrubbed a kitchen (even the dust bunnies that were normally stuck to the chair feet had been evicted) would go next.

I knew where I'd go—bed. With that in mind, I walked down the hall to the room recently assigned to Dana.

She was there, but she wasn't sleeping. Somehow in the last four hours, in addition to her baking, she'd found a can of paint, pan and roller, and brushes. She was halfway around the room already.

Even if I hadn't seen her *givnomai* on the Internet, I would have guessed it. No one but a bee, maybe a beaver, could be this diligent.

She turned when I entered. A streak of purple ran down her nose and dots of white adorned her hair. "You're done. Did you want some lunch? I made a quiche."

I'd never had quiche in my life, wasn't 100 percent sure I knew what it was.

"Uh, no, actually I wanted to talk to you about something." Facing her beaming eagerness made bringing up the Web site that much harder. Made it hard to believe the drunken girl I'd seen on the Internet and this one were one and the same person.

Finally, I just said it. "I saw the Web site."

"Oh." She picked up the brush and dabbed at a spot where the old institutional green was leaking through the purple. "Do you like this color? I thought about pink. It's my favorite, but Harmony didn't think it was a good idea." She wrinkled her nose. "I'm not sure why."

"Because of the baby?"

She patted her stomach. "What about him?"

"*Him.* He's a boy."

The wrinkle morphed to a full-face frown. "I know."

I took a breath, then let it go. The kid was going to be the first boy in history raised with a family of Amazons— a pink or purple bedroom was sure to be the least of his differences.

I paused, wondering if he, like many Amazons, would inherit skill sets from his grandmother. Pisto was a warrior and Dana a hearth-keeper. I had no idea which was more common in their line. Could a boy be a hearth-keeper? Of course, common belief was that males didn't inherit any of the Amazon strengths, had normal mortal life spans and no powers; skill sets or lack of them should follow this same rule . . .

"Is it okay if I paint the furniture too? I was thinking white."

Purple walls, white furniture . . . if the boy did get a skill set, I prayed to Artemis it was warrior. Or maybe on his thirteenth birthday I'd just gift him with a badger tattoo like the one Nick had been drawing. He'd need the added toughness to survive junior high.

Dana picked a plastic bag off the floor and pulled a white lace baby gown and bonnet from it. "I got this from Goodwill. What do you think?"

I rethought the tattoo. It would take more than a badger to handle the ribbing this kid was going to endure, even in liberal Madison.

"Pretty. I might have some of Harmony's old stuff stashed somewhere too." And none of it was pink or frilly.

"Really?" Dana pulled the gown to her chest and twirled. "I can't believe how happy I am. Nothing could ruin this. Nothing."

Just hearing those words made me cringe inside. I'd felt that way once, but I'd learned that things had a horrible way of twisting around and around again until the one worst thing you never dreamed would happen did.

And current times were far from certain. Still, I wasn't going to stamp on Dana's fluffy image of life. Maybe she was right. Maybe her life would be perfect from now on.

"About the Web site. I was wondering if you could tell me who put it together."

"Oh, the one of our tattoos? I really don't know. We went to a couple parties after the bar closed, and someone was passing around a phone. Most of the pictures we took ourselves."

"You didn't even know whose phone it was?"

She picked up a roller and started coating the wall in purple. "Didn't seem important. It was just for fun."

Fun. Some fun. I couldn't help myself, my "mother" voice kicked in. "You know you shouldn't show people your *givnomai*."

Dana frowned, almost a scoff. "Everyone does."

The importance of guarding your *givnomai* had been pounded into me by Bubbe, into all Amazons by their elders, I had thought. Yet another example of teenagers deciding they knew better. I wanted to shake Dana, then and there. Shake Alcippe or whoever had fallen down and not warned these girls about guarding their *givnomais* too. Of course, it went past that, showed how much the Amazons needed to change. The world was changing; if the Amazons didn't change with it, they would be destroyed by enemies they never knew existed.

Who was I kidding? That's exactly what was happening. I made a mental note to talk to Zery, to insist she get the older Amazons educated on today's technology and the benefits and dangers that could come with it.

I tightened my jaw and resisted my desire to lecture Dana until I ran out of words and voice. I knew from experience with Harmony that reaction would just shut her down, make her see me as the enemy rather than the cool friend she could trust. And for now I needed to be that friend.

I let it go.

"So, how'd you even find out the pictures were on the Web?" I asked.

She took a step back to admire her work. "Same way. People at a party were talking about it."

"But no one claimed the page."

She filled in a spot of white with a quick hard turn of the roller. "Not that I heard."

I left her alone, happy and sucking up paint fumes. She had been very little help, except to tell me she was no help so I could move on to step B—whatever that was.

Back in my office, I stared at the computer screen. I had told myself if I couldn't figure out who had set up the page, I'd call the police—Detective Reynolds, to be exact. But now old loyalties were warring with that resolve.

Should I talk to Zery first? What if she didn't want to tell the police? But if I couldn't think of a way to track down the page's owner, how could Zery?

I toyed with calling the social site and demanding their assistance, even went so far as to click around their "contact" page. There were all kinds of links to report abuse, but none that indicated they'd be willing to reveal who had set up a page. I had a feeling it was going to take a lot more than one parent's outraged call to get that information out of them, especially since the pictures in question would garner at most a PG rating.

Which brought me back to Zery and Detective Reynolds. I was savvy enough to realize calling the detective would focus his attention back on me as a possible suspect—not that his attention had wandered too far from that direction anyway. I also realized Zery was stubborn enough and arrogant enough to refuse to let the police into what she saw as Amazon business. Knowing the queen as I did, she'd put together some kind of war party, march to northern California, and storm the site's corporate offices first.

That would be lovely—computer programmers held hostage by a troop of six-foot-tall Amazon warriors.

Amusing as the image was—it also rang horribly possible.

I jerked open my desk drawer and rummaged for the card Reynolds had given me on his first visit.

So far as Zery was concerned, better to ask forgiveness than permission. Okay, not so much with a warrior; you might not survive the forgiveness stage. But since I was damned sure I wasn't going to be gifted with permission, it was the only option left to me.

I picked up the phone.

Detective Reynolds was in.

"I found something I think you need to see," I said, my eyes focused on the bear *telios*. If I concentrated on the girls, I wouldn't think so much about how angry Zery was going to be when she found out I'd gone to the police before her.

"Really?" He sounded bored, but it was an act. There was a little lift on the "L" that gave him away. "And what would that be?"

"You near a computer with Internet?" At his affirmative, I read off the URL. "Scroll down to the third row, then over two pictures."

"How'd you find this?" Tense—not bored at all.

"A client sent it to me. She liked one of the tattoos and wanted to see if I could replicate it. I recognized the bear and leopard from the pictures you showed me." Peter had tried the story with me and it hadn't worked. Didn't mean it wouldn't work with Reynolds.

"Quit the bullshit."

Or not.

"You're welcome," I replied.

"Welcome, my ass. When are you going to come clean? Who are these girls and why won't you tell me?"

Amazons, and because it wasn't really my secret to give up. But maybe it was time, and maybe I could convince Zery of that . . . maybe.

I twisted in my chair and turned my back to the tattoos on my screen. For some reason I couldn't face them right now. "I didn't know those girls. I swear that."

"But you know more about them than I do. I've run every check I can think of and come up with diddly—and not much of that. What do you know?"

I took a deep breath. I wanted to tell him. I really did, but . . . "I don't know those girls. I had never laid eyes on them—" I cut off what I was about to say.

"Had never laid eyes on them? That didn't sound complete." He took a breath. I could tell he was struggling for control. "You had never laid eyes on them before what? That's what you were going to say, isn't it? Finish the sentence."

He was leaving something unsaid too—or else. Tell

him what I knew or else . . . he'd arrest me? Question me? Make my life living hell? I didn't know and didn't want to find out. Still . . . "Before you showed up with those pictures."

There was a muffled curse, then the sound of his phone being slammed down. I listened to the angry buzz of the dial tone, then slowly slid the handset back on the receiver.

Well, the ink was injected there. No going back.

Now to prepare Zery.

Chapter Eighteen

I sought strength in a piece of quiche before facing Zery. It was good. Having a hearth-keeper around really had some benefits—at least until hearth-keeper junior showed up. I guess I'd see if having fresh-baked quiche for lunch balanced out waking to a baby screaming at two A.M.

After picking the crust off the quiche that was still in the pie plate and popping it into my mouth, I squared my shoulders and went in search of Zery.

She was on the phone and, lucky for me, she looked happy.

"We found another girl who went to that bar and she named two others. The first is at the Florida safe camp. The other two are somewhere between Illinois and California. When they arrive in California, the queen knows to keep them there. We'll find out what they know and keep them there, watched and safe."

"How are you going to do that?" The Amazons had a complex structure. Each Amazon had loyalty to their family group, identified by their *telíos,* and to the six reigning queens—especially the queen whose safe camp they were visiting. But for the most part, we hadn't changed a lot from our nomadic past. We had tribe loyalty and were constantly pressured to follow tribe rule, but I'd never heard of an Amazon (outside of the queen and high priestess) being grounded to one safe camp. It went against one of our basic tenets of survival and our history as nomads—keep moving, never settle in one place too long.

"We'll do it." Her expression dared me to say otherwise.

"You think that does it? You think the killer was only targeting the girls who went to the bar?" I was truly curious. I wanted to believe rounding up the girls and keeping any others from visiting the bar would stop further killings, but I just didn't know.

"Pisto's taking another group to the bar tonight. Dana told her about parties they went to after the bar closed. Next party, we'll be there."

And what? Beat each and every person there until they admitted to being the killer?

"The parties are probably on the weekends," I said for lack of anything else to add.

"Maybe." Her eyes narrowed. "Why are you here?"

I ran my finger over the top of a file cabinet that sat by the door. It came back coated in dust. I wiped the dirt on my jeans. "I need to talk to you about something."

She stood up and walked around to the front of the desk. "Talk."

"I . . ." Despite the fact that most of the tribe still despised me, Zery trusted me right now. I didn't want to say anything to endanger that, but her trust also meant maybe she'd at least listen to me when I suggested it was time to bring the Amazons out into the open.

"Like I said before, the police contacted me. Earlier, before you moved into the gym."

She tilted her head. "You mentioned that. They thought you might know something about the girls' tattoos."

I nodded. "He'd taken them to some Milwaukee shops. Artists told him it looked like my work."

"And?" She hadn't moved an eyelash.

"And nothing. I told him I didn't know anything."

Her posture softened, but her gaze didn't. If anything, it became more piercing. "But you didn't tell me. When you saw those tattoos, you had to know the girls were Amazons. Why didn't you warn me?"

She knew as well as I did that I had told her—that I had left the stone fetishes at the safe camp. She was giving me a second chance to explain that. I ignored her offer.

"We didn't exactly leave things on the best of terms."

She started to say something, but I barreled on. "Point is, this cop, I've gotten to know him some. He really cares. He really wants to find the killer, and I was thinking that we haven't been making a lot of headway. Maybe we . . . you . . . should talk to him."

She pulled back like I'd slapped her, or tried to. "Have you been gone that long? We don't work with humans. And we can certainly police our own problems—we've been doing it for millennia."

"But the Amazons have never had to deal with a problem like this. No one has ever preyed on the Amazons. And you seem dead set on not believing Alcippe could be involved. Who does that leave?" I didn't wait for her to state the obvious: me. I kept going. "If it isn't someone in the tribe, it's someone outside of it. Outside of your reign. You'll have to deal with humans sooner or later." *If the killer wasn't Alcippe.* But no matter what, I still believed the Amazons opening to the outside world was the right move—that ultimately their insistence on a closed community was what had led to the girls' deaths. And I didn't want Amazons to reveal everything about who they were, just be more open, stop looking down on people who weren't Amazons, be more aware of how the world had changed.

Her lips thinned; the skin surrounding them turned white. "We can take care of our own."

I took a step forward. "I never thought you'd let arrogance cost Amazons their lives. The police can get information we can't. Why not use that?"

"You're pointing fingers at me? What about those fetishes? How did you get them? Maybe Alcippe is right—

you too, for that matter. Amazons have never been 'victims.' We've never had to fear anyone because, loose as our structure is, we respect tradition—know what being an Amazon means, know how important keeping ourselves separate is. But then you leave, mingle with humans, live as a human, raise your *daughter* as one.

"As your friend, I can't believe you killed your own kind. I can't." Her eyes were huge and her voice rough. "But as queen, I have to consider that you seem to value being human more than you ever valued being an Amazon. Is there a side to you I'm just not seeing? Is our friendship blinding me to your guilt? Did you kill those girls, or know who did?"

Anger swelled to a roar inside me. "We have been over this. If I was the killer, why would I let you stay here? Why would I be encouraging you to talk to the police? Why would I be here at all? Why wouldn't I have run by now?"

She wrapped her fingers around the edge of the desk. I had the uncomfortable feeling it was to keep from grabbing onto me. "Why indeed? Maybe I'm not the only one who's arrogant."

I left without replying.

Zery wouldn't talk to the police. I couldn't make her.

I stepped out of the gym and into glaring sunshine. Four Amazons sat on the ground outside, talking. When I walked out, they stopped and followed me with their eyes. Their animosity was tangible—worse than before. I guessed they'd heard of my run-in with Pisto or seen the evidence. I doubted Pisto would have run home and tattled. Not her style.

I felt their gazes like stones attached to my back as I walked away.

Damn them. I was not the enemy. Why couldn't they see that?

Over dinner I realized a hole in my thinking. I couldn't make Zery talk to the police, not of her own free will. But I could bring the police to her. I could tell the police about the Amazons without revealing who and what they truly were.

Half truths. A new art I seemed to have mastered.

I went to bed with the knowledge I was going to make use of it tomorrow.

I called Reynolds first thing the next morning and got voice mail offering a cell-phone number. I called it. He was already in his car and on his way over. It would have been flattering if I hadn't gotten the distinct feeling he was fingering his handcuffs as we chatted—and not in a let's-have-some-fun way. When I told him I was ready to talk but wanted to do so on neutral ground, he named a coffee shop not far from campus.

"I was a member of a cult."

Reynolds set his coffee cup down without taking a drink. "A cult?"

"Well . . ." I twiddled a plastic stir stick between my fingers. "I wouldn't call it a cult."

"You just did."

"I know." I tapped the stick against the paper cup. "It's just hard to put a term to it."

"Closed group with a charismatic leader who keeps the members cut off from outside society?"

I bit into the stick, flattening it with my teeth, then dropped it back into my cup. "The point is—I was part of a group that's a tad shy."

"Secretive." He reached in his jacket pocket and pulled out a notepad.

"They don't surround themselves with barbed wire or anything." Wards were a lot more effective. "And members come and go all the time."

"So do Hare Krishnas."

I snorted. "Believe me, none of these women are selling flowers at the airport."

"They sell fortunes instead?" He looked at me without raising his head from the notepad.

"That's not illegal."

"Depends on how it's done."

"Listen." I swished the stir stick around a few times, then jerked it out and dropped it on the table, leaving a little snake of coffee in its wake. "Do you want to hear what I have to tell you or not?"

He leaned back, one arm propped on the back of his chair, and made a circular motion with one hand. "By all means. That's why I'm here."

"I left the group ten years ago."

"Any reason?"

I gave him a glare. He held up his hand in surrender. "Tattoos are . . . important to the group. Everyone has them. Girls get them sometime during puberty—preferably right at the beginning. When you brought me the pictures . . . I didn't recognize the girls, but I recognized the tattoos, the style anyway. I knew they were from the group."

"But you didn't do them?"

I shook my head. I couldn't tell if he believed me or not.

"Address?"

"For what?"

He lowered his pencil. "The whatever you called it . . . camp."

"You don't need to go there." I wanted him to talk to Zery, not drop in unannounced on Alcippe and company. My horror must have shown.

"Why not? What could happen?" He had that tense look again, like the barista behind me had pulled a gun and he was trying not to show he'd noticed.

"Nothing. I mean, some of the group, the leader, in fact, is at my shop."

"I thought you left."

"I did, but with the girls . . . some bonds are hard to break, okay?" I sounded frustrated, guilty, and apologetic all at once. And I was pretty sure all the emotions were targeted not at him, or even the Amazons, but at myself.

"Why didn't they come forward before this?"

I sighed. "They didn't know."

"Didn't know what? That the girls were missing? How do you not know that? One of those girls looked about fourteen."

He was showing his age. To me she looked every one of her seventeen years or more; to the bartender who served her downtown, she must have looked older. Even the greediest of bar owners wouldn't serve a fourteen-year-old, fake ID or not.

"Or that they were dead?" he continued. "They not watch the news . . . read a paper? It's been everywhere. If my teenage daughter went missing, I'd be scouring every inch of ground from here to the borders—of the U.S., not Wisconsin. And if I didn't find her, I'd keep going. You mean to tell me they saw all the coverage and didn't even think it might be their girls? What are they hiding?"

"You have a daughter?" I asked. It was an inappropriate question, cutting off his passionate diatribe, but I was curious. I hadn't seen him as having kids, or a wife.

He blinked. "Two. One's married. One lives with her mother—in Rockford."

Divorced. That intrigued me too. Since Amazons never committed to a relationship with a man, the whole marriage thing confounded me. I'd have loved to ask what drove him to commit, then what drove him—or her—to walk away. But I didn't. I had used my one inappropriate and personal question for the day—maybe forever.

There was no reason to think Reynolds and I would

have any kind of conversation after today. I would introduce him to Zery. He'd understand what a tiny role I'd had (or was pretending to have) in this mess, and he'd back off. Go back to doing whatever he did to solve this crime.

He rapped his notebook against the table. "So, he must know about the girls now—if he's staying with you."

"She." The pronoun came out harsher than I'd meant it to, but it annoyed me that he'd assumed Zery, the person with power, was a man. It was an unfair judgment on my part; he was victim to his own society's norms, not the ones I'd been raised with. And I had my own issues—obviously.

"She?" The corners of his mouth curved down, in surprise or thought . . . whatever, it was obvious he hadn't expected the female bit.

"The entire group is."

Still digesting my previous revelation, it took a minute for him to catch my latest.

"Is what?"

"Female. No men."

"No men at all?" His expression morphed from surprise to shock. "How do they work that? I mean there are kids, right? Or is it a new group? Only been around a few years?"

"No, not new." I really hadn't foreseen the need to explain the Amazons like this. I was beginning to get a sick feeling in my stomach. "It's just a group, okay? None of that matters, does it? You just needed to know how I was connected, and I told you. Now you know where the girls came from, maybe it will help you with the case."

He raised a brow. "It doesn't work like that. You don't get to tell me what you want me to know and expect me not to ask anything else. Two girls were murdered."

"I know." I sat against the back of my seat hard. "Listen, I want to stop the killer. I have a daughter too, you know."

"Are you worried about her?"

I almost threw my coffee on him then. Of course I was worried about her—some things didn't need to be said.

"When we started, I asked if I gave you something if you could give me something in return. I gave you something—two somethings." I picked up the printout from the Web site that I'd brought with me.

He didn't move, just stared back at me with his eyes shuttered, not giving away any of his thoughts.

"I want to know who put those pictures out there." I held out the printout.

"Why?"

I opened my mouth, then closed it.

"You're not involved, right? And even if you were, there's no reason for you to know that. You or one of your not-a-cult friends wouldn't go looking for the person, right?"

I shifted my eyes to the side and took a breath. When I looked back, I was calm, kind of. "I want the killer stopped. We all do. It's about the only thing me and my 'group' have in common anymore. But I don't want them harassed. They're private. If I'd thought you were going to dig into every aspect of who they are, I wouldn't have told you about them."

He smiled, his eyes understanding, but sad. "I get that, but it doesn't matter. You don't get to pick and choose what I use. I don't even get to pick and choose. I just follow whatever lead I can."

I stood up and walked out of the shop, leaving him with the dirty cup and my chewed-on stir stick. I was pissed, but nowhere near as pissed as Zery was going to be.

I needed to get home and prepare her. Little did Reynolds know he might have another murder to investigate—mine.

Chapter Nineteen

I beat Reynolds to my shop, but barely. I'd rushed into the gym to grab a few minutes with Zery, but she was being stubborn, ignoring me while she stood huddled with Pisto and a few other warriors. The group sent to scout for new parties, I guessed.

By the time she had turned to look at me, I knew it was too late. I could feel Reynolds standing behind me. Could see it on Zery's face too.

She pulled a knife from her belt as she walked and threw it the length of the room. It slammed into a wooden pillar about four feet to my left. Stuck there. I didn't turn my head, didn't drop my gaze from her face.

Message sent and received.

Reynolds stepped forward, the entire length of his body pressed against my side. I could feel tension vibrating through him. His hand was on his holster. I don't know what stopped him from pulling his gun—street smarts? Some sixth sense that told him Zery wasn't a threat at that moment? Or was it a simple matter of speed? Zery had performed the entire act in only a few seconds. Cop or not, it had to seem surreal to him—she'd moved that fast; maybe he thought it was all an act. It wasn't, of course. Zery was deadly serious.

As Zery ground to a halt in front of us, I didn't bother to further analyze the reason for his lack of overt action. I was just grateful for it.

"What are you doing?" Zery asked. The question was directed at me. She had yet to let an eyelash flicker in Reynolds' direction.

The detective stepped forward, went through his whole "I'm a detective investigating the murders" routine. I'd heard it before, blocked it out. Besides, I was busy soaking in the betrayal in Zery's eyes and the pure hatred in Pisto and company's.

As Reynolds' introduction wound down, the group of warriors around Zery grew. None of them touched a weapon, but they didn't have to—the promise was obvious. If Reynolds felt it, he didn't react, gave no sign that he knew the dozen or so women now surrounding him—they'd come up from behind too—wanted him, us, gone.

Done with his spiel, Reynolds crossed his arms over his chest and waited.

Zery didn't move, and none of the warriors would until she did.

It could be a long wait. Not wanting the detective to get impatient and force an action all of us would regret, I took a step forward, into the gym. "The detective just wants to ask a few questions about the girls . . . who they were, where anyone saw them last, that kind of thing." I prayed what I said was true, that he wouldn't start digging into Amazon life.

Zery held my stare for a heartbeat. It felt like a lifetime. Then she raised her left hand, told the warriors with that one gesture to back off, scatter. They did, but they didn't wander far. One twitch from Zery and they'd be back at her side, their weapon of choice pressed to my or Reynolds' throat within seconds.

Reynolds unfolded his arms. "Is there somewhere we can talk?"

"The cafeteria," I responded and started walking, taking the short route through the main gym. Either way, we had to walk past warriors. Might as well get it over with as quickly as possible.

While we moved ahead, Zery took a minute to speak with Pisto. The Amazon had been staring at me since I'd walked into the gym, eyeing me as if measuring me for a hole—although I doubted she was worried about accuracy of the fit, just depth.

"Interesting group," Reynolds said as he held the door open for me. I closed my eyes and walked into the cafeteria. I didn't want to know if any of the warriors were watching as I let him get away with what to him was probably just a show of good manners, but to them . . . no telling.

"We just caught them at a bad time. They're training for a celebration."

"With knives?" His gaze floated over the room, cataloging everything he saw there, I was sure.

"Celebration's the wrong word. More of a demonstration," I replied.

His eyes focused on me. "You have a hard time hitting the right word, don't you?"

I walked over to a table and pulled out a chair. "I'd offer you coffee, but . . ."

"You won't." He sighed. "I'm doing my job, Mel."

I shrugged, then turned so I could look out the window at the walkway between the cafeteria and my shop.

Zery arrived, saving me from getting completely pissy—at least for a few seconds before they both told me to leave. Even then, I had to swallow my ire. Arguing with either of them in front of the other might reveal more about me and my life than I cared for either to know.

After an angry stare at each, I strolled out the door. Somehow, as I walked out, a small rock got kicked into the space near the hinges, keeping the door from closing.

I was leaning against the doorjamb, straining to hear what was being said, when Peter stepped around the corner from the front of the building. He glanced from me to the window.

It was lighter outside than inside. I didn't know if he could see Reynolds and Zery sitting at the table, and I didn't want to step away from the door to find out—didn't want them to see me, or Peter for that matter.

Realizing I had no other option, I moved away from the door, toward the basement steps where I was fairly sure we wouldn't be visible from where Zery and Reynolds sat.

"Is there a problem?" I asked.

He raised both brows. "Not with me." He glanced over my shoulder, back toward the parking lot. "Looks like you have a visitor. Is he in there?" He nodded toward the cafeteria.

I stared at him, remembering our kiss and his questions about Reynolds. The air around us seemed to thicken, and I was suddenly uncomfortable in my skin, like I needed to move, get away from something. But I held firm. I wanted to know what happened between Reynolds and Zery. I wouldn't let my conscience drive me away.

Besides, I had nothing to feel guilty about—at least not regarding Peter.

"Why's he here, Mel?" He brushed my hair from my face.

My body, traitorous hunk of flesh that it was, edged forward. It was cool today, and my fleece wasn't enough to keep the chill at bay. I suddenly realized how warm he would be, how nice it would feel to lean up against him.

I took a step back.

"It doesn't involve you or the shop," I replied, keeping my voice firm and businesslike. "Don't you have a client?"

"No, actually, I was looking for Dana. Have you seen her?"

A band tightened around my heart. "No, how long's she been missing?"

He frowned, real concern showing in his eyes. "I didn't say she was missing. Just that I was looking for her."

"She isn't upstairs?" I couldn't help it; panic was building. Dana had been at the bars. Zery had the other girls who had been there under watch—why hadn't I thought to do the same for Dana?

Reynolds and Zery forgotten, I headed down the stairs, skipping as many as I hit. When I jerked open the door, what—make that who—I saw there stopped my heart cold.

Alcippe.

The old bat was standing in my basement, dressed in some flowing purple number that seemed to fluff up when she saw me—like a cat expanding its fur. Bubbe stood next to her. I could tell by my grandmother's iron-stiff back that they'd been arguing.

That was enough for me. I entered the room ready to battle.

Bubbe held up one hand. "Stop."

I did what she would have done, kept moving. "Get out of my house," I said, my feet coming to a stop less than a foot away from Alcippe. Her robes billowed again, flapping over my foot with the whisper-light touch of silk.

She glanced at me, then away as if I didn't exist—or was too inconsequential to mess with.

"Melanippe. You forget yourself and who you bring with you." Bubbe pointed toward the door I'd entered through. Sauntering down the steps came Peter.

This Alcippe noticed. She spun to face me. "Men? Have you fallen that far? You look to men for safety?" She made a face like she wanted to spit.

My hands itched and a space behind my eyes pounded. I wanted to pummel her—with magic and my fists, show her where I looked for safety. As if anything about her brought me fear.

Peter glanced around; I could see the confusion on his face. Bubbe began to mutter, but it was too late. He wouldn't forget what he had seen here, but luckily he hadn't seen anything too strange—yet.

"Is Dana here?" I forced my arms to relax at my sides, to present a less aggressive image, at least from Peter's angle. For Alcippe I didn't bother but let every ounce of aggression I felt pour out of my eyes. "What have you done with her?"

In answer, the high priestess turned and held up one hand. "Dana, are you ready? We'll leave now. My business is done, for now." She angled her face to mine, let her own animosity show—didn't try to hide it either, not even from Peter.

The door to Mother's weight room crawled open and Dana, her eyes red and her shirt covered in paint, crept into view. I spun on one foot, my hands flying up, my only thought to stop the high priestess from doing to Dana what she'd done to me.

"Melanippe." Bubbe's hand shot upward too. Wind smacked into my face; I fell backward onto my butt.

As I clambered to stand, Peter moved. Within seconds he was beside Dana, his arm wrapped protectively around her shoulder. He murmured something to her. I couldn't hear his words, but I could see their effect on Dana. Her shoulder lost the rounding of defeat and her chin rose.

Glad to have someone on my side, even if it was just a man and a hearth-keeper, I faced Alcippe and my grandmother. "You can't make her go against her will."

"It isn't against her will. She wants to go. Don't you, Dana?" The door to outside was wide open; Pisto stood this side of it. A light breeze shifted her hair. I couldn't stop myself from imagining the breeze growing, until it clawed at her hair, wrapped around her, and jerked her out of the basement, left her defeated and winded outside on the dirt.

As if reading my thoughts, Bubbe moved again, this time casting as she did. A bubble clamped down around me. I couldn't see it, didn't think anyone else could either, but I could feel it—and I could see the expression on my grandmother's face. Whatever she was doing was costing her.

Guessing at her game, I twitched my fingers, tried to reach the wind—nothing. Bubbe had shut me off, dropped me into a vacuum.

I pulled in a breath, ready to fight dirty if necessary, but then Peter moved behind her, reminding me we weren't alone. What Bubbe had done was subtle. What I would have to do to break free wouldn't be. Was I ready to expose myself and the Amazons that completely?

Pisto stepped farther into the room. "C'mon, Dana. Time to go home." Her hand lowered to her sais, two tridentlike weapons shoved into her belt. She pulled one out, spun it around so the long end ran parallel to her arm and the forked end was concealed by her hand.

Peter murmured something else to Dana, then the pair turned and started walking away from Pisto toward the main stairs that led to my shop and living area instead.

Alcippe thrust out an arm. A curtain of dirt, jerked from every corner of my unswept basement, rose from the floor. The noise was deafening. It was like being part of a landslide, except the earth was moving sideways, then upward.

Her arm out straight, Alcippe held the wall, cutting off the path Peter and Dana had been about to take.

"Pisto, get your sister," Alcippe ordered. Then she looked at me. "I won't let you tear us apart again."

That was it. I'd had enough, and the dirt wall Alcippe had set in front of Peter pretty much gave away the whole magic thing anyway. I sucked in a breath and prepared to blast my way out of Bubbe's bubble. As I did, I realized I didn't need to. My grandmother had quit chanting, let whatever had been cutting me off disintegrate.

I jerked my attention to her, but she had her back turned and seemed to be concentrating on Peter instead. He looked dazed, lost. His arm was still around Dana, but I could tell he had no idea where he was . . . what was happening around him.

I wondered briefly if Bubbe had teamed with Alcippe to stop Peter's exit with Dana, but as quickly as the thought appeared, I dismissed it. My grandmother was a cat at heart. Most high priestesses were. They didn't work as a team.

Bottom line, she was more concerned with shielding Peter from learning something he shouldn't, something that might cost him his life later, than in keeping me from battling with Alcippe.

Maybe she even wanted me to finally face my old nemesis.

I pulled in a breath and prepared to blow Alcippe's curtain back to the four corners of my home.

My lungs had just started to fill when the outside door creaked and a voice filled with authority called out, "What's going on here?"

Detective Reynolds stood in the doorway, a gun in his hand.

Pisto whirled. I didn't stop to think, just made a swiping motion with my hand while I released the little bit of air that I'd gathered. The wind wrapped around her feet, tripping her.

She fell, her sais smashing into the cement floor. To my right Alcippe moved too. Her wall of dirt collapsed as she did, clouding the room until all of us were coughing and choking, fighting our way through the dust storm caused by my wind and Alcippe's dirt. Somehow, through the mess, Peter found me. His hand gripped me by the arm and he dragged me forward toward the door. My tennis shoes slid over loose dirt. I almost lost my footing but, head down, he kept pulling. As we reached the door, I realized he had Dana by the arm too.

The three of us stumbled up the steps into the clean air. Dana collapsed on the grass, her hands on her belly, her eyes huge. I dropped to my knees beside her, assured her she was okay, that her baby was okay.

Behind me I could hear Pisto yelling, demanding I step away from her sister, but I ignored her. I didn't know who or what was keeping her from launching herself onto my back and I didn't care. I felt Dana's fear like my own. I wasn't going to leave her here to wallow in it alone.

Finally, with Dana cradled in my arms, her face pressed against my chest, I turned my attention to what was going on around us. Peter, his normally casual posture abandoned, stood with his feet shoulder-width apart, his body coiled as if ready to spring. It was an alert, almost aggressive stance I'd never witnessed him take.

It was unsettling—like he was an entirely different person from the one I thought I'd come to know, but also disturbingly reassuring. It was nice to have someone else on guard, to be able to concentrate on comforting Dana without worrying about an attack from behind. It was nice not having to be the strong one. A piece of me screamed at the sacrilegious thought, but I couldn't deny that another part of me almost sighed with relief—even if it was for only a few moments.

The sound of Pisto screaming again, this time just a general cry of outrage, pulled my attention away from Peter and to the chaotic scene playing out in the small space between my shop and the gym. Seemed like everyone was there—Amazons, my employees, and a few customers. Even the dog had reappeared. He sat in the back as if unsure whether to dive into the melee or run for cover.

But the real sight was the main players—those who had been in the basement when the curtain fell. Reynolds, Bubbe, Alcippe, and Pisto, all coated in dust, stood on the other side of the basement stairwell.

Dirt continued to spiral out of the open basement door; it made seeing exactly what was going on a challenge. But I couldn't miss Pisto's yells or the fact that someone or something was keeping her from coming over the open stairwell at me.

Giving Dana one last reassuring pat, I stood. Enough of letting Peter carry the load. I needed to be ready to fight.

At this angle I could see that Mother, looking calm and clean, had Pisto gripped around the waist. The Amazon lieutenant leaned forward, a crazed look in her eyes. Somehow she'd lost her sais. I could see them lying on the ground a few feet away. One side of her face also appeared to be swelling, making me guess Mother's calm demeanor was deceptive.

To their left, Alcippe and Bubbe seemed to be involved in a battle of their own. I couldn't tell if magic or only wills were involved, but it was obvious the two were attempting to gain control of each other in some manner.

Reynolds stood facing all of them. He'd lost his jacket and his gun was back in its holster. He had his back to me, so I couldn't see his face, but his hands were shaking. By the way he held them, I had to guess he was trying to decide if holstering his gun had been a wise choice. But from the basement doorway, all he'd seen was an explosion of dirt and now coughing, if tense, people. I doubted if, on paper, either would look like a justified reason to pull a gun.

The door to the cafeteria opened and Zery stepped out. She, like Mother, appeared calm, but I knew she was holding an iron fist around her emotions. She always did.

Reynolds spotted her and moved that direction in controlled, even strides. As he approached, five Amazons moved to block his progress. He froze. Every line of his body showed he was aware of their intent, but he didn't lose his cool or reach for his gun.

His and Zery's control were a stark contrast to the raging Pisto behind him.

Zery called out an order and the Amazons folded back like geese moving into a new formation. Her movements smooth and unhurried, she brushed past Reynolds and took his former position in front of her lieutenant and high priestess. Without a word from Zery, both ceased their struggles—Alcippe taking a step back and lowering her head, Pisto jerking her body from Mother's grip and moving to stand by her queen's side.

Her countenance dark, she watched me.

I folded my arms over my chest and stared back.

Beside me, Peter moved closer, completely cutting off Pisto's view of her sister. Her shoulders stiffened, but she didn't shift her gaze from mine. It was me she blamed for this, and she was making sure I knew it.

In another situation she would have called me out, but with Reynolds, my employees, and their clients watching, Zery wouldn't stand for it.

Another time, Pisto's expression said.

As Zery moved back toward Reynolds, so did Pisto. Anger still rolled off her body. While Zery and Reynolds talked, she kept her eyes focused on something over his shoulder, seemed to be ignoring them both.

At one point, Zery turned to her and barked out some short order. Pisto hesitated, then pivoted and cantered off, around the corner and out of sight.

Zery swiveled back to Reynolds, who was watching the warrior leave. After another word to him, Zery stepped around him and followed Pisto. With her exit, the remaining Amazons, including Alcippe, Mother, and Bubbe, followed. After I raised my eyebrows a time or two at my employees, the area cleared of everyone except Dana, Peter, Reynolds, and me. Even the dog, who had sat still through everything, loped off.

Reynolds just stared at me.

I turned with the idea of helping Dana to her feet, but Peter had beaten me to it. Instead, I grabbed her hand, squeezed, and whispered in her ear for her to go upstairs and get showered. Then remembering my resolution to keep an eye on her, I held onto her hand, keeping her from leaving.

"She'll be okay. I'll walk her up." Peter held out his hand.

I paused, unsure.

His hand didn't waver. "Your mother went toward the shop when she left. I can ask her to play guard dog, if you like. Then I—" he glanced at the approaching detective—"can come back down here."

I gave Dana's hand another squeeze, then slipped her fingers into Peter's. "I'll be fine," I murmured.

Reynolds came to a stop a few feet away.

"Oh, I know that," Peter replied. "Still might come back down." He stared at the other man as he spoke.

Reynolds arched a brow but otherwise didn't respond.

After one last stare, Peter and Dana left.

"What was that about?" Reynolds asked, pulling a

white square of material from his pocket and handing it to me.

At my questioning look, he mimicked dabbing at his face. "You have a spot."

I glanced down at my dirt-coated body, then at his. "Yeah, you too." I tossed him back the square, bent at the waist, and shook a small sandstorm of dirt from my hair.

When I'd resumed an upright position, he was leaning against the banister, looking patient and expectant at the same time. "So, you going to tell me anything?"

I went through the motions of knocking dust off my arms and laughed. "Seems I'm the one who's been doing all the telling. I think I'm done."

"It doesn't—"

"Work that way. I know." I stepped toward the sidewalk. I was finished. I didn't know what he'd seen or thought he'd seen in the basement, but I doubted I'd be able to affect his perceptions. Let him worry it out on his own. His conclusions couldn't be any more detrimental to me or the Amazons than the truth.

And I had a hearth-keeper to protect.

"What if I tell you what I find out about the Web site?"

That stopped me. I turned.

"Would you?"

He shoved the cloth into his front pocket and walked over to where I could now see his jacket lay on the ground. "I might."

I laughed again. "I'm starting to think you don't get the whole barter system."

He picked up his jacket, let it dangle from two fingers at his side. "It's the best I can do."

I shook my head. "And what is it you want from me for this 'best you can do'?"

He glanced at the basement steps. "Tell me what I saw down there."

I pulled in a breath, held it for a second. "Nothing. You saw nothing." Then I walked to the front, and he didn't stop me.

Chapter Twenty

Midnight I was jolted awake—this time by tiny sniffles. The dead girls were back. I didn't pause this time, didn't wait for them to approach me, just shot out of bed and headed to Dana's room. At least this time I was dressed. I'd taken to sleeping in my clothes, never sure when I'd be awakened again, or by what.

Her door creaked as I pushed it open. The noise jolted me into realizing I was unarmed, without even a ward ready to protect myself. I paused, but only for an instant. I was too close. I wasn't waiting for my mind to slow down enough to think of a spell. If the killer was waiting for me, I'd have to come up with something while on my feet.

I pushed the door the rest of the way open, and heard the soft rustling sound of movement in the bed.

"Dana?" I whispered. "Is that you?"

More rustling, then the sound of a hand feeling around in the dark.

"Dana. It's Mel."

A groan, and a lamp clicked, blasting the space in a blinding yellow glow. A tousled head appeared from behind a mass of covers. "Mel? What's wrong?" Dana shoved her body to a sitting position.

"Nothing. Nothing. I just thought I heard something." I backed from the room, pulling the door shut behind me. Then stood there with my heart pounding.

False alarm.

Or was it? Harmony . . .

I took off in a run, my bare feet pounding against the wood floors. It was a short trip, and this time I didn't bother with the niceties. I slammed into the door, twisting the knob as I did. The door banged into the wall and I didn't stop, kept going until my legs smacked into the bed and I'd jerked the covers back revealing my daughter, her eyes round and a scream ready, staring up at me.

I jerked her into a hug.

She panted against me, not resisting as I began rocking forward and backward, pulling her with me as I did.

"Mom, are you okay?" she finally got out.

I stroked her hair and squeezed my eyes shut, refusing to let the tears I could feel there spill out.

"Mom, seriously. You're scaring me," she whispered, her voice still rough with sleep.

I was scaring myself too, but I couldn't let go . . . wouldn't.

"Melanippe?" Bubbe stood in the doorway, her hair wrapped in a turban and a staff in her hand. I'd never seen my grandmother carry a weapon of any kind. That scared me too.

"Let the child go. She has school. Needs sleep."

I nodded and tried to relax my arms, to release my daughter, but somehow my grip tightened and my face got lost in her hair.

"Mel. That's enough." Mother this time. Her hand touched my shoulder, then my hair.

A sob escaped my lips, and I knew they were right. I was losing it, but I couldn't, not around Harmony. I dropped my grip on my daughter and pushed her lightly back against her pillow. Murmuring words even I couldn't understand, I tucked the covers around her and pressed a kiss to her forehead. She stared up at me and I knew I'd screwed up—scared her when I wanted her to feel safe. I wanted to say something to fix what I'd done, but at that juncture my mind was a blank. I let Mother take me by the hand while Bubbe stayed with Harmony, probably casting some spell to make her forget what she'd seen, to keep her from realizing her mother was insane or close to it.

With Harmony's door shut and Dana tucked back into bed too—she'd wandered into the hall when I'd exploded into my daughter's room—Mother led me into the kitchen and put a kettle of water on the stove.

Mother cooking. Things were worse than I'd imagined.

After a few minutes, she set a mug of hot water and a packet of instant cocoa on the table in front of me. I shook the packet and poured it into the water, more for something to do than because I wanted the cocoa.

Mother pulled out a chair across from me and sat, just watched me while I stumbled through stirring the mix into the water with a dirty spoon still on the table from dinner.

"There's something you aren't telling us," she announced after I'd finally submerged the last of the mix into the cup.

"There's much she isn't telling us." Bubbe walked into the room, her staff tapping with each step. She stopped next to the table. "Good she starts with the spirits who circle."

My head snapped up. My grandmother held my gaze. How long had she known?

Mother straightened, her eyes shifting back and forth between Bubbe and me. I glanced at her, then down at my cup.

"I thought the killer . . ." I wrapped my hands around the cup, let the warmth seep into my fingers. "They came when Zery . . . I was afraid."

"Who are they, Mel?" There were lines on Mother's face I'd never noticed before.

I looked at Bubbe. She took a breath. I didn't need to

tell her. She knew. "How can we help, if you don't trust?" she asked.

I grabbed the cup tighter and started to talk. I told them about finding the girls, about releasing their spirits and moving their bodies. I told them about going to the safe camp and delivering the totems, about trying to break into Bubbe's office to learn more. I told them everything—except why I hadn't told them before.

I saw the hurt and confusion on their faces, the realization that I didn't trust them. Suddenly, I couldn't look at them anymore. I dropped my gaze to my cup, stared at the hot cocoa my mother, the warrior, had made for me.

"Both of the girls who were killed went to this one bar, and were pictured on the Web site. Three other girls were too. Dana was one of them. When the girls' spirits came back, I panicked."

"You didn't try to speak with them?" Bubbe moved closer, placed her gnarled hand on mine.

"No, but the last time they came was when Zery—" I looked up. "Zery."

I shoved my chair back and headed for the steps. Mother and Bubbe were right behind me. The trip down the stairs felt longer than it ever had before. The ridged metal strips attached to the edge of each step cut into my feet.

I reached the doors first, didn't wait for my family, jerked the doors open and fell onto my knees. A body . . . blond, face turned away from me, lay on the cold concrete porch. My hands shaking, I couldn't bring myself to touch her, didn't want to live this again . . . didn't want to know . . .

"Mel! What? Who?" Zery stood a few feet away, a sword held in a halfway position, like she was lowering or raising it, I couldn't tell which.

"Zery?" Relief hit me. A laugh exploded from my constricted chest. My hands dropped and brushed the body before me, reminded me Zery might be safe, but someone else wasn't.

Zery raised her sword higher, crossed the few paces between us. "Step back, Mel."

When I didn't move, she pointed the blade at my throat.

I lifted my hands and edged my body backward.

"Who is it?" she asked.

I shook my head. "I don't know. I thought it was you—was afraid—"

She shook her head in return, her hair moving around her face as she did. "Don't say anything and don't move. Whatever you do, don't move." Her voice was shaking. There was a slight tremble in the blade as well.

Behind me the doors creaked open. Bubbe and Mother. I could feel them, smell the scents of my home drifting out and mixing with the night air. It should have been comforting, but it wasn't.

Couldn't be.

My best friend was holding a sword to my throat, and she meant to use it.

"Put it down." Mother, her voice strong, missing the deference she'd normally show a queen, was back to the voice she'd used on Zery when we were little and got caught messing with Mother's weights. Rolling them across the room. Staging races.

Bubbe ignored them both, moved forward to place her hand on the woman's shoulder and carefully roll her onto her back.

Pisto, her face peaceful, lacking the hate I'd seen sketched there the last time she'd looked at me.

My breath caught and my gaze shot to Zery. The sword moved up and down, as if she'd forgotten she held it. Mother jerked me backward, behind her.

The action seemed to knock Zery out of her trance. Her arm stiffened. She took a step forward.

"Why?"

Mother stood between us, and despite my efforts I couldn't get around her. "She didn't do it."

"I saw her, and she laughed. She sat over Pisto and laughed."

"From relief. I thought it was you." I darted far to the right, out of Mother's reach, made it past her to a spot not far from where Bubbe murmured over Pisto's body. With my grandmother and Pisto between us, I stared at my old friend, willed her to believe me. "I didn't care for Pisto, but I didn't kill her."

"Like you didn't kill the other girls? How did you get their totems? Alcippe said you brought them to camp; I didn't believe her. I convinced myself she'd made a mistake, that her dislike of you was coloring her perceptions. But it was you, wasn't it? You killed them and now Pisto. Tell me why." Her sword arm was stiff, her stance stiff too, rigid with anger.

"There is no why. I didn't kill them, any of them." I took a breath, prayed she'd believe what I was going to tell her. "I found them, like this, on my front porch."

"On your front porch?" She shook her head. "I know you. You can do better than that."

I held out my hands. "I can't. It's the truth. I don't know why, but the killer brought them to me—woke me with a rock tossed at my window. I came down and they were here. The first one . . . when I realized she was an Amazon . . . I didn't know what to do, had no idea who to trust." I rubbed a hand over my forehead. "What would you expect me to do? What kind of greeting would I have received if I'd shown up at the safe camp with a dead Amazon teen in my truck? I convinced myself I had no choice, took her totem, released her spirit, then left her somewhere I knew she'd be found, so the police would be called in."

Zery looked away, at the brick wall of my shop. I was sure she wasn't even seeing the dusty red bricks and cracked mortar, that her mind was spinning as out of control as mine.

"The second . . . well, I realized the tribe might not even know. I had to do something to alert you. So, I brought the totems."

"So, you brought the totems," she repeated, like some kind of automaton.

"But the dead girls, they've been visiting me. They came tonight. I knew something had happened. I just didn't know what." I looked down at Pisto then, the full reality that she was dead setting in.

Bubbe brushed hair off the dead warrior's face, started to fold her hands like I'd done with the others, then with her fingers posed above Pisto's right breast, Bubbe paused and looked up at me.

I pressed my hands together in front of my lips, in a praying posture. "Like the others," I murmured.

New creases formed on my grandmother's face. I could tell she was disturbed. I wanted to ask her what she thought it meant, why anyone would mutilate the girls so, but as the question formed in my mind, Zery sprang back to life. She paced forward, her sword extended.

"You have to come with me, back to camp."

I glanced at the shop where my daughter and Dana slept.

Dana. Pisto.

I swallowed. The young hearth-keeper had just lost the last of her immediate family. Pregnant and the end of her line—except for the baby boy the Amazons wanted her to give up.

I shook my head. "I'm not leaving."

"We're not giving you any choice." As if solidifying from mist, Alcippe stepped out of the shadows.

"What are you doing here?" I asked.

"Making sure a killer doesn't escape." She swept the long skirt of her dress out of her way and stalked forward.

Seeing her now brought forth every suspicion I'd ever had. I started to move too, toward her. "That's a good idea. Why don't you tell us what you know about the killings?"

"Me?" She laughed. "It's over, Mel. Your hatred has gone too far."

"Mine or yours? Both girls broke the rules, didn't they? Snuck up to Madison without your permission. Did they like what they saw here? Were they questioning the need to stay hidden? Is that why you killed them, to preserve the precious Amazon way of life?"

Her hands disappeared into the sleeves of her kaftan.

I took another step, barely noticing that Bubbe had stood, that the staff she'd held earlier was back in her hand. "You tattooed them all too, didn't you? Is that why you took their *givnomai*, taking back what you gave them, denying them their right to be Amazons by killing them, then stealing their personal power?"

"What?" She and Zery said the word at once.

Zery began to walk toward Pisto, her gaze locked on her lieutenant's T-shirt-covered breast.

Alcippe pulled her hands from her sleeves, shoved them up into the air. Grass that had been flattened under my bare feet seconds early shot upward until skinny green tendrils curled around my thighs, pulled on me.

I cursed and clawed at the weeds, managed to jerk one leg free just to have it captured again as soon as I set my foot back onto the earth. Past trying to hide any of my skills, I pulled in a breath and exhaled.

A gale erupted from my lungs. Fed by my emotions, it knocked into the high priestess. Her kaftan molded to her body. Her hair whipped free of the braid she'd contained it with, snapped like something alive into its full length behind her. She stumbled, and her face . . . her expression, the shock that I was doing this to her . . . it was worth the wait.

Her magic forgotten, nothing but weeds to be trampled under my feet, I stalked forward, inhaling as I went, spinning my arms with each step. I was going to do what I should have done ten years ago—would have if I'd had the skill. I was going to blow her so far and so deep across the earth, there'd be a trench from here to the Gulf of Mexico.

I was strong, powerful, and unstoppable. I held the breath, felt it in my lungs. Then as I opened my lips to set it free, I saw Bubbe move, saw her staff swing toward me.

There was no time to do anything except watch as the hard polished end of my grandmother's staff collided with my forehead.

My knees collapsed and the world around me faded . . . the power in the breath I'd held fading along with my consciousness.

. . .

I woke in the cold and the dark. Something about the space seemed familiar, but it took a few minutes to realize I'd been locked in my own basement—in the boiler room with my dirty laundry and Harmony's outgrown toys. The front of my head pounded. I touched my fingers to the pain and quickly found the reason—a ping-pong-ball-sized lump.

Who knew Bubbe packed such a wallop?

But at least she'd hit me and not responded with magic. My head probably wouldn't have survived that.

I allowed myself another few seconds to become accustomed to the knowledge that my five-hundred-year-old grandmother had KO'd me with a staff, then I tried to stand. My head tilted left and right, like some demented bobblehead-doll, my stomach, though, surely empty . . . I'd lost all track of time . . . clenched . . . I made it as far as my knees before giving up, at least somewhat.

On all fours, I crept to the door, then, my head still down, reached up and twisted the knob. As I'd guessed—locked. I fell back onto my belly and lay there with my nose pressed against the one-inch crack under the door.

"Shit." Not my favorite curse, but it fit my mood.

A staff rapped into the floor on the other side of the door. "She's awake," a female voice I didn't recognize announced.

"I'll get Alcippe," replied another.

"No. I put her here. I'll talk to her."

The voice of my conqueror, all five hundred years of her.

The guards, at least I assumed they were guards and not my own personal servants waiting for me to awaken so they could serve me lemonade and cookies here in the luxury of my boiler room, must have agreed to her demand because the next thing I knew the door had whacked me firmly in the side of the head.

With a groan I rolled over, giving Bubbe ample space to squeeze into the room—or at least as much space as I was willing to give at that moment.

The door snapped closed behind her, and she peered down at me. "How are you feeling?"

From this angle she was upside-down, and I couldn't tell for sure if she was smiling or frowning. I knew which I was doing. "Peachy," I replied. "You could have killed me."

"I could have, but you were a difficult labor. My daughter wouldn't appreciate it if I dispatched her efforts so easily."

I humphed and rolled again, making it back to a sit. "So, what's happening?"

She slipped a glass of cloudy liquid into my hand, then walked to the nearest pile of laundry and began rooting through it. "Harmony is at school. She was not happy you left on your trip without telling her."

"My trip?" If I'd been able, I would have stood. Instead, I choked down a gulp of whatever she'd put in the glass and grimaced as I swallowed the nasty brew.

"Trip. You have to stay here—" She jerked Harmony's

favorite pink jeans from under a stack of sweats and towels, then sniffed them. With a grimace she dropped them back onto the stack. "And she will make do."

"What about Dana?"

Bubbe sighed. "She has been told."

"But . . . where is she?" My head was beginning to clear, the pounding to lighten to a rap.

"Here. I won't let Alcippe take her against her will. I won't let them take her baby." She dropped her attention back to the laundry. She was leaving something unsaid. A "but" or something seemed to hang in the air.

Her fingers tightened back around the jeans. "Zery has taken Pisto to the safe camp. Her funeral will take place there. Cleo and I will take Dana and bring her back home."

"And what about me? What about Alcippe? You know she has more reason to have done this than I do."

"Alcippe has no reason to have killed Pisto."

But I did. Bubbe didn't say that, didn't have to.

She took a breath and kept talking. "Alcippe doesn't live in Madison, didn't find the bodies and keep them from the tribe. Alcippe didn't bring men into our midst."

Alcippe was damn near perfect whereas I was a complete and total fuckup. But I wasn't a killer. "I can't stay in here," I said. "The killer"—*Alcippe*—"is still out there. Dana is still at risk. Harmony could be at risk."

"You will stay here." She started to move toward the door, the jeans gathered in her hands.

I managed to stand. Wobbly, but on my feet, I put a hand next to hers on the denim. "I have to do something. The *givnomai*. The killer is taking them for a reason. I know Pisto's was missing too. I could see it on your face. If I tell you what hers was, will you bring me the totem? It and her *telios*?"

"You'll call on Artemis?"

It was what she wanted more than anything—me to admit my connection to the goddess, to work on my priestess skills in the open. She'd seen what I could do when I attacked Alcippe, guessed that I'd unwound her serpent ward, but I'd yet to openly admit any of it, to say I would at least try to follow her path.

"I've done it before. I told you about the girls."

"But you didn't put all your trust in the goddess. She would never have guided you to make the choices that got you here."

I licked my lips. "My power has grown."

She smiled, but not with the joy or pride I expected, more like you smile at a child who tells you her favorite color is red or that the sun felt warm on her face—like she wanted to pat me on the head. "But you don't believe, haven't trusted. If I bring you the tools, will you try?"

I had no idea what she was asking of me. I'd always believed. I'd grown up believing. As for trust . . . I didn't trust anyone, hadn't for a long time. Still, I agreed.

She frowned, but nodded. "They will bring you food soon. You'll find what you need on the tray."

Chapter Twenty-one

I spent the next hour or so jumping at every sound out-side the closed door. I'd considered trying to blast my way out, but couldn't think of how that would help. Right now at least, the other Amazons didn't see me as a threat and thought I was locked down.

I'd wait for Bubbe to get me the totems and see where the ritual took me, see what Pisto's *givnomai* told me. My stomach had just started to growl and my patience to wane when I heard voices outside—my guards chatting with someone. Based on the smells making their way past the locked door and stench of Mother's workout gear, I cleverly deduced it was someone bearing a tasty meal.

I stood up to greet her.

Holding a tray covered with a blue cloth and flanked

by two scowling warriors, stood Dana. The smile on my face vanished.

Dana. It made sense a hearth-keeper would be sent to deliver my meal, but Dana . . . I hadn't expected her. The Amazons claimed I'd killed her sister. Did she believe them?

She entered with her eyes downcast. Behind her the guards moved shoulder to shoulder, forming an Amazon door. I understood why they wouldn't want to leave me alone with her—not believing what they did. It hurt, though. I'd come to care about Dana. I identified with her desire to keep her son, but also saw her as the young girl she was . . . not all that much older than Harmony.

The thought that she might hate me sent my appetite fleeing.

She scuttled in, her gaze never rising from the tray.

"Dana—"

One of the warriors made some grunting noise, cutting me off. I shot a glare at the pushy giant.

When I looked back, Dana hadn't moved. She was staring around the small space, apparently looking for some flat surface on which to leave the tray. I stepped forward, shoving a pile of dishrags off the washer and onto the floor.

Still not looking at me, she slid the tray onto the dented metal top and turned to leave.

"I'm sorry about Pisto," I murmured.

She stopped, and ran her palms down the sides of her jeans.

I wasn't going to say anything else. She deserved her sorrow, didn't need me proclaiming my innocence and getting in the way of what she was going through.

Her shoulders began to shake. A sob escaped her lips.

I looked at the warriors, stupidly expecting one of them to step in and help her out of the room. The terra-cotta warriors of Shi Huangdi showed more empathy.

Risking a kick to the head—if they managed to show life—I moved closer to the distraught hearth-keeper, but kept myself from touching her. Just yesterday I would, without question, have pulled her into my arms for a hug, had in fact, but today . . . I just stood there, let her know she wasn't alone.

She pulled in another breath, and whispered, "What happened? They're saying . . ."

She asked. I had to answer—was burning to answer. "I didn't hurt her. I didn't hurt any of them. I wouldn't do that. You know that?"

She licked her lips, raised her eyes enough to glance at the warriors who showed some signs of life by shifting from one foot to another.

A loud sniff, then she turned and fell against my chest. I staggered to keep from falling.

"I didn't believe them. I told Alcippe you didn't do it—couldn't. Just because you and Pisto fought. She and I fought, but I'd never . . . I'd do anything . . ." Her hand found its way to her stomach.

I placed mine over hers. "It isn't your fault—don't

even think like that. You can't afford it. He"—I patted her hand against her abdomen—"can't afford it."

She nodded, the up and down motion of her head tight against my shoulder, pulling at my shirt. "I know." She let out another snuffling breath, then pulled back. Her eyes were red and swollen and her nose was running.

I searched around for a cloth to wipe her face, but came up with nothing I thought would meet her more particular needs. Finally I jerked out the tail of my shirt and stretched it toward her.

She laughed, just a light twitter of sound, but I relaxed a little. She was going to be okay. It had to be tough, losing her sister, but she'd get through it.

"Can I stay here?" she asked, after retrieving a roll of paper from the toilet positioned between the wall and laundry sink.

"Here?" I motioned to the dingy space filled with smelly laundry.

"No, I mean here . . . your house. Alcippe is trying to get me to go back to the camp and I'd like to go . . . for a while, for Pisto's—" She blew her nose on a length of tissue, placed a new piece against her eyes. "But I don't want to stay. I know Pisto wanted me to, but . . ."

I pulled off another length of toilet paper and handed it to her. "Of course you can stay. I told you that already."

"But with you here." She glanced at the warriors. "I

didn't know how your family would feel about me. Pisto was my sister and you were the one who invited me."

I waved the strip of paper in the air, cutting her short. "Nothing has changed—not as far as my offer. And besides, with me"—I searched for a term—"out of commission, they're going to need someone to take care of them. You can do that, right?"

She nodded, the first spark of life I'd seen lighting her face since she'd walked through the door. "And I can stay here too, for a while." She picked up the snarl of clothes I'd tossed onto the floor and nodded to the washing machine. "Harmony was looking for some of her things this morning. Your grandmother . . . she was . . ."

"Incredibly sympathetic?" I chimed in.

Her confusion obvious, Dana frowned. *Sarcasm doesn't work with her.* I waved my hand in a *never mind* gesture and slid the tray off the washer. With Harmony at school and Mother and Bubbe busy—trying to get the Amazons to see sense, I hoped—Dana had to be feeling alone.

I glanced at the warriors. Obviously they weren't going to do much to make her feel better. Besides, once she got the wash going and left, I'd be free to work my spell with the added camouflage of my third-hand washer clanking away, covering my chant.

With no objections from the warrior twins, I settled down to eat my lunch while Dana sorted and pretreated the wash, in general giving our clothing more care than it had seen since being shoved in a bag and brought home from the store.

While she loaded the first pile into the washer, I palmed the leather bag Bubbe had hidden under the cloth and slipped it behind a stack of socks so ripe I didn't think even Dana would brave moving them.

Twenty minutes or so later, Dana had everything laid out in neat color-coordinated piles and had thoroughly instructed me on their proper bleach/no bleach/detergent mix. She looked a little sad when she took my tray and left. I liked thinking it was caused by leaving me, but I suspected it was more about not getting the joy of folding and fluffing all to herself.

After she left, the warrior twins showed me some teeth. It was not in the form of a smile, at least not one seen anywhere except on the face of a hyena before it lunged at your throat. I returned the gesture with a full peep at my own impressively healthy set of choppers. They growled and grunted, but left.

Alone, I pulled out the leather bag and worked the tie open with my teeth. Two totems, some twigs, a handful of acorns and a lighter fell onto the floor. I glanced at the door, afraid the twins might have heard, but after a few seconds turned back to my task.

I swept up a pile of dirt with my hand, then used it to outline a circle. That done, I placed the two totems in the center—a horse for Pisto's *givnomai* and a lion for her *telios.* I paused, my fingers still touching the stone representation of the lion—the same family group as Zery. The groups had developed over the first few hundred years of the Amazons' existence. It didn't mean Zery and

Pisto were closely related, but it did mean they probably felt some kinship, some loyalty based solely on sharing a *telios.*

Perhaps I could use that loyalty to make things easier on Dana. A vote from a queen would go a long way toward easing her life if she did choose to mingle with Amazons aside from outcast me and my family. And maybe that tie would make Zery more willing to stand by Dana than our lifetime of friendship had. I swallowed the bubble of hurt and went back to my work, added the twigs and an acorn to the circle's center.

It took a few tries, but soon I had the twigs smoldering. A tiny wisp of smoke snaked upward. I leaned forward, closed my eyes, and called on Artemis.

This time the vision came hard and fast, almost knocked me back against the wall. Pisto—trapped and angry. I could feel her energy as clearly as if she stood in the room next to me. I sat lost for a while, caught up in the power, forgot that Pisto was dead—that the energy I felt so clearly couldn't be hers. I had hoped to somehow tap into where her *givnomai* was now, get some feeling or guidance from Artemis, but this direct link . . . it was impossible. Pisto was dead, and her *givnomai* was no longer attached to her body. The emotion radiating from the combined totems could only exist if the combination were still attached to a live form—but they weren't. Couldn't be. Before an Amazon was allowed to choose her *givnomai,* a priestess checked to see if the pairing existed already. If it did, it couldn't be used—not until that

Amazon died, freeing the *givnomai* for another in her clan. Perhaps there was some slim possibility a priestess had screwed up, reused Pisto's pair, but . . . I closed my eyes, let the energy flow through me, red-hot boiling anger . . . outrage . . . Pisto. There was no mistaking it.

Somehow the power in Pisto's *givnomai* still lived.

But if it wasn't attached to Pisto, if she didn't have control over it—who did?

I smothered the remnants of the fire with my hand and sat there staring at the two totems—almost afraid to pick them up. What I suspected wasn't possible. It couldn't be.

I don't know how long I sat there. Long enough that I'd rolled everything around in my mind multiple times, come back to the same well-worn possibility over and over.

The teens being delivered to me—to throw suspicion my way? To force me to face the Amazons?

Zery being staked out in a clear show of priestess and artisan skill. Skills I had, although none had known it, but skills others in the tribe, Alcippe, for example, possessed too.

Alcippe trying to force Dana to abort her baby. Alcippe angry when I got in her way. Alcippe appearing moments after we found Pisto—when she should have been miles away, back at the safe camp.

But why? Why kill the first girls—because they didn't obey? Had they shown ideas of wanting to be free of the

Amazon rules? To leave the safe camp, not just for a night, but forever? But then, why not kill Dana too? Because she knew the girl was pregnant, hoped in the beginning the child would be a girl, would pull Dana back closer to the tribe?

And then, when the baby had been a boy and Dana had come running to me . . . had the priestess snapped so thoroughly she'd gone so far as killing Pisto, knowing I would be yet again the obvious target of the Amazons' wrath?

Was staking out Zery also because of me—punishment for her believing me?

Was all of this because Alcippe had lost control of the tribe, saw that mixing with humans was coming, and blamed me? Hated me?

I jumped to my feet and began banging on the door.

I'd started to wonder if the twins had left me when finally the doorknob began to twist. I stepped back, breathless from my whole-bodied attack to get their attention.

Bubbe stepped into the room. In her hands were my favorite hiking boots and the keys to my truck. Behind her the basement was dark and empty—no twins.

"What's happened?" Bubbe's face and the missing twins told me it was something bad.

"Zery. The police have her." She shoved the boots into my hands.

The news set me back, but I took the hikers and put them on. "The police?" I asked.

"She was taking Pisto's body to the safe camp. They

were almost to the beltline. Alcippe was following her in another car. That detective pulled Zery over."

Boots on and keys in hand, I stood and stared her in the eyes. "He pulled her over?" Could he do that? A Milwaukee detective pull over a car in Madison for no reason?

"There were other cars too. A group of Amazons were driving down. But only Zery was pulled over. Alcippe tried to stop, but Zery waved her on."

"So, where's Zery now?"

"They found Pisto's body in Zery's car. They took her away in shackles."

Handcuffs. The police had hauled an Amazon queen off to human jail in handcuffs. This was very bad.

"The warriors?"

"In the gym. Without Zery or Pisto . . ." Bubbe shook her head. "Cleo is trying to settle them, stop them from their stupidity."

"They want to attack the jail, don't they?" Of course they did. Most of them had spent their entire lives dreaming of fighting a real battle with a real cause. Freeing their queen from human clutches? What could be more noble?

"That is the talk now, but there have been other mentions." Her gaze was sharp.

Me. They wanted me—dead, I was sure. Nothing like facing a mob of Amazon warriors to liven up a dull imprisonment.

"Harmony will be safe." Bubbe shoved open the door. "We will bring her to you when things have settled."

I stared at the open door, unable to do much more. She wanted me to run, to leave my daughter. She knew me better than that—surely. My gaze traveled back to my grandmother. She raised her hands, started to mumble.

I strode forward, stepped into her space. "Don't even think it. I don't care how strong your powers are. They won't get me to leave Harmony."

Her eyes narrowed. Her lips drew together in a pucker. "You will both be safer if you aren't here."

"Not if the killer is still out there. I know who it is—who it has to be."

Bubbe relaxed her lips, moving from a purse to a twist.

"It's Alcippe. And all of this is about her losing control of the Amazons and her hatred of me. If I leave and she can't get to me and I leave Harmony behind, she'll go after her, because Alcippe knows that would hurt me more than anything. Would kill me."

Bubbe shook her head. "Alcippe lives for the tribe."

"And that's why she hates me." I ran through everything I'd worked out in the last few hours. When I was done, Bubbe looked no more convinced, but she didn't start chanting either. She moved to the side and stared at the wall—let me walk past her into the basement, her gaze never wandering from whatever spot she'd focused on.

I jogged through the basement to the outside door. Once past that, I crept up the stairs. I could hear voices arguing—or at least one voice, male. I peered over the stairwell.

Peter stood at the corner of my shop, his back to the gym. In front of him were the twins, fully armed with swords, staffs, grenades . . . maybe not grenades, but they were loaded down with weapons and even wearing some kind of padded Kevlar type vest.

I could only imagine what Peter was thinking.

As I watched, they pointed toward the parking lot. I crouched down a little lower. They didn't turn to look, but Peter did. He saw me. I could feel his gaze, but before I could think what to do, he turned back to the twins and began to argue louder.

"The shop is open. I just left for lunch." He stepped to the side, to his left, forcing the twins to turn too, move so their backs were to me. "I have appointments."

The twins seemed to broaden from behind, but didn't say much, at least not much I could hear. Peter looked past them, at me. His eyes said *run*.

I didn't stop to think why he wasn't questioning what was going on or how he seemed to know I needed to escape without the twins' noticing. I just vaulted up the stairs and sprinted to my truck.

I had to get to my daughter. I had to make sure she was safe.

After I pulled up at West High, I sat in my truck for a few minutes, let it idle—technically against the law in Madison, but far from my biggest worry at the moment.

I wanted—no, *needed*—to know Harmony was safe, but I also knew I couldn't just drag her out of geometry or whatever and race away.

The killing had gone on too long, and it was tied to me. I had a responsibility to stop Alcippe, especially since no one else believed the killer *was* Alcippe.

Then there was Zery. I couldn't traipse off and leave her in jail. I was the only Amazon equipped to talk with the police, to maybe get Reynolds to bend. I had to go back, had to face Alcippe and the Amazons.

I drove to a nearby neighborhood street, where I deserted the truck and took off on foot. I would check on my daughter, reassure myself she was safe, then I'd do whatever I had to do to stop this disaster.

I checked my watch. It was almost two—right before sixth period. Harmony should be on her way to English. Luckily the classroom was on the ground floor. I didn't want to worry my girl by interrupting her class. I just wanted to see her. It took three tries before I found the right class.

The period had already started by this time, but the kids were still milling around. Harmony was facing the window. A slender boy stood in front of her, his back to me. Her eyes did some angle thing I'd never seen before, and she flicked her hair over her shoulder. My girl was flirting.

Seeing the obvious display of interest from my daughter shot fear of a new kind through me, but the relief at seeing her at all—happy and healthy, if focused on some boy whose face I couldn't see—quickly knocked that aside.

My fingers gripping the concrete sills that topped the brick, I soaked up the sight.

Rachel appeared, shot the boy and then Harmony a sidelong glance. She saw the attraction too, seemed to approve of it more than I did.

I tapped my fingers against the sill. I'd wanted a normal human daughter. Guess that's what Artemis was giving me.

At that moment a line of cars pulled up to the four-way stop near the school. I dropped to my knees in the dirt to avoid being seen. Being arrested for spying on students, or even just being outed as a crazy stalker mom, was not part of my plan.

By the time the cars had pulled off, the class had settled into their seats and I didn't dare risk peering at my daughter again.

She was safe.

As long as I found Alcippe and stopped her, Harmony would stay that way.

Chapter Twenty-two

Back in my truck, I realized I didn't know where Alcippe was. Bubbe had said Zery waved her on, but had she continued to the safe camp or returned to the gym?

Zery was jailed somewhere in Wisconsin, and Alcippe thought I was locked in my basement.

I bet she didn't go far. I drove home.

From the outside things looked pretty normal, in other words, quiet. The twins were nowhere to be seen. I stood on the sidewalk between my shop and the gym, undecided on what to do first.

Someone grabbing me from behind made the decision for me. An arm snapped across my chest, pinning my arms to my side, and my attacker began walking backward, dragging me with each step.

I reached out, gathering power without thought. The process was becoming easier, second nature. A spell was on my lips, wind building in my lungs, when a rough voice whispered in my ear. "Too damn stubborn. You were supposed to leave."

Mother.

"I'm taking you to your truck and you're going to get in it and drive. Head north," she ordered.

I let out my breath and released most of the power. "Where's Alcippe?" I asked.

She squeezed me, mumbled something under her breath that I didn't think was exactly an endearment and kept dragging.

I relaxed against her. Fighting would have just wasted energy. Besides, she obviously didn't intend to hog-tie me and drive me somewhere herself, so this whole exercise could only have one conclusion: her letting me go and me heading right back.

You'd think she'd have known me better by now. Ten feet from my truck, she took a hard left. "My truck's over there," I said, letting my impatience to end the farce show.

She kept dragging. That's when I got suspicious. I twisted, or tried to. Her arms held—as surely as titanium bars.

Another of her long-legged paces, even moving backward she could eat up ground at twice the pace I could, and we were beside a battered van—the windowless kind serial killers use to troll parking lots. Bubbe and one of the hearth-keepers I'd seen working in the cafeteria stood beside it.

I dug in my heels. Mother didn't even slow her pace. The ground tugged on my boots as I jammed them into the earth. I pulled in a breath, my brain spinning through spells like cards on a Rolodex, searching for something I could use that would force her to release me without killing either of us.

"Melanippe." Bubbe held up a hand, her face calm . . . understanding.

Hell no. I sucked in instead of blowing out and went limp, fell. The trick worked. It caught Mother, who was prepared for my fight, off guard. I slipped through her arms. She'd moved two giant steps backward before she realized the loss. By then I was jogging to the front.

I got as far as the corner, paused, again weighing shop or gym. And again, I didn't have to make the choice. Someone made it for me—actually, a mob made it for me.

Amazons began pouring out the front, Alcippe in their lead. She took one look at me and yelled. Twenty pairs of angry feet pounded toward me. Instinctively I spun. Mother and Bubbe were a few feet behind me, both waving for me to come toward them, to run to the van and disappear. I leaned in their direction, my body automatically moving to safety. Then I remembered why I was here, that someone needed to face Alcippe, and that someone was me.

I turned back to the crowd and began mumbling the

first spell that sprang to my brain. It started to rain—hard. Drops fell from the sky like lead balls, big, too big to be natural, and hard, edged with ice. My shirt and pants clung to me. The Amazons racing toward me slipped on the instantly saturated ground. They piled one on top of the other in an almost comical display. I might have laughed if I'd known what I was doing, if I'd felt like I could stop the deluge I'd beckoned. Instead, I listened to my teeth chatter and watched, wild-eyed, wondering what to do next.

Alcippe clung to the corner of the gym, her long dress hindering her movement. She started to raise her arms and, again without thought, I blasted out a breath. The rain changed direction—moved almost diagonally, right in her face. She had no choice; she raised her arm to block the onslaught, to keep from drowning while standing up . . .

I snapped my lips shut. The wind stopped, but the rain continued. Alcippe placed her arm over her head, like a visor blocking the moisture. Heat and hate poured from her eyes.

I realized then I could kill her. I had her off guard, had the upper hand. The thought was tempting. I even pulled in a second breath, but as I did, my gaze drifted upward, to Harmony's window, to those stupid bottles of nail polish lining her sill.

I'd left the Amazons to make my daughter a better life, to make her a better person. If I killed Alcippe like this, what would that prove? What would it change? Alcippe would be gone, but she'd also be a martyr—brought down by evil me. She might die, but her message, "The Amazons can't change," would live on, even grow.

I couldn't kill Alcippe. Not like this. I had to discredit her—show the rest of them the old ways weren't the only ways. And there was only one way to do that.

I closed my eyes and found the switch, or faucet, whatever it was that controlled the power I held but didn't understand. The rain stopped suddenly, as if we'd just stepped under an overhang—no gradual lessening or softening, just gone.

The Amazons scrambled in the mud, sliding and gripping each other to help themselves stand. I crossed my arms over my chest and waited. They'd remember me soon enough.

Alcippe recovered first, of course. She slogged forward, her dress sagging, revealing withered cleavage. Her sleeves clung to her arms, and her skirt wrapped around her ankles. Finally, she gave up trying to get to me and shoved her hands out, ready to call on a little magic of her own.

A wolf, translucent but deadly, appeared from nowhere. His feet splayed, his head lowered, and his ears back, he snarled at Alcippe. I blinked, not sure what I was seeing was real—but it was. When I opened my eyes, the wolf still stood there, his lips raised, revealing his gums and teeth, the ruff on his neck standing at attention.

Alcippe's gaze shot to me, then just as quickly behind me.

Bubbe and Mother, both surprisingly dry, stepped forward, one on each side of me.

"You can't protect her." Alcippe flicked her attention from the wolf to my grandmother and back.

"That was not my plan." Bubbe twitched two fingers and the wolf sat. "Melanippe can care for herself. Better than I knew."

The sky was clear now, but the air cold. Goose bumps formed on my flesh, but by sheer force of will I stopped myself from shivering. I glanced at my grandmother, tried to read what she was thinking, but everything about her looked relaxed, unworried.

"She attacked us. Me, a high priestess." Alcippe's voice was strong, but her gaze darted to the wolf again and again.

I'd never seen this particular piece of magic held this long and visible to all. I'd seen the serpent, but only after immersing myself in the spell. I glanced at the other Amazons. All of them stood rigid, their stares locked on the wolf.

They all saw him. He was real.

"Call off your *telíos*," Alcippe ordered.

Bubbe tilted her head back and forth, studying the animal. "He's causing no harm." She raised her chin, her voice grew stronger. "Yet."

Alcippe's eyes drew together; her hands balled at her sides. "What do you want?"

"Melanippe?" Bubbe turned to me, her voice back to her normal tone, but sweeter—much sweeter. "What is it you want?"

I licked my lips, weighed my options. What did I want?

"The truth. I want the truth."

Surprise flitted across my grandmother's face, but was quickly gone—replaced by a smile. She looked back at Alcippe. "Not too much to ask."

"The rite of truth," I added.

Every eye turned to me.

It was bold, but the only choice I had—and I had nothing to hide, nothing to fear. Not anymore. Beside me, Mother stiffened. My grandmother was more subtle, but I could feel a shift in the energy surrounding her.

But when she spoke, she was calm, resolved. "The rite of truth."

Alcippe hesitated, as I knew she would. By agreeing, she risked her life. Whoever won the battle also won the right to demand one truth of their choice. If the loser spoke a lie or refused to answer, Artemis would forfeit her life—and worse, to Alcippe anyway, that Amazon would die an outcast.

It was the worst fate she could face—and everything I wanted. The smile on my lips came from deep inside.

Alcippe saw it, recognized it. Her eyes narrowed, and her fingers straightened. She'd made the choice. She was going to accept. I widened my smile, concentrated on her lips, waited for them to open.

"I accept the challenge." The right words, but from the wrong direction. I spun, stared at my grandmother.

"You can't," I responded.

"I did. I asked what you wanted. You said, and I accepted." She held up her hand, waved, and the wolf was gone. "But inside." She moved forward, her steps even, almost floating.

Alcippe stepped in front of her. "She challenged me."

Bubbe shrugged. "Perhaps, but the truth she wants is mine to tell." Then she kept moving, enigmatic and frustrating as ever.

I followed Bubbe into the gym, the other Amazons, Mother, and Alcippe filed in too. Bubbe had already taken position at the far end, near the stage. Leaving me the space by the door. Alcippe took center court. Mother and the other Amazons formed two lines flanking us. Normally there would have been a circle of Amazons surrounding us, but in the rectangular space available, the lines made more sense. Plus, the rite normally would have been performed outside—the walls of the gym more than made up for the lack of Amazons completing the customary circle.

Alcippe waved her hand. The doors slammed shut behind us. I sensed they wouldn't open until we were through.

My grandmother stood the full length of the basketball court away. Her arms at her sides, she looked completely at peace—like she hadn't just twisted my challenge, forced herself into the position I'd meant for Alcippe.

Why had she done it? Frustrated, I stalked forward, got to the center before hitting an invisible wall of power.

I cursed and turned to face Alcippe. "This isn't what I asked for. I didn't challenge Bubbe. I challenged you."

"I didn't hear a name, only a request. A request I answered." Bubbe didn't even bother to look at me as she spoke, concentrated instead on folding the arms of her sleeves up past her wrists.

I wanted to scream, could feel it growing inside me. I did not want to fight Bubbe, but her cold indifference to what she had done was infuriating me, and she knew it. Damn her. She was pushing my buttons, trying to get me to forget myself.

I took a deep breath and adjusted my own sleeves, pulling them down until they brushed the top knuckle of my thumb.

The Amazons stood like stone statues beside us. No one except me seemed concerned that Bubbe had twisted the rite as she had. Fine. I'd fight my grandmother. And I'd try to beat her. Get whatever truth I could from her, even if it was just why she had stepped in to protect Alcippe.

That was certainly a question that was burning inside me.

Alcippe raised her arms, lifted the wall, and I faced my grandmother in a way I never had before. I waited, thinking the entire thing might be a put-on show, a way to make me see the light—or the light as my grandmother saw it.

As I stared at her, she looked different, old, frail.

Bubbe never looked old, not really. I frowned. I couldn't do this. I started to turn, to tell Alcippe it was over, I'd admit defeat and give up whatever truth they wanted. As I moved, color flashed from the end of the room—Bubbe moving her arms. Suddenly I was surrounded by eleven of the twelve Amazon *telioses*: bull, lion, stag, fish, dog, hawk, serpent, hare, leopard, boar, and bear. Each as real as the wolf outside had been, and each just as deadly.

I looked at Bubbe, surprised. I'd been the one to issue the challenge, meaning she got to choose the battle, but I hadn't expected this.

"Never underestimate, *devochka moya*." She slid her gaze to the first *telios*—a bull. Hereford by the looks of him. You never could tell with Bubbe; she liked to mix old with new. For whatever reason, I got a bull known more for burgers than fighting.

Might have been some kind of insult. The thought had barely formed before he started trotting forward, horns high and ears erect.

At three thousand pounds it didn't matter what he was bred for, he was damn intimidating.

My bullfighting experience was pretty much limited to one rodeo I attended back in my Amazon days. And I wasn't the one fighting him, my designated one-night stand had been—well, riding him, actually. Still, it was all the experience I had to go on.

I rubbed my palms on my jeans.

"Mel." Mother broke ranks long enough to slide her

sword across the gym floor. I watched it twirl in circles, like some crazy game spinner. Where would it stop? Whose move?

Lucky me. It was mine.

The bull lowered his head and snorted. I somersaulted across the floor, stopping next to the sword, and picked it up with both hands. It took a minute for my arms to adjust to the feel of it. It wasn't heavy, not like some movies and fantasy novels would have you believe, but I wasn't used to it. Swords were never my thing.

The bull seemed to sense that. He charged.

I tried to position the sword, to pierce the animal in the neck where I calculated I would do the most damage with the least effort, but my movements were awkward and I stumbled. As the creature pounded toward me, sense won out over looking good or doing things right. I deserted the sword and leapt out of his path. I could smell the sweat on his body, feel the air move as he raced past.

I let out a ragged breath, my knees crumpling beneath me.

Telios. Why *telios*? The rite of truth could be fought any way—with magic, hand-to-hand combat—hell, as far as I knew, two hearth-keepers could stage a bake-off. And my grandmother, who I'd thought carried at least some fondness for me, chose the Amazon *telioses* embodied. I was glad Artemis hadn't had a fondness for dragons.

My breathing still labored, I pressed my fingers into the floor to keep from tumbling and looked at Bubbe.

Her face was calm, almost unlined. All appearances of frailty and old age were gone.

The old fake—I should have known better. The beginnings of anger pushed me to a stand. Her gaze behind me, Bubbe twitched a brow. I turned, but too late. The bull stampeded, his head down. There was no time to dodge, no time to think. On instinct, I murmured a prayer and blew out a breath. His steps slowed, his head lowered further—as if he were pushing against a wall instead of charging across the open gym floor.

I blew harder. He slowed more until finally he seemed to lose all steam, slowed to a stop, then stood there, head hanging and his body colored dark with sweat.

I placed my hand over my heart, felt the thumping inside my chest, then picked up the sword and strode forward. Staring my grandmother in the eye, I stabbed the weapon through his neck, severing his spinal cord. The *telios* shimmered and vanished, back to nothingness . . . air. The sword clattered to the ground.

I'd felt the muscle as I'd shoved the sword into his neck, felt the heat of his body and his breath. He had been real . . . but now he was gone. Air . . . nothing but air. Only my grandmother could do that. No sooner had the thought come than the bull reappeared—just as solid and intimidating as he had been originally.

I bent to retrieve the sword and did my best to hide the sinking feeling in my core. I weighed the weapon and my options. Obviously, in my grandmother's rule book I hadn't bested the bull. I took a step toward him, hoping some new idea would come to me before he gored me in the stomach, but he seemed uninterested in me, frozen, in fact. I frowned and began moving in a circle, pivoting slowly on one foot to study each animal for movement.

Behind me another *telios* came to life. I recognized the feeling now, a kind of tingle, like something was creeping up on me—which it was.

I supposed I should have been grateful Bubbe was launching the creatures at me one at a time rather than releasing them in some kind of Amazon blood orgy but, as I turned, I saw the gaping jaws of a lion as he yawned into life. No words of thanks sprang to mind—just a few well-worn curses.

I didn't bother reaching for the sword. I knew nothing about fighting a lion, but doubted holding a sword would provide me with much advantage.

Again Mother came to the rescue, sliding a shield and spear across the floor. I was thinking something big and loaded with bullets would be a lot more practical, but Amazons didn't do firearms. Besides, pulling a trigger probably wouldn't teach whatever lesson my grandmother had gone to so much trouble to relay to me.

I picked up the spear, tossed it up and down, testing its balance . . . muttered to myself. I was tired of having to defend myself . . . prove myself even to my own family.

The anger began to build again, this time with no direct focus. I was angry at all of them.

Zery was locked up and a killer was on the loose—

standing in front of me, actually. I tossed the spear again, glanced at Alcippe. I'd tried playing this the Amazon way, convinced myself that would be best—and found myself caught in this trial by *telios*. Maybe it was time to take things back into my own hands.

I turned my grip, readied myself to throw the spear.

Chapter Twenty-three

The lion lunged. All thought of Alcippe fled. I spun, threw the spear without pausing to aim or think about the best target. To my shock, it hit home, embedded into the lion's head. Like the bull he shimmered, then was gone. The spear fell with a clatter to the floor. I just stared at it. Again my heart pounded. My pulse jumped at my throat. My gaze shot to my grandmother. She was unmoved, unruffled.

I took a step forward. "What the—?" The lion reappeared, but like the bull, frozen. I snapped my mouth closed and searched for my next opponent. The hare, stag, and fish all came to life.

On the surface, none of these animals seemed particularly dangerous—but I knew better than to relax. I didn't understand this game, but I knew one was under way—and I needed to learn the rules fast.

The three animals wandered around the court, seemingly unaware of my presence. I glanced at Mother, but no weapon was shoved my way. The first two had saved me from being gored or eaten, but they hadn't won the game. Perhaps that was all she'd been doing, buying me time to figure things out. Or perhaps she was as perplexed as I was. Either way, I was on my own.

The sword was within reach. And with no better idea leaping into my mind, I picked it up and started toward the deer. He didn't startle, just lowered his head to munch on imaginary grass, then twisted his neck to rub his antlers on the floor. I raised the sword, ready to sever his spinal cord like I'd done to the bull, but as my arm raised, he shifted—grew, until his rack was an impenetrable maze reaching from floor to ceiling. I lowered the sword anyway, felt the impact as it hit bone all through my body, but the stag didn't disappear, didn't even move.

I jerked the sword free from the antlers and stared at Bubbe. Like the deer, she seemed unmoved. I thought about tossing the sword to the side then, admitting defeat, but my fingers wouldn't let go.

Damn it. I wanted to beat her; I was going to deliver everything I had.

I stalked to the fish, grabbing the spear on the way. I stabbed at him. He slithered right, then left, darting as if swimming with the current, as if my spear were inconsequential—of no threat whatsoever. I dropped it, tried to grab him with my hands. I had him or thought I did, but as my fingers closed, he slipped through, slid out of reach.

Trying to hide my growing frustration, I moved toward the hare. He was gray, his eyes like black marbles. I stayed back, waited for him to do something. He sat up on his haunches, rubbed his front paw over his nose, and studied me in return. Then he winked.

Winked. That's when I got it—a trickster. The hare was a trickster—a lot like my grandmother. She'd set me up, known I would believe the way through this challenge was through direct battle, known Mother would throw things at me and like an idiot I would follow her lead.

I pivoted, strolled to center court, and sat down. I needed to think, not act. My gut always got me moving before my brain had time to weigh things. And Bubbe knew that.

I needed to gain control, needed to think.

Bubbe had called on the *telios* for a reason. Each had a special gift or message, but I didn't think that was the point here. Not really. This was my grandmother's message, and what was her favorite lesson to lecture me on?

Being an Amazon, accepting who I was.

I stood up. Around me all the *telioses* had come to life. I ignored them, walked past the leopard pacing to my right, stepped over the serpent that threatened to slither over my foot. Went directly to a table where Pisto had kept paper and pens for charting which Amazon was leading in what competition. I jerked the cap off a marker with my teeth, shoved up my sleeve, and started drawing.

To win you had to battle with your own weapons, define the fight for yourself.

I needed to play on my strengths. I was an artisan. This was how I had to battle.

I drew snow and a den. Mountains and trees. A spring-fed stream and a field filled with clover. I drew everything the *telios* needed to thrive, then one by one I approached them.

I reached for the fish first, felt the cold splash of water as my hand dipped toward him. Wiggled my fingers, let him swim toward me through my splayed digits. I wasn't there to catch him or destroy him. I was there to free him. As he shot past my hand, for the briefest of seconds the stream I'd drawn on my arm appeared. He lunged forward. His body whipping back and forth, he went with the current until he reached the edge of the court of our defined battle zone, leapt into the air, and disappeared.

The bull let me approach, followed me to the field, put his head down, and charged out of the court. The leopard leapt into a tree, prowled along the branch until the limb misted away above the line of Amazons' heads. The hawk soared into a mountain sky. The stag trotted into a forest. One by one all the *telioses* left, and it was just

Bubbe and me alone in the center of the court. By her side stood the wolf. She was smiling.

"Only one left. Do you know what this *telios* wants? How to free him?" she asked.

He was gray and tan, rangy. His eyes were golden. He sat by my grandmother's side, completely at peace. He was familiar and beautiful. I suddenly realized I had no idea what he wanted, what would make him feel free. I could fool the other *telioses,* but I couldn't fool my own. Couldn't convince him the fake image of trees or hills were real. Couldn't make him disappear.

I held out my hands, but he didn't come. Just watched me with an intelligence that made me doubt everything I'd done, everything I'd ever believed.

Finally I dropped my arms to my sides, too tired to keep playing this game. The desire to beat my grandmother wasn't enough to keep me going. I wanted a truth from Alcippe, not Bubbe. I was done, let her beat me.

"You know I don't," I replied.

"Don't or won't?" Bubbe dropped her hand to the wolf's head, ran her fingers over his fur. At her touch, he looked up. My body tensed, and I knew she was right: I was afraid of facing my own *telios,* of facing that very important part of who I was.

Her hand dropped to her side, and the wolf disappeared. "You've won. Declare your truth," she said.

I raised my brows. "Me? I didn't master the *telios.*"

"No, you didn't do as I wanted. As I said, you beat me. I give up. I can't make you accept who you are. You win."

I grunted. No one could twist words and events like my grandmother. As much as I had wanted to beat her, this wasn't victory. It was almost like a whole new kind of loss.

"I say you won," I replied. "Tell me what you want to know."

Her hand drifted to where her dress closed in the front. She stroked the silk trim. "There is nothing for you to tell me, Melanippe. I know you. I trust you."

We stared at each other, she with the same relaxed patience she'd shown through the entire ordeal, me without it.

Alcippe stepped forward, raising both hands as she did. "With no clear victory each can demand a truth." She nodded at Bubbe.

My grandmother studied me for a second, then asked, "Have you ever killed an Amazon?"

The question was direct and one I could answer easily. She could have worded it much more broadly, forced me to admit my connection to the crimes, but she didn't, and I recognized that, although the Amazons still lining the court didn't seem to. Every eye was focused on me, every finger tightening around some weapon.

"No."

The exhale of air was audible, the disappointment and confusion tangible. It startled me, made me realize how thoroughly they had wanted me to be guilty. I was an easy target—no longer one of their own, but not completely foreign either. I was the safe choice, the only one that would mean nothing in their lives would truly change—and with one word, I'd blown that dream to hell and back.

I turned, ready to leave.

"You have a question for me."

I looked back. Bubbe lifted a brow. "Make me answer it."

I frowned. What did she want me to ask? What truth did she think needed telling in front of witnesses?

The questions I'd had for Alcippe rushed to my mind. Are you killing the Amazons? Did you kill my son?

Too specific. Yes-and-no answers seldom gave you the full truth.

I licked my lips, concentrated on what I could ask that would tell me something I needed to know and needed to know was true.

"Why did you take this challenge from Alcippe?" It was a simple question, one very likely unrelated to anything, but it was the one that I couldn't answer alone, couldn't fathom by myself.

Bubbe smiled; a quick light of victory gleamed in her eyes. "I told you. I'm the one who has the answer to your question."

I closed my eyes. I'd let her trick me, given her a question she could answer truthfully without revealing anything at all. I didn't have time for this, had wasted enough as it was. Perhaps now that the Amazons knew I wasn't the killer, they'd listen to my case against Alcippe.

I turned to face them, but Bubbe wasn't done.

"Alcippe didn't kill your son."

My breath stopped; my eyes focused on nothing.

"He isn't dead or wasn't, at least, when I left him at a human hospital."

There was a whooshing in my ears, a decade of hate rushing up to greet me. I could barely hear the rest of my grandmother's words—how she'd used magic to make him appear stillborn, taken him from my arms, bundled him up, and delivered him to some human hospital. How no one but she had known. How she'd done it because she loved me, loved Harmony, and hoped with my son out of sight and mind, I'd settle down, get back to who I'd been, accept being an Amazon.

After that it was just static, the annoying buzz of misplaced trust and false love swirling around me. I stumbled from the gym, or felt like I did. I didn't fall, and no one came after me. I wandered alone to my truck, got in, and drove.

I hadn't even made it to the first stoplight before flashing lights glared at me from my rearview mirror. Madison cops aren't big on traffic stops; I was instantly wary. I pulled over anyway.

Reynolds stepped out of the unmarked car. I stayed in the truck, my fingers gripping the steering wheel so tightly I was surprised it didn't snap from the pressure.

"What are you doing?" he asked.

I stared out my windshield; a new crack was forming where a rock had hit it on my last journey to the safe camp. I should have had it filled. Too late now.

Too late for a lot of things.

"Mel?" He angled his body, looked from me to the car he'd left. I wondered briefly if he was signaling to someone inside, if I was going to be surrounded soon. "Mel." This time he leaned forward, almost into the truck, inches from my face.

"Nothing. I'm doing nothing," I replied.

He breathed then, but didn't back off. "You raced out of your lot pretty fast," he commented.

"Yeah, well, I needed to get away." I looked at him. "Still do."

He cocked a brow. "Not the best thing to say to a police officer." His lips twisted toward a smile.

I didn't return the gesture.

He sighed. "Listen, you're obviously upset. If it has something to do with the case, I need to know."

The case. Zery and the dead girls. I'd almost forgotten. Turned out my brain could only concentrate on one tragedy at a time.

I pursed my lips—forced my voice to stay calm, to hide the emotion whipping through my body. "It has nothing to do with the case." Or did it? I'd been so sure I knew what had happened to my son. Knew Alcippe had killed him—and I'd been wrong. What else was I wrong about? Was Alcippe innocent of the girls' deaths too? If not her, who? Who else had high priestess and artisan skills? Had a reason to target me and motive to kill Amazon teens?

I pressed my fingers to my brow, completely blowing my facade of calm.

"Mel." Reynolds glanced back at the car again. "There's something you aren't telling me. I think we need to go back to your shop."

I dropped my hands, stared him in the eye. "Where's Zery? How's she doing?"

His tongue made a bump in his cheek. It was obvious he didn't want to answer. "She's in Milwaukee."

"But you're here." Was that good or bad?

"I questioned her earlier. She refused an attorney."

"She didn't tell you anything." I'd be shocked if she'd given him so much as her name.

He cleared his throat. "It would go easier for her if she would."

I wrapped my hands back around the steering wheel. "She won't."

He watched me for a second. I could feel his eyes studying my profile. I wasn't sure what he was looking for—the killer's name tattooed on my cheek?

His hand smacked against my truck door. "I'm going to your shop. You can follow or not."

I watched him walk back to his car, his legs eating up the space with long determined moves. I turned the key in the ignition, determined to keep going. Let him go back to the shop. Let him find the Amazons acting on whatever the hell idiotic plan they had brewed up.

It wasn't my problem.

His car sped past me, performed an illegal U-turn right before the light changed and released a flood of cars all in a hurry to go Artemis knew where. I started moving, took a right on Glenway, then slammed on my brakes to the annoyance and honks of a VW Bug behind me. I twisted the steering wheel to the left, gunned my way through a tow place's parking lot, and took another left back onto Monroe.

Damn Reynolds for already knowing me so well.

Reynolds was leaning against his car, which was parked on an angle, taking up two places, when I arrived back at my shop. I hopped out of my truck and slammed the door. It needed the extra force to latch, but it felt good too.

"This is a waste of your time." I shoved my hands into my front pockets and stared at the detective. I didn't want to walk down that sidewalk right now, didn't want to risk seeing Bubbe, or any of the Amazons. The knife that had been shoved in my back was still there, throbbing, making it hard to breathe.

He slowly pushed away from his car and sauntered toward the sidewalk.

After blowing out a breath, I followed, but I didn't hurry. Just putting one foot in front of the other was hard enough. He'd reached the midway point—at the crosswalks that led to the basement door on the right and the cafeteria door on the left. He paused then, his hands on his hips, and looked up at Harmony's window and the tree, then over to the roof of the cafeteria/gym. Again I wondered what he was expecting to see, but shrugged the thought aside. Fact was, there was no telling what he *might* see.

As I came within a few feet of him, he spun toward the cafeteria door and paused again. "Do I have your permission to enter?"

I realized then he needed my permission—at least for anything he saw inside to be usable for his case. I chewed at my lip, struggling with old loyalties and newly discovered deceit.

Up ahead, something moved.

Bubbe stepped out from behind the gym, onto the other end of the sidewalk. Her arms hung at her side, her shoulders rounded. She looked old and tired.

She'd pulled this trick before. She didn't fool me—not this time.

"Do you allow me a mistake, *devochka moya?*" she asked.

I shifted my gaze, the lump in my throat making it hard for me to swallow, the sudden pounding in my chest making it hard for me to stand there, not to run away

Reynolds turned, but slowly, like he was afraid of startling us. I ignored him. Whether he entered the building or not, discovered what we were or not, didn't matter. Nothing mattered.

I turned too, but away. There was nothing for me here now. No trust, no love. The shop I'd built, been so proud of, the mother and grandmother I'd believed in, none of it meant anything. The only thing left was Harmony. I was going to go get her, take her and leave.

Florida. There was a camp there, but it was a big state. We could keep away from it, from Amazons, and Harmony would like it. What teenage girl didn't dream of living near the beach?

"Some things you can't run from. Some things follow."

I came to a stop. Was she saying she'd follow, like she and Mother had the last time? I turned back.

"Don't. I won't take you in this time."

"I did what I thought was right. What was best. Have you never made a mistake? Done something that later you knew hurt others?"

The dead girls. One, then two. Slipping their bodies from my truck, rolling them into the grass. Zery staked out in my yard. Then Pisto taken too . . . dead. Were my silence, my actions, the cause?

My hands started to shake.

"I can't take it back. I can't do it over." Bubbe didn't move, and her voice didn't change, but I could feel her sorrow . . . her regret.

I stared at the tip of my boot, at a brown scuff on the black rubber.

I didn't want to understand what she had done. I didn't want to forgive her.

Reynolds stepped off the sidewalk into the grass, moved toward my grandmother. I didn't know what he was thinking, why he was approaching her, but suddenly I did know, angry as I was, much as I wanted to hate her with all the abandon I'd hated Alcippe, I couldn't.

"No," I said.

Reynolds stopped. His eyebrows rose.

"You don't have my permission to go inside. There's nothing in there for you. Nothing that will help you with your case."

Then I turned to my right and walked down the steps, into my shop's basement.

I wasn't ready to forgive Bubbe or even talk with her, but I wasn't running either. Not this time.

Chapter Twenty-four

I made it to my office and was in the process of shutting the door when a hand thrust against the other side, stopping its closure. My thoughts shot to Reynolds.

"I didn't give you permis—" I jerked the door open, and stared into the chocolate brown eyes of Peter.

"You didn't give me . . . ?" he asked. His tone was teasing, but his eyes were dead serious. I knew instantly another shock was coming my way.

I left his question unanswered, moved to my desk, and collapsed into my chair. He followed me, reached down, grabbed me by the forearms, and pulled me back up. My chest was pressed against his and, in any other state of mind, I'd like to think I would have shoved him away, but I didn't, I just let him hold me there, and when his lips lowered to mine, I didn't object.

His kiss was firm, reassuring—like he knew the turmoil I was going through and wanted to make it right. I wanted someone to make it right, maybe that's why I let him kiss me, why I leaned against him just a little, opened my lips beneath his.

His tongue found mine and my hands found their way around his neck. His hair tickled my fingers. I wanted to stand there, and forget everything for a while. Pretend I had no bigger issues to deal with than the risk of another employee or a client walking in and finding me hanging on him like an adolescent lost in her first make-out session.

He pulled back just a smidge, enough that our lips separated but our bodies were still pressed together. My breath was ragged and my heart was pounding, but this time it felt good. I felt alive, was happy I'd come back.

"I need to tell you something."

And like that, my happiness fled.

I loosened my fingers, took a step back, ignored the sudden feeling of loss. "Why'd you do that?"

He ran a hand down my arm, caught my fingers in his. "Because I knew I might not be able to again, not after we talk."

A ball of dread grew in my stomach. I sat down, more to get away from him, to keep myself from touching him, than to relax. There was no hope of the latter.

He exhaled and walked to the other side of my desk, to the window that overlooked the cafeteria and gym. "I know about the Amazons."

I stiffened, but then forced myself to relax—or appear to relax. "You mean the women renting the gym? Is that what they're calling themselves now?"

"I know about you . . . that you left the tribe, that you were pregnant, but never appeared with the baby."

My fingers curled around the arms of my chair. He'd been eavesdropping.

His gaze turned on me then, and I knew it was more than that—he knew more about me than I'd ever dreamed possible; he was involved somehow in my life. "Where is he, Mel? What happened?"

I stood, didn't think about it, just did. "Leave."

He shook his head. "Bad start. Sorry. It's just . . . we've wondered for so long. We've been able to track almost all of the others, but your child—the one we had the most interest in, he . . ." He looked at me. "It was a he, wasn't it?"

I couldn't answer, but I didn't want him to leave. I wanted to hear what he had to say. The hand I'd raised when I'd ordered him to leave drifted back down to rest on my desk. "Who the hell are you?"

He stepped away from the window. "I'm an Amazon."

I laughed without humor. He was crazy. "You are not an Amazon." I'd felt the evidence of just how male he as when we'd kissed.

"A son." He watched me then, waited.

I blinked, confused. "A son?" What he was saying sank in then. "You are the son of an Amazon?" I asked.

He nodded, his eyes still alert.

I looked at my computer screen, black and covered in a coating of dust that didn't show when it was on. I wasn't sure how to play this—if I should play this.

"There aren't a lot of us—not as many as there are Amazons, but we're growing, finding those who don't know their heritage, bringing in those who we can."

I leaned back and let my chair rest keep me vertical, hoped my upright posture hid the shock that threatened to send me sliding to the floor. "But why? Why would the sons gather together? What do you want?"

He frowned, an angry line forming between his brows. "Heritage. Support. Understanding."

"But Amazon sons . . ." *Took after their fathers. Weren't Amazons.*

"I'm as much an Amazon as you are . . . or"—a strange look flitted over his face—"most Amazons anyway."

There was something about his tone, the way his eyes didn't quite meet mine. "What do you mean *most* Amazons? Why single me out from the grouping?"

"You were the first."

"The first what?" I was feeling queasy, didn't want to hear more, but also couldn't help myself from asking.

"The first child of a son and an Amazon."

"What?" I couldn't keep the confusion out of my voice, and outrage, what he was saying . . . It was possible, of course, the Amazons didn't keep records of the male lines, but to say my mother . . . I shook my head. The odds were too great. Part of the benefit of moving around like we did was to avoid the type of inbreeding he seemed to be insinuating.

"This is ridiculous." I shoved my chair back from my desk.

He moved forward, leaned over my inbox. "Not that. I'm not saying your father was your grandfather or whatever you're thinking. I'm saying your father was a son of an Amazon—a different Amazon, not your grandmother or your mother, a whole different line. *Telios*, right?"

I snapped to attention then. He knew about the *telios*.

He turned around, lifted his shirt up to his shoulders. A fox peered at me from the center of his back. The animal's paw was poised above the stream, like he was about to dip it into the current, search for a fish. It was a beautiful tattoo, alive and real enough it could have been a *telios*, but it was wrong—the wrong animal, in the wrong place, and on a male back.

"That isn't a *telios*," I replied.

He pulled his shirt the rest of the way off, high on his right shoulder was another tattoo, a lynx. Again the vibrancy of the colors, the way it seemed to glisten and move as if alive, gave it the appearance of a *givnomai*, but it was also wrong.

He pointed at it.

I shrugged. "Nice." That's all I was giving him. I didn't know where he'd learned as much as he had, but I wasn't giving him any more.

He stepped closer. "Touch it."

His arm moved. The skin under the tattoo shifted,

making the lynx seem to move too—but it was an illusion, that was all. There was no magic in that ink. There couldn't be.

"It won't bite." He grinned—a challenge.

I placed my palm on his arm and immediately jerked back, stunned. The tattoo had pulsed under my hand, vibrated with power.

I stared at the lynx, half expecting the tiny animal to jump off Peter's arm onto my desk. I'd seen . . . survived . . . stranger things in the last eight hours.

Peter held out his arm again, in an impossible to miss invitation. I swallowed my hesitancy and placed my palm to his skin. There was no missing the power in that ink. I pulled my hand back a second time, but slower.

Peter turned, presenting his back. Prepared this time, I stroked the line that formed the fox's head, followed it down his back to the orangey-red, then white, then black stripes on his tail. Throughout, Peter stood still, but I could sense him reacting. His muscles tensed, as if the skin were sensitive, as if he were containing some response.

When he turned, his eyes were almost black, dilated. My body reacted in return. I licked my lips and tried to stop my mind from wondering how it would feel to have his fingers stroking my *givnomai* and *telios*. Did he feel my power when I touched his?

But what he was saying wasn't possible. Mother would surely have noticed something as obvious as *telios* and *givnomai* tattoos on any man she was intimate with.

I tapped my fingertips against my palm. "Even Mother wouldn't have missed those."

He stared at me, as if reluctant to be pulled out of the moment. Finally, he yanked his shirt back over his head. "*You* missed them."

At my startled look, he continued, "When you were fathered, not everyone had the tattoos. As I said, you were the first. We've grown a lot since then, learned a lot."

I couldn't let his earlier statement go. "But you said, *I* missed them? You and I, we never . . ."

He smiled, that sexy slow smile that had drawn me to him in the first place.

"Not me, Harmony's father . . . and your son's."

"Michael?" There was a quaver in the word.

"Did you think it was strange they kept their shirts on, didn't let you touch their bare backs or shoulders?"

I frowned, thinking back. It was true both men had worn shirts every time I'd seen them . . . been with them. And Michael . . . he'd preferred a position where my hands couldn't reach his back, not easily. Harmony's father . . . he'd held my hands, something I'd thought was sweet and sensitive at the time.

I looked up at Peter, knew he saw the realization in my eyes. "So, Harmony and . . . ? " I paused. My son. It suddenly occurred to me he was alive somewhere. I'd been so focused on my grandmother's betrayal, I hadn't taken time to consider what it meant. But if what Peter said was true, if the sons were organized, kept track of each other . . . maybe somehow they could help me find him. Joy shot through me. My son. I might be able to meet him.

"Second lineage." Pride shone from Peter's eyes.

I frowned. There was something I was missing here, something important. "Was it planned? Did Michael and Harmony's fathers seek me out?" An ugly, dark feeling crept over my skin, dimming the joy I'd felt just seconds earlier. "What are you doing? Selective breeding?" The queasiness was back.

"It isn't like that."

I curled my lip. "What is it like? These 'sons' sought my mother and me out, planned for us to get pregnant. Who does that? And why?"

"I think you have this backward. Your mother and you—all the Amazons—seek out men with the plan of getting pregnant. And you have criteria when you do. Don't lie and say you don't. Has any Amazon you know picked a man who didn't fit some 'ideal'?"

Dana. Dana hadn't, but he was right. Most Amazons picked their men based on the obvious genes they'd bring to the match. Physical strength being number one in desirability. We were shallow because it didn't matter. We didn't plan on building a life with this person. I started to say as much, then realized there was no way to make that sound good.

"Maybe it's in our DNA," he continued, "but the Amazons' sons want the same thing. We want our children to be as strong as they can be—we just had a different set of ideal traits."

"And all of them had to come from Amazons."

He raised a brow. "We weren't interested in getting stronger—not physically. We were interested in regaining some of what the Amazons have lost over the thousands of years since being fathered by Ares."

No mention of Otrera, mother of the Amazons, I noted.

"And what's that?" I asked.

"Ares was a god—immortal, magical, all powerful."

"You want to be immortal?" This was beginning to sound like a bad villain speech. He just needed a mustache to twirl.

"No." He hesitated, averting his gaze for a second before looking back. "We want to rejoin the Amazons—to be seen as equal, not something to be tossed aside."

It felt like all the oxygen had been sucked from the room. I couldn't catch my breath, couldn't believe I was having this conversation. "All the sons. They want to join the tribe?"

"Not all." He moved his gaze again—a move I'd seen my daughter use just last week when she had wanted to go to the mall with Rachel and "claimed" all her homework was done.

"What do the rest want?" I asked, tension coiling inside me.

"The sons who survived have been through a lot. Best case they were abandoned by their mothers, worst they were killed or maimed." He touched his right shoulder, where the lynx was.

"Your *givnomai* . . . ?"

"Is on the limb the Amazons seemed to prefer when they mutilated their sons."

The right arm, made sense. It was the arm Amazons most often broke or removed to keep their sons weak. It was also completely sick and made me once again despise where I'd come from. And in an even sicker way, those Amazons of old had been right. They'd mutilated their male offspring to keep them from growing up strong, from becoming a threat.

But Bubbe and a few others of her generation had put a stop to that.

Bubbe. How would she react to this?

Unable to take any more, I sat. Confusion, twisted loyalties, ancient truths that weren't—all of it swirled around me until I couldn't sort one thought from another.

Then suddenly everything fell into place. "Finish. What do the rest want?" But I didn't need to hear his answer. What would I have wanted? What had I wanted?

His lips thinned. "We've tried to track down every son, to tell them who they are if they are old enough to understand. The little ones . . . we position ourselves in their lives. Train them without their adopted parents finding out."

At my questioning look, he continued. "Teachers, softball coaches, even babysitters. We take whatever job we can to get close to them and gain their trust."

"And?" He hadn't got to the ugly part yet, and there was an ugly part—uglier than what he'd told me so far. There had to be.

"But there are sons who don't agree with us. Some work openly against us, finding Amazon children before we do, accusing members of our group of all kinds of things to keep them from getting close. Then working with the boys themselves.

"And in a few cases, boys we've trained have turned— either joining the other group or just walking away."

"That's not bad, though." That was what I had done.

"Maybe not." But his face said it was.

"What brought you here, Peter?"

I didn't believe he'd come here to seduce me. That had been my initial thought, but if that had been his purpose, revealing himself to me now would have made no sense. Then I thought about what he'd just said, about getting close to the children of Amazons. Until now it had all been boys, but until I had left the tribe, the only Amazon offspring out and about in the real world were boys.

I was back on my feet. "Harmony. How long have you been watching her?"

"She's special, Mel. The first child to be second generation. We had to watch her."

Something dark and elemental wove through me, made my hands open and close, made my mind begin to shift through the magic at my disposal.

"Keep away from her. Go back to your little nest and tell the others. No one trains my daughter but me."

"But you haven't been training her. She's fourteen, almost an adult. You hadn't even given her her *givnomai* yet."

I shook my head, my body shaking too. It was none of his business, no one's business but mine, what I shared with my daughter or didn't, when or if I trained— "What did you say?"

He stared at me, confused. "You haven't trained her. You don't even know what skill sets she has."

I stepped around my desk, moved to within an inch of him. "Her *givnomai*. What did you say about that?"

"You hadn't—" Then he realized his slip. I could see it on his face. He stepped back, held up one hand. "She needed one. You know that. If she'd waited much longer, it might not have worked."

The *givnomai* was given during puberty when powers were thought to be forming. The *telios* came later, when the girl . . . or boy . . . became an individual, symbolically left her family, but through the tattoo kept their strengths with her.

And there was a killer out there collecting them. A killer who knew who I was, who had some kind of perverse interest in me, and had already attacked one person I loved. My hand formed a fist. I pulled back my arm and slugged Peter, or tried to. With the reflexes of a lynx, he caught my fist in his hand. Stared at me, his eyes wide.

"She needed one, Mel."

My body was shaking—anger and fear for my daughter crowding out all rational thought. "Not your decision." He'd touched my daughter. I wanted to kill him.

"She'll be safer now. Her powers will grow."

She wasn't safer. She was in danger. It was all I could think of. I couldn't even concentrate on my rage, on the desire to blast Peter to tiny bits. All I could think of was Harmony, and the killer.

"I have to get to her." I was mumbling to myself, but out loud. I turned, Peter all but forgotten, until he grabbed my arm.

"She's fine. Why are you panicking? You're a tattoo artisan. I know there's some reason you hadn't done this yourself, but now that it's done, can't you see that it's a good thing? And Harmony wanted one. She came to me."

She came to him. Like that justified anything. My anger began to bubble again, to break through the surface of worry. How could he even begin to think that made this okay? Or did he?

I took a step back, looked at him with new eyes. What did I know about Peter? Obviously not very much. But I'd seen his tattoo work, knew now that he had Amazon blood, bore tattoos with power. What else? Did he have priestess . . . priest . . . skills too? Could he be the killer?

Of course he could.

Chapter Twenty-five

I closed my eyes and tried to hide the emotion racing through me.

Peter's hand grazed my arm. I took another step away, this time toward the window. Once there, I shoved it open, felt the cool, slightly damp air of a day that had turned gray flow into the room. The wind pushed my hair away from my face—I welcomed it.

I didn't know if Peter had priestess skills, but I was about to find out.

I pulled in a deep breath, then turned. Peter was staring at me, his brows lowered, a line between his eyes. He held out his hands as if about to say something, ask something.

I didn't wait to hear his words. I let go, let the wind blast from my lungs. The force of it almost sent me reeling backward out of the window. I dug my fingernails into the old wood of the window's frame to keep from falling. My fingers ached and my back snapped against the top of the double-hung frame, but I stayed in the room, my gaze glued to Peter.

The wind should have hit him full strength. I'd done nothing to signal my move, but he still seemed to have known. As the air rushed across the room, less than a heartbeat from when it would have hit him, he dropped to a crouch—stayed there, balanced on the balls of his feet and splayed fingers.

My initial inhale spent. I grabbed the first thing my fingers reached, a terra-cotta saucer that had sat under a long-dead plant and now gathered dust and loose change. I whirled it across the room, aiming a foot or so higher than Peter's head, instinctively guessing that he wouldn't sit still and wait for my missile to hit. As it left my fingers, I spun them in the air, adding momentum.

I didn't wait, didn't watch to see if my impromptu Frisbee would hit its target, I started grabbing everything I could find—books, painted rocks, even a Xena Warrior Princess doll my employees had given me as a joke— never realizing how close to the mark they'd hit. All went flying.

I could hear them hit, could feel the floor shake as Peter leapt to escape. An old tattoo machine in my hand, I pulled in more air and glanced in his direction, ready to spin a shield if he threw magic my way.

He was crouched again, his gaze on me and his muscles

tense. I could see the question on his face—like I was the one doing something wrong, who'd gone crazy

I threw the machine, let go of a blast of air at the same time. For one second he was trapped—between where I'd aimed the blast and the machine.

Indecision shone in his eyes, and I knew I had him— that he was about to reveal his true talents. I expelled the air out of my lungs, moved my hands in a circle, and chanted, using the air to form a barrier between me and whatever magic was about to be propelled toward me. And as I did all of this, I kept my gaze on Peter. My chest tightened; I knew once he attacked I'd quit playing, attack him for real—kill him rather than let him kill another girl.

He leapt again, toward me, blurred as he moved. I squinted, unable to make out what was happening, what he was doing. Suddenly he was back in focus, but it wasn't Peter flying toward me. It was a lynx—just like the one I'd seen tattooed on Peter's shoulder.

Stupidly, I dropped my hands, dropping the shield as I did. The cat hit me square in the chest, knocking me back against the wall. My fingers wrapped in its gray-brown fur. I pulled on its head, tried to keep its teeth from sinking into my neck.

I slipped and we fell, tumbling to the ground and rolling. The lynx's front paws wrapped around me and its feet wedged against my stomach. I could feel its breath on my neck and I tried not to panic, knowing the claws on those back feet could tear into my gut, easily do as much damage as its teeth. I groped around the floor as we moved, frantically trying to find something . . . anything I could use to fight the creature.

My fingers wrapped around a metal ruler and I pulled back my arm, determined to somehow thrust it through the animal's throat. Then the creature began to blur again. I froze, fixated on what was happening, unable to process what I was seeing . . . or not. And suddenly, lying on top of me, staring down into my eyes, was Peter.

"What the fuck?" I said, dropping the ruler and shoving against him with every ounce of strength I could muster. I quickly realized my hands were pressing against bare skin—that Peter was completely naked.

He rolled off me and moved to a sitting position. His leg was bent, hiding anything too shocking, but with the amount of bare skin revealed, I couldn't stop myself from dropping my gaze to the floor.

My heart was pounding as if it might explode from my chest. Peter had turned into a lynx; my mind skittered trying to understand that.

I exhaled, no magic this time, just a way to release some of the confusion swirling inside me. "What . . ." I looked up, stared at his face. "What did I see?"

He moved one shoulder. "Me." He tilted his head, studied me. He wasn't even winded—looked cool and calm, analytical, even. "So, it's true. Amazons don't shift? You haven't seen that before?"

I dropped my face to my hand, let my fingers drag

across my skin as I looked back up. With them closed and still lying against my lips I answered, "No. I've never seen that before." I'd planned to force him to reveal his skill, and I had, but it hadn't been what I'd expected, not at all. A lynx hadn't killed those girls, not that Peter couldn't have other skills as well, but . . . I shook my head. I didn't believe he was the killer, not anymore.

The corners of his lower lip pulled down; his head nodded. "That's what I'd heard, but . . ." He shrugged. "We didn't know for sure. There's a lot about the Amazons we don't know." He walked over to where his clothes lay in a haphazard pile.

I couldn't find the strength to follow him, to stand, to do anything but sit on the floor and stare at him. Too much adrenaline had shot through me, too many certainties proven false in too short of a time. I felt deflated, lost like a balloon blown away by the wind . . . floating.

"The sons can all shift, but not until after we get our *givnomai.* That's one reason I thought it was so important for Harmony to have hers."

"You think Harmony will be able to shift into her *givnomai?*" I couldn't imagine, or worse—I could. I wanted to ask what tattoo he had given her, what animal I could expect to face the next time I banished her to her room, but I didn't. A *givnomai* was personal. She'd tell me when . . . if . . . she wanted to.

It hit me then. I was beginning to accept the idea of Harmony with a *givnomai,* beginning to think of her as a young Amazon, and not just the little girl I'd spent the last ten years protecting from everything that even hinted of Amazon.

Peter had pulled on his pants, stood barefoot and bare-chested while he answered. The lynx on his shoulder seemed bigger now, impossible to ignore. I forced my eyes to look away.

"We don't know, but since she's second generation, we think it's possible—or it might be a trait that's gender based. There's no way for us to know."

Standing there, he was glorious, all male with his long firm muscles, even his tattoos had a masculine look that the same animal and scenery wouldn't have had on a woman. I couldn't put my finger on what the difference was, but it was there—and I was drawn to it, but I was still angry too, and wary.

"What other skills do you have?" I asked. I had to check.

His shirt bunched in his hand; he frowned. "I'm an artisan. I figured you knew that."

"No . . ." I twisted my mouth to the side, not sure of my word choice; finally giving up, I went on, "Priestess skills?"

"Magic?" He lowered the shirt, frowned. "You have both, don't you? And not just shades of both. You can truly use both—compete as either."

He seemed fascinated by me again, watched me like I'd just shared some new pain-free technique for tattooing.

"Are you sure you don't shift? Have you tried?" he continued. The expression in his eyes was so intense, I couldn't help but place my hand over my *givnomai*. Even through my shirt, I could feel the power that had been put in the little creature pulse.

"No. I don't shift and I wouldn't even know how to try. I never realized . . ." I let the words drift off. I had never realized the possibility existed.

The creature under my fingers seemed to move, swish its tail. I curled my fingers over it, silenced it . . . or more accurately, my imagination gone wild.

Peter wanted to know if I'd tried shifting. He didn't know how useless shifting into my *givnomai* would be. I wouldn't gain any great strength or athletic prowess, but then . . . I'd be able to blend anywhere, hide out in the open.

Again, I wondered what Harmony had chosen.

"Did you tell her? Tell Harmony? Or does she think she just got a tattoo?" I asked.

He finished tugging the shirt over his head. "Just a tattoo. It's not my place to tell her about the Amazons. I can't imagine she would have believed me if I had. But I did tell her she had to keep it secret, that no one could find out she had one . . . that you could lose your business."

I shook my head. Oh yeah, my daughter wouldn't tell anyone she had a tattoo. I believed that. Obviously, Peter had no experience with teenage girls, especially one who would see a secret tattoo as some kind of victory over her too-protective mother. Which brought me right back to where I started. Harmony had a *givnomai* and there was a killer somehow connected to me, or drawn to me, who was collecting them.

Peter was dressed now, but his feet were still bare. He lounged against my desk, relaxed, apparently willing to stay there all day and chat. Seemingly unaware that he might have put Harmony in the path of any danger.

But then, while he knew about the killings, I didn't know if he had realized the victims were Amazons. And he couldn't know what I'd been hiding—their delivery to my door, or their missing *givnomais*. Couldn't know unless he was the killer, and frustrating as the realization was, I didn't think he had killed anyone. I really thought by giving Harmony a *givnomai* he believed he had been helping, doing what was right.

Not his choice to make for my daughter or my family, but I couldn't fault his motives. Truth be told, Mother and Bubbe would have applauded his motives, maybe even his actions—if he hadn't been a man.

Looking up at him was beginning to make me uncomfortable. I stood. "There's something you don't know."

"There are all kinds of things I don't know." He shoved a piece of broken pottery across the floor with his foot. It came to a rest next to mine.

"The girls, the ones found dead near Milwaukee? They were Amazons."

He looked past me, to a spot on the wall.

He knew.

"The girls on that site you showed me? The one of the tattoos? Two of them were the victims."

Again, nothing.

I picked up the pottery shard and threw it at his feet. "What don't you know? What else have you been doing besides tattooing my daughter and—" I clamped my lips shut before "tempting me" could come out.

"You asked why I came here. A big part was Harmony. We hadn't been able to get close to her before, at least not as close as we wanted, and with her age and the need for a *givnomai* . . . well, when you advertised for an artist, we couldn't let it pass by."

"How did you know she didn't have a *givnomai*?" Ugly scenarios were playing out in my head. My hand tightened on the tattoo machine I'd thrown earlier. This time I'd figure out a way to use it more effectively.

His brows lifted. "We didn't for sure, but we'd been in your shop, heard the two of you arguing. It seemed pretty obvious."

I pressed the tattoo machine against my leg, felt my heart slow a little.

"But after I was here, I noticed things. Things that worried me. That's why I called in Makis."

"Makis? The art teacher?" The art teacher . . . "The wheelchair? You don't mean . . . ?" The mutilations. They'd been horrifying enough when they'd just been in theory, something that had happened long ago, but to realize someone I'd met . . . "He's a son," I finished, unable to say more.

"*The* son or our leader anyway. Makis is one of our oldest. Both of his legs were broken, then he was left on a church doorstep. Medical care wasn't much back then, and no one wanted a crippled baby, but he survived. As he grew, he realized he was different, started finding others like him, and slowly pieced together who we were, where we came from."

"He must hate us." I said the words without realizing their significance at first, just voicing what I felt.

"You would think, but he doesn't seem to," Peter replied, but I barely heard what he said.

"He must hate us," I repeated. I dropped the machine back on the floor, took two giant steps forward, crushing another chunk of pottery under my boot as I did. "Is he a priestess?" I was too focused on my suspicions to worry over terminology this time. "Can he do magic?"

Peter lost his casual posture, stood erect. "Yes, but he doesn't hate Amazons. I don't know why he doesn't. He has every reason to, but he doesn't."

"He's a priestess and an artisan." Again, to myself. I headed for the exit.

"Where are you going?" I could feel Peter moving behind me, heard him curse as he stepped on another shard of pottery or some other debris left on the floor. Still, he followed me.

I raised my left hand, blew air over my shoulder, and slammed the door in his face, mumbled a spell and twisted my fingers—using compressed air to turn the lock.

He'd get out eventually, but at least I had a head start. I didn't think Peter was involved in the killings, but I didn't need him arguing with me, slowing me down.

My life was a mess, but none of it mattered—not compared to stopping this killer.

I met Reynolds on the steps. I tried to walk past him. He stepped in front of me. My body shook with the need to get past him, to shove him out of my way and sprint down the stairs.

"I didn't give you permission to come in here," I said.

"This place is open to the public. I don't need your permission." He placed his hand on the railing beside me.

My jaw tensed. "I'm leaving. You do need something to stop me."

One finger tapped the wooden rail . . . once, twice, three times. "Depends. Maybe I think you're acting"—his gaze drifted over me—"suspicious. I have reason to suspect you, you know?"

Sane Mel, the Mel who wanted so much to blend, would have stood there and argued, would have played the game, but that Mel had disappeared when she'd realized her daughter was on her way to meet a killer, and that Mel wasn't coming back—not for a long time, maybe never.

I kicked him in the groin.

The look on his face, the way his eyes rounded, then squinched together as he doubled over, would have been comical, if I hadn't actually liked him, already regretted to some small degree the need for the move. But any humor or pity was lost as he fell to his knees and reached for his gun. I started moving, fast.

"Stop."

I looked back. He was hanging onto the railing with one hand. In the other was a black handgun, and it was pointed at me.

I shook my head. "I can't." Then I turned my back on him.

Behind me, he cursed. I could hear him rustling, forcing himself to stand, I guessed. I quickened my pace, made it to the front door, and jerked it open.

"Mel," he yelled. He was closer—too close. I sped through the door, thinking I'd have to lock it behind me, play the same trick on him I'd played on Peter, but as the breath seeped from my lips, a grayish-brown body streaked around the corner of the building toward me.

Open window, tree. Didn't take a rocket scientist to figure out how Peter had escaped.

"Mel," Reynolds yelled again.

Peter stared up at me, his eyes still his, just in the face of a cat.

"Please" was all I said. I didn't have time to fight Peter and Reynolds too. Didn't have the mental wherewithal to stand there and argue either. I needed to get to my daughter.

Reynolds' shoes squeaked on the floor. He was almost to the door. I glanced back, could see him lunging forward, his gun still drawn.

Peter saw it too, leapt past me and into the building.

Reynolds yelled a curse. A shot fired, hit the door as the breath I'd been holding shoved it closed behind Peter.

I broke into a run.

Chapter Twenty-six

It took less than three minutes to get to the address on Makis's business card. It took twenty to find Makis's class space.

I thought I knew the building where Harmony had been taking art classes—I'd driven by it thousands of times. But once I parked the truck and jogged toward it, things got fuzzy.

I found myself standing in front of the address, suddenly unable to remember where I was going, what had driven me here.

I turned, started to shuffle back to my truck and, just as quickly, my memory returned, my panic with it, but increased.

Three steps forward and the fog returned. I blinked.

An older woman wandering past asked if I needed a drink. I refused, stumbled again to my truck.

I slammed into it, my palm smashing down on the hood. Harmony. How could I . . . ? I stared back at the building, focused on the door that bore the same numbers as the card in my hand.

A ward. Makis had some kind of ward on the door, something akin to what Bubbe had cast over my front yard when the Amazons were gathered there trying to save Zery, I guessed.

I had no experience with the spell, no idea how to combat it. I forced my heart to slow and my gaze to wander over the building front. Through the glass door I could see ferns and vines hanging from seventies-era macramé hangers. The mass of plants blocked my view deeper into the shop. Murals, a scene of the Capitol, one of some cows, and a group of football fans wearing white and red, covered the front windows.

Makis had managed to provide his shop with complete privacy in a way no one would think to question. I glanced around, looking for inspiration—considered tossing a rock through the Badger fan's red jersey, smashing the window, and maybe the ward. But there were too many people around. And a move like that would only alert Makis to my presence and state of mind.

The roof was flat. A one-story, probably with no attic, not even a crawl space. I glanced back at the plants, at their junglelike growth. Plants needed sun, and painted-over windows didn't provide much.

I had an idea. I left my truck and jogged around the end of the block, into the alley that ran behind the shops.

A Dumpster was set a few feet away from the building's back wall. It was an easy jump from there to the roof. I paused, checked my grip on reality. I still knew where I was and what I had to do. Makis hadn't been guarding against someone trying to break into his shop, just been trying to stop the casual passerby from entering.

Letting out a relieved breath, I crept toward the front and the upraised white square I prayed was what I thought it would be.

I stopped next to the skylight, a grin breaking across my face. I allowed myself less than a second of self-congratulation before hunkering down next to it and peering inside.

It was darker than normal outside and lights were on in the shop, making the scene below well lit, if small. The window was only a couple of feet wide. Even leaning side to side, I could see only a small piece of the shop below, but it was enough. Directly below me, a paintbrush in her hand, stood Harmony.

My palms pressed on the window's edges, I leaned forward, tried to see what was happening below—to decide what my next move should be. Makis had had access to Harmony for over a week. There was no reason to believe tonight was the night he would target her—not that I wanted to take the risk and leave her alone with him. But I also didn't want to do something that would send him over the edge, cause him to attack if he hadn't planned to.

For the first time I wished I'd given in to another of Harmony's demands—for her, us, to get cell phones. I had just never seen the need. But now, staring down at her, so close, but so impossible for me to reach without crashing through the glass, I did.

When we got out of this, I was taking her to the mall. I'd be supermom for at least a day. The thought made me smile, and as I settled down next to the window where I could keep an eye on my girl, I relaxed.

Until I saw the wheelchair behind a bookcase, visible to me, but not my daughter. The chair was turned over, its occupant sprawled across the floor.

Makis's face was pale, his arms and legs akimbo—unnatural. And three feet away, completely unaware, sat Harmony, painting.

Something was very wrong.

I lifted my fist, ready to rap on the glass, but as my knuckles lowered, a figure stepped into view—a boy, brown hair, slim build. The boy I'd seen Harmony flirting with at school. The boy she'd been mooning over with Dana, I assumed.

He angled his head as he talked to her. A diamond stud winked at me from his ear. He moved again, to stand behind Harmony. He wrapped his hand around hers, the hand that held the paintbrush. Together their hands moved up and down in broad strokes, slow, sensual, almost sexual.

As his arm moved up, his T-shirt shifted, revealing the edge of a tattoo. My already tense muscles squeezed tighter. My fingers dug into the edge of the skylight, until the tips became numb. Another upward, then downward stroke and the tattoo was revealed—a dog, a hound, black and tan. Just like the stray that had followed me around my shop, followed Zery into the shower, watched Pisto jerk off her shirt.

The boy pressed closer to my daughter, his face so close to hers his breath stirred her hair.

The skylight creaked, the casement coming loose under the pressure of my grip. The boy and Harmony looked up, revealing his face.

Nick, the boy I'd offered a job to, who'd shown up but left and never came back.

I saw him, knew him, realized I'd been wrong more than right—but it was too late. He'd seen me too.

He grabbed Harmony by the arm and threw her to the ground, reached behind him, and grabbed the notebook I'd seen him sketching in that day on State Street.

I stood and jumped at the same time, praying the glass would give. My feet hit the pane, cracked but didn't give.

Harmony struggled to her feet, her hair falling free around her shoulders. Her eyes rounded and her face paled when she saw me. I screamed for her to run, to get back, to find cover, then jumped again, this time adding a rush of air.

The glass shrieked and gave beneath me. I plunged downward, trying to weave a bubble of protection around me as I did, but only succeeding partially. Glass tore at my jeans, caught my shirt, ripped into my shoulder. I fell to the ground, landing in a squat—not the best position unless you're a cat.

Pain shot through my ankle. Without thinking, I pressed my hands onto the floor for balance. They came back up bloody, pieces of glass protruding from my palms.

I glanced around, looking for Harmony . . . Nick. To my left there was the sound of fighting, bodies bumping into furniture, paintbrushes or pens scattering to the floor. Then Harmony, yelling, "What the fu—?" The rest was muffled, by nothing more than a hand, I prayed.

I clawed the bigger pieces of glass out of my palm, and scrambled through the debris. The shop was like a maze, file cabinets and drafting tables with their tops flipped up formed walls that cut right, then left. I whirled around one corner, only thinking of getting to my daughter as quickly as I could, and tripped over the downed Makis, grabbed his fallen wheelchair to keep from tumbling onto him.

His olive skin was ashen, his breathing shallow. My heart told me to crawl over him, continue toward Nick and Harmony, but as I moved my foot to step over him, I stopped, placed two fingers against his throat. A pulse strong and steady beat under his skin.

Deeper in the shop, Harmony yelled, but her voice was strong, angry. Something crashed. She yelled again. My girl was putting up a fight, holding her own.

I pulled my hand away from Makis and folded my fingers into my palm. He was unconscious, but not dead. I couldn't help him now, but I could set him back in his chair, roll him somewhere out of the line of fire. It took only seconds to right his chair, a little longer to get the dead weight of his body into it. Then I shoved it into a nook, behind a double-wide steel file cabinet I thought would stay standing, even through the tsunami I was prepared to unleash in this place to free my daughter.

Then I crept forward, hoping my quiet had confused Nick, led him to believe I was too injured in the fall to follow—that it was just Harmony he had to battle now.

They stood in the back, twenty feet from a door that led to the alley. Nick had her by the arm, was trying to drag her toward it. Harmony picked up a jar filled with clear liquid and threw it at him with the intent and speed of a major league pitcher.

Nick twisted, his arm extended, his fingers curved and stiff, and slapped the jar off its trajectory, into a wall. The jar smashed, liquid splattered, and the room filled with the stench of turpentine. Harmony seemed undeterred, grabbed for something else—a stone pestle, but I froze. Nick's speed and grace, the power with which he swung, even the shape of his hand—it wasn't human.

He jerked Harmony, spun her into his body, so her back was against his chest. She flailed the pestle behind her trying to strike him, but he grabbed her wrist, shoved her hand to her side. He whispered something in her ear, then wrapped his fingers around the pestle, crushed it to dust in his fist.

My daughter's eyes rounded, and I could feel her panic like a spear to the chest. She'd got it now—that Nick wasn't normal, not just a crazed boy. But she couldn't know what I knew, that he was a son of the Amazons and somehow he was calling on the powers of the *givnomai* he'd stolen—the speed and grace of a tiger, the strength of a horse . . . at least one more yet to appear, maybe more. Who knew when he'd decided to start depositing his gifts on my doorstep—how many girls he might have killed before?

His fingers that had just crushed stone to sand trailed down her upraised arm in a gesture so clearly predatory and sexual, every fiber of my soul contracted. Rage soared through me.

I sucked in a breath, but held it—frustrated. Harmony was squeezed against him, her body between his and mine. I couldn't touch him with the wind building in my lungs, not without catching Harmony in the gale too.

His fingers tangled in her hair; he pressed his lips to a spot on her neck, right behind her ear. Then he murmured something else, something that made my daughter's body stiffen, her eyes harden. Her hands formed claws, not literally, but they might as well have been the talons they mimicked. She reached behind her, blindly raked her bubble-gum-pink nails over his cheek—leaving four bloody welts in her wake.

He shrieked, shoved her away, sent her reeling into a bookshelf. Papers, metal cans filled with paint, chunks of uncarved marble and stone smashed to the ground around her. She lay on the ground, heaving for breath, scrambling for a new weapon. I moved forward, instinct urging me to her side, but as I did, a creak overhead drew my attention. A huge chunk of granite, once destined to be carved into art, teetered on the shelf above her head. As I watched, it tumbled down, straight for my daughter's head.

I let out the breath I'd been holding, batted my hands, and prayed I'd hit my target.

The stone, falling one instant, was smashed backward the next. The force I'd created drove it into the wall, into the plaster, through lath, until it barely jutted out like a foothold on a climbing wall.

Nick and Harmony both turned—stared at me. With the same speed he'd shown earlier, Nick was back at her side, his fingers around her wrist, dragging her through the rubble that littered the floor.

I launched myself at him, landed on his back in a move driven by nothing except sheer outrage and passion. My arm wrapped around his neck and I squeezed, wished for the strength to pop his head off and send it rolling across the floor. Wanted to stand over his body and kick it until it stopped moving, until not even a reflexive death twitch was left. Rage—hot, cold all-encompassing—dropped over me until I didn't know my own name, didn't even know why I needed to kill this boy, just that I did.

I was an Amazon, and I was going to make him pay.

I felt him shift in my arms, heard his clothing tear as his body grew. Suddenly he slipped from my hold, my fingers running over fur. Then he stood facing me . . . not Nick, the skinny boy, but Tiger prowling, snarling, warning me to get away from his prey.

Harmony gasped. I didn't look down at her, just gestured behind me, telling her to get out. For the first time in her life she obeyed me without argument.

Tiger roared as she ran, leapt toward me . . . and Harmony. A wall of air released from my lungs forced him back, sent him sliding across the floor. He clawed at linoleum, his claws gouging, a growl rumbling from his chest.

He stood, paced left, then right, watching me, deciding his next attack. I didn't care. I reveled in his indecision, knew that every minute he wasted, Harmony was getting farther away. As long as she was safe, I could take my time deciding how to kill him, die in the process if need be. All that mattered was that my daughter had left.

"Mom?"

I froze, didn't look, but didn't have to. I knew the voice, knew the title, and knew by the tiger's intent stare that Harmony was standing behind me.

"Get out," I ordered, slashing my hand and releasing more wind to send a bookshelf smashing to the ground, forcing Tiger to jump backward out of its way.

"Makis. He gave me something." She shoved something cold and smooth into my hand. I glanced down, just long enough to see a double-faced totem, male on one side, female on the other. Both carrying a child and spear. At the feet of each sat a bird and a chisel. Amazons and their sons, both hearth-keepers, warriors, priestesses, and artisans. The imagery wasn't lost on me, but it offered nothing either. I tossed the stone to the side.

"Get home or call Bubbe and Mother, anything. Just get out of here. Now." I felt like I was screaming, but couldn't be, my teeth were clenched too tightly.

Harmony stepped around me, bent to retrieve the totem. A tentacle, long and coral in color, wrapped around her, jerked her across the floor. I glanced up, to where Tiger had been. He was gone and in his place was the third *givnomai,* not one used by many, Octopus.

The creature pulled her closer until she was almost engulfed in his body. She went limp, her arms and legs falling loosely toward the floor.

Chapter Twenty-seven

I grabbed a palette knife from the mess on the floor, and raced toward the monster, plunged the dull blade into what I guessed was his head, or neck. The creature heaved, dropping my daughter. I pulled back, ready to sink the weapon in again, but it slapped me to the side, sent me spinning and sliding like I'd sent Tiger a few minutes earlier.

My side rammed into a file cabinet and I scrambled back to my feet, searched frantically in my mind for a spell or weapon that would force the thing to release my daughter. As my crazed gaze danced back to Octopus, I saw something . . . the notebook Nick had carried. Octopus held it too, one tentacle caressing it. Getting strength from it, I guessed.

I leapt again, this time aiming not for the center of the

beast, but the far tip of one tentacle—for the notebook that I guessed held three dead Amazons' *givnomais*. *Givnomais* that Nick was somehow leeching of power. My foot on the corner of the notebook, I jabbed the knife into coral flesh and shoved backward with my foot. The tentacle rose, reaching for me, and the notebook went flying. I dropped and rolled, evading Octopus's reach, then belly-crawled toward the notebook that had slid beneath a shelf. Behind me I heard a thump. I glanced over my shoulder, saw my daughter sprawled on the floor, pale and lifeless. Octopus was gone, but Nick, naked and bleeding, was rising to his feet.

I jerked the notebook free, held it to my chest, and stared at the bleeding boy.

"Give it to me," he said.

"Don't," a voice beside me spoke. Makis. He was slumped in his wheelchair, but the tires spun, moving him forward.

I didn't care what either of them wanted, only that Harmony was all right. As if reading my mind, Nick looped his arm around her waist, pulled her up beside him. "She's alive. I wouldn't kill her. Not like this. I never intended to hurt her anyway. Not until you showed up, attacked me."

He frowned, his eyes pulling down like a confused little boy. "Why are you fighting me? I thought you understood."

Harmony stirred, or was it just her body swaying, an illusion of life?

Still, my grip on the notebook loosened; the tightness in my chest lessened. "Understood what?"

With Harmony so close, within his grasp, I couldn't move too fast, wasn't even sure what to do with the notebook now that I had it. If I destroyed the pages, set them on fire, or shredded them into the wind, what would happen to the girls' spirits? Would they always be trapped between two worlds?

"What I was doing. Why it was right." Something flashed in his hand and he held a knife—short-bladed and sharp, not at all like the dull tool I'd plunged into the octopus's neck. "The Amazons threw me out like trash— killed your son with no more thought than they'd give to stomping on a roach. Even him—" He jerked his head toward Makis. "Look what they did to him. But he was weak, wanted to go back to them, after everything. Thousands of years of disrespect, pain, death, and he wants to blend with them. Can you believe that?" His lip curled. "But you, you did what no other Amazon had. You walked away. That's why I thought you'd understand. Why I've watched you for so long, tried to please you." He shook his head. The knife glimmered. "I brought you gifts. Then I tried to warn the others off—to get them to leave you alone. I even offered you their queen, but you turned her down. I tried again. I knew Pisto would please you. She fought against us, was everything we're trying to stop. Why aren't you happy?

"Is it because I didn't join you at the shop? I couldn't. I saw Dana, knew she wouldn't understand. But I didn't leave you—was there in my dog form. I wasn't rejecting you. Can't you see that?" He lifted his arm, caused Harmony's weight to sway.

Makis wheeled forward, not far, just an inch. He wiggled a finger, pointing to the ground where the totem he'd given Harmony lay.

I placed my hand over it, slid it closer. Trapped inside my closed fingers, the figure began to throb like a tiny beating heart. I clenched it tighter, tried to keep the surprise from showing on my face.

"Harmony," Makis said low, but Nick still heard.

"I said she's okay. I don't want to hurt her. I love her—like Dana. Dana's happy now, right?" He looked at me. I couldn't reply. "That's the problem with the sons. They weren't selective. They took any Amazon they could."

I swallowed the saliva that seemed to have pooled in my mouth, the nausea his words created.

Makis gestured again; this time he leaned forward. Hidden in his chair, behind his back, was a throwing knife. I shook my head. Harmony was too close.

Makis shifted his gaze to the notebook, then Nick. My fingers slid in between pages and cover, brushed over something warm and alive—skin. I shuddered, then forced my fingers back to the spot, recognized the power pulsing there—a *givnomai*, Pisto's. Feeling as if I might retch, I jerked the book open, yanked the pages free of the binding, and tossed them in the air.

Nick dropped Harmony to the floor and lurched forward, grabbing at the pages as they floated downward. I whirled my hands overhead, creating a tiny cyclone to keep the pages out of his reach, then raced to my daughter. She had a pulse, but her lips were blue. I pressed my ear to her heart, began blowing into her mouth.

"The totem," Makis urged.

I ran my finger over the figure, not sure what I was supposed to do with it, how it could help Harmony. Then I stopped thinking, just put my trust in Artemis and believed. I shoved the tiny figure into my daughter's hand, kept my fingers wrapped around hers, prayed and breathed into her mouth. Breathed for her, in and out.

The pulse I'd felt in the figure began to grow until I could feel it creeping up my arm, through my shoulder, into my chest, until my heart matched the rhythm inside it. I wanted to drop the thing, get away from it, but knew if I was feeling this, Harmony was too, if my heart was beating with it, so was hers. On cue, she opened her eyes. They were round, alive, and more aware than I'd ever seen them.

There would be no hiding her heritage from her anymore. No hiding anything from her anymore. It was time I let her grow up and make decisions for herself—at least some. I jerked her to my chest, whispered a prayer of thanks into her hair.

Nick jumped, grabbed at another notebook page.

Makis threw the knife he'd had tucked behind his back, but Nick had already begun to shift. The knife missed, hit a file cabinet, and clattered to the ground. The blur of air that was Nick transformed into a horse, then just as quickly moved again back to the boy. He picked up the knife he'd held before shifting. Threw it. It sliced into Makis's shoulder, pinned him to his chair.

The old man flinched, tried to jerk the blade free. Nick stalked forward, to the sink tucked in the corner. Death in his eyes, he twisted on the spigot, began to chant and move his fingers. The water began to morph, until it changed into a hangman's noose. The water-and-magic-formed rope dropped to the floor, slithered across the vinyl tiles like a cobra—headed toward Makis's chair.

Harmony pushed me away and shoved the totem into my hand. I didn't pause to question the move. I lurched to Makis's chair seconds before the noose would have reached him, yanked the knife from his shoulder, and without stopping to aim, threw the blade.

It struck, plunged into the center of Nick's chest. He crumpled to his knees, shock and betrayal on his face.

It isn't pretty watching someone die, and despite my lust for Nick's blood earlier, he was no different. Harmony crept to him, through the puddle of water that had been his last weapon, and pulled his head onto her lap. I wanted to tell her to stop, not to touch him, but she hadn't lived with his evil as long as I had, had known a different side of him.

And even he deserved some company in death. Or that was what I tried to tell myself when the Amazon in me roared, demanded I jerk her away, curse him as he took his last breath.

He'd threatened my child, killed others. I didn't know what he'd endured to get to this place, but right now I didn't care . . . doubted I ever would, at least not enough to forgive him.

I waited to make sure he was truly dead, not a threat, then I stalked to the front of the store. I needed a minute alone to calm the monster inside me, to convince my still-raging adrenaline that he was dead, Harmony was safe, and the entire nightmare was over—or just about.

There were still a lot of loose ends to tie up, Zery to free, Peter to kick out of my shop and life, and a grandmother to . . . I clenched my jaw. I didn't know what I was going to do with Bubbe or Mother, or . . . any of it. Not right now.

But I didn't have to think about it, not for a while. Makis's wheelchair whirred behind me. He had a paint-and-blood-soaked rag held against his shoulder. The sight reminded me of my own wounds, my bloody palms and shoulder. Lost in the fight, I'd forgotten them. I picked at my shirt where it clung to my shoulder, winced when the thickened blood released its hold, pulled at the wound. I put that aside and turned instead to my palms, prodded a bit to see if glass lay hidden beneath the blood.

"I'll dispose of the body," Makis interrupted my self-exam.

I must have looked surprised. He rapped on the wheelchair. "Don't be deceived. I make do, and there's a . . . group to help."

"The sons," I inserted, wiping a sliver of glass I'd dug free with my fingernail onto my jeans.

His face turned solemn. "Peter told you?"

I quit worrying about my wounds. They didn't matter.

Instead, I stepped closer to the front window and peered through a slit of clean glass not covered by the mural. "It's dark. Harmony and I need to go home." The words sounded idiotic even to me. I turned back, embarrassed by my answer. "The police need to be called. They need to know Zery wasn't the killer."

He tapped his fingers on the arm of his chair. "She's my granddaughter."

I frowned, surprised. "Zery?"

"Harmony."

I swayed, hit one of the plants. Water dripped onto my shoulder—the good one.

"I want her to know."

I slowed the swinging plant, tried to slow my spinning brain. Grandfather. Of course he was. My life wasn't complicated enough.

"Where's her father?" I had to ask, had to get all the skeletons dug up, so I'd know what I needed to worry about burying.

"Dead."

"Dead," I repeated. Seemed I had a record going.

"He was our first casualty." A shadow hovered behind Makis's eyes.

"Casualty? That sounds like some kind of war's going on."

He pulled the rag away from his wound, glanced down at the bloody tissue. "It is. This isn't our first skirmish with the others."

Skirmish? This nightmare I'd been caught in—three dead, four if I counted Nick, Harmony almost taken—it was a hell of a lot more than a skirmish to me. I didn't comment on that but questioned the last word instead. "Others? I thought Nick . . . I didn't get the feeling he was part of a group." In fact, he'd screamed *loner* to me. If anything about this made sense, it was that. Nick seemed like every alienated boy I had seen on TV who for some twisted reason turned to violence to make him feel whole.

"He didn't get his ideas on his own. And his talent"—a hollowness seeped into Makis's eyes—"so varied and strong. We had no idea."

Meaning what? There were others like him out there? Sons of Amazons with skills I'd never dreamed existed— with a thirst for revenge? That I could never relax? That life would never feel safe or secure again?

Harmony wandering toward us, her arms wrapped around her body, her eyes dazed, saved me from asking . . . from learning something I wasn't ready to deal with yet.

"He's dead," she said. "You killed him."

It wasn't a judgment, just a statement. Like she needed to say it to understand it, to believe it.

I held out a hand to her, let my fingers trail down her arm. I wanted to hold her, to tell her it had all been a bad dream, but it hadn't and I was done lying to her. "There are a few things we need to talk about," I said.

Her eyes, dark and round, stared at me. "You think?" Then shaking her head, she walked past me, out the door and to my truck.

I smiled. Harmony was going to be okay, which meant I'd be okay. I could survive anything as long as I had my family. I needed them. I huffed out a breath.

Which meant Bubbe and I were going to have to have a long talk.

A week later I was sitting on the front steps looking through Harmony's artist notebook. My daughter and I'd had a long talk after the scene at the studio. We'd stayed up most of the night, in fact. Luckily the next day had been Saturday. My girl had needed a few days to adjust before returning to her life. It wasn't often a girl saw her mother kill her hoped-to-be-boyfriend. At least I hoped it wasn't going to be an everyday thing. With almost four years of high school left, who knew?

Anyway, she knew who she was and where she came from. Bubbe and Mother were thrilled—with that, at least. They were not so thrilled with Makis's claims.

Bubbe had babbled on about genetic tests, but she was blowing smoke. She knew without any help from science that Makis was telling the truth. Bubbe just knew things like that—at least once the possibility had been plopped down in front of her. Without Makis staring her in the eye and making a claim, I don't think she ever would have acknowledged the relationship on her own.

But he had and she did and that was that—although his appearance had already added a new dimension of conflict to our home. He and Bubbe would work it out eventually—or not.

I wasn't getting involved. At least not until one of them blew my house down around me.

Makis and I'd had a long chat too. He told me all about Harmony's father, how he died, why he'd searched me out. And he told me about Michael. His affair with me hadn't been part of the plan, but how the sons had been happy when it happened. How Michael's death was another casualty of their war, how they now suspected Nick/Tim had been the dog who'd killed him. That Nick's fascination with me may have started then.

I struggled with coming to terms with that, that my rebellion had given sons like Nick fuel, but I got past it. Finally accepted that I wasn't responsible for others' insanity, could only do what I thought was best . . . just. And leaving the Amazons, standing up for equality between men and women, hearth-keepers, warriors, artisans, priestesses, all of us that was right.

After sorting out those issues, I'd had my talk with Bubbe, visited my son's fake grave, and driven to the hospital where she'd left him so long ago. I hadn't gone inside. Hadn't talked to anyone . . . yet.

He was out there, and I was going to find him, but he

was now ten years old. Me popping up and claiming him as mine wasn't going to be simple. I needed to think about it, prepare myself, and decide when I did find him exactly what I was going to say, how much truth I was going to tell this child. I'd spent so long lying to the first one. Lies had almost become more natural than truth—but that was over.

Harmony knew all—her heritage, her brother, even Bubbe's betrayal—and, superball that she was, she'd rebounded with barely a flicker of disbelief. I suspected she was the one not telling me something now, but I was letting it go for a while. I owed her that—at least until I thought her secrets put her in danger.

Now I sat on my front steps, flipping through my daughter's notebook, admiring her work, and feeling grateful my life was back to normal, almost.

Detective Reynolds stepped around the corner. He was dressed casually in jeans and a Packers sweatshirt.

I flipped the notebook closed and lay it on my lap.

He stopped a few feet away, next to the banister, cocked one hip against it. "Kind of weird how everything wound up . . . all neatlike."

The sun was battering down with all the strength it could muster on a fall morning. I squinted as I looked up at him, but didn't raise a hand to block it. The warmth felt good.

"Has to work out that way sometimes, I guess," I replied.

"Does it? Doesn't seem to." He moved his hand on the railing. "How's Zery?"

I lifted one shoulder. "Don't know. We don't talk much." After being released from jail, she'd gone straight back to the safe camp. I told myself she was needed there, that after learning about the sons, the Amazons had a lot to sort out, but it still hurt. Of course, I could have called her, or gone to see her when Bubbe and I visited my son's faux grave, but I hadn't. I guessed Zery and I both needed time before facing whatever our relationship had become.

"She came with the mothers when they claimed the bodies," he said.

And Dana, she'd gone with them too, but she hadn't mentioned seeing Zery.

"You know what happened to the missing skin?"

The question caught me off guard. He'd never mentioned the missing patch where the girls' *givnomais* had been removed. Now he was acting like I'd know exactly what he was talking about. Which, of course, I did.

Makis and the sons had left Nick's body in his apartment along with his notebook and knife, but they had removed the tattoos, given them to Alcippe so she could complete the ceremony to release the girls from this plane. They'd set things up to look like he'd attacked another girl, one who got away, but not before shoving his own knife into his chest.

"Any leads on the last girl?" I countered.

He stared behind me, at the shop's front door. I'd

heard a creak a few seconds earlier, knew someone was standing there listening.

"Not a one," he replied, then slapped his palm against the railing and turned. "I've got tickets to the Badgers next weekend. You ever been?"

I shook my head.

He stepped away from the railing. "Saturday, noon. We'll tailgate. Wear something red." He slipped one last glance to the door, then strolled around the corner.

"You going?" Peter stepped through the door, onto the concrete behind me.

He looked good, relaxed in a pilled fleece and jeans with a tear in the knee. What was it about worn-out clothes that was so damn sexy?

"What are you doing here?" I'd fired him before racing off to save my daughter. Or thought I had. Maybe slamming him into a wall, then peppering him with tchotchkes hadn't been direct enough. I hadn't seen him since then, although I'd picked up the phone more than once.

"Guess he survived our little encounter okay." His eyes were focused on the spot where Reynolds had disappeared around the side of the building.

"You don't sound too excited about that. What happened, anyway?"

Reynolds and Peter had both been gone when I returned with Harmony. I figured Peter had gone to help Makis. I'd expected to hear from Reynolds, with a warrant in his hand. I had kneed him in the groin: assault on a police officer. But I guess he got sidetracked, what with finding his serial killer with a six-inch-deep gash in his chest and all.

When he'd shown up today, I'd thought for sure he'd bring up our last meeting, but he hadn't.

Maybe he was saving it to discuss over beer and brats.

"What did he tell you?" Peter asked.

I snapped my attention away from my musings. "Nothing. We hadn't talked until just now."

He slipped his hands into his pockets and wandered down a step—still far enough away I didn't have to strain my neck too much to look up at him.

"I jumped on him. He fired and missed. I slapped his gun out of his hand, then ran up the stairs—back out the window."

I nodded. Pretty much what I'd figured.

"So, you going with him?" he asked again.

I arched a brow. "I might."

He walked closer then, sat down beside me, and stared out toward Monroe Street.

I faced the front too, placed my hands on Harmony's notebook. Traffic was light today, but it was Sunday, not much going on.

"I can help you find your son, now that you know what happened to him."

My fingers straightened, splayed out stark white against the notebook's black cover. "Why?"

"It's what I do." He placed his forearms on his knees and laced his fingers together. "And I want to help . . . you."

I didn't reply for a while. Felt my breath entering and leaving my lungs, realized just how hard and cold the step was beneath my butt.

"You want your job back?" I asked.

"I hadn't left. Check the schedule. I had the week off."

I shook my head. Next time I'd have to throw something bigger at him, maybe my truck. "I haven't forgiven you for Harmony. I don't trust you."

He slid his hands up and down his thighs. "I know, but you will. I'll make sure of it."

I looked at him, expecting to see a grin or at least a smile, but his expression was dead serious. "In the meantime, are you going to let me help you?"

I gripped Harmony's notebook, thought about the little boy out there somewhere growing bigger every day. Days I'd never get back. "You can help."

Then he smiled. "Good."

And it was. It was all good. Things weren't perfect, but they were out in the open—or as out as they were going to get for a while—and I had friends, family, and two men who seemed inexplicably willing to put up with my crap.

And somewhere I had a son. I couldn't wait to meet him.